SWEET DREAMS

Jo Ullah grew up in a small village in Dorset, where she was fed on a regular diet of horror and the supernatural by the inventive mind of her mother. Being dyslexic, reading and writing were always a difficult mountain just waiting to be scaled. Luckily the view from top is much better than it was from the ground.

Jo lives in Bristol with her family and other creatures great and small, practising her writing, gardening and love of art.

Keep up to date with news of Jo Ullah's books and artwork via her website –

www.joullah.com
Or follow her on Twitter at –
@JoUllah

Also by Jo Ullah

The Locksmith

SWEET DREAMS

Jo Ullah

Scabious
Press

SWEET DREAMS

By Jo Ullah

Published by Scabious Press 2020
Bristol, Somerset, England

Disclaimer - The author wishes to state that although EFT and Matrix Reimprinting are powerful tools for the purpose of mental and physical healing, they have been portrayed in this novel as achieving faster and more dramatic results than would be expected in normal circumstances. This is for the sake of a more interesting and exciting narrative, as these techniques achieve the best results through a certified practitioner and over a more gradual period of time.

Cover design by J D Smith
www.jdsmith-design.co.uk

ISBN - 978-1-9999065-1-1

To Christine, whose work inspired this novel.

1

When I was about twelve I had this dream – it was the first of those kinds, the ones that happen.

I was watching a circle of little girls dressed in pink with blonde hair, like fairy witches. They stretched their arms out at their sides to touch their clenched fists with their neighbour, and then they brought them back to the front of their bodies, before repeating the gesture over and over. One girl stood in the centre of the ring, turning in a slow circle.

And that was it. I woke up and thought; *wow, that was weird.*

A few days later I went to a birthday party. It was for Becks' little sister. Becks wanted me there so she could have a friend, and I said I would help out with the sandwiches and stuff. I had only just got to know Becks that year, year eight at secondary school, but her house was already my second home. Anyway, there were all these little girls, aged about seven or eight years old and they were dressed in varying shades of pink – Becks said that was the norm for primary school girls – and they had blonde hair.

I stood and stared as Becks' mum organised a game I'd never seen before. She'd made a long loop of string with a fat plastic red ring threaded onto it and got the girls into a circle, with one child standing in the centre. The children passed the ring from hand to hand along the string, hiding it from the girl in the centre. This child turned slowly around looking hard at the clenched fists of all her friends trying to guess where the ring was.

Gobsmacked is a good expression to describe how I felt, it was just like my dream. Maybe that meant I was going to develop superpowers or something? I didn't tell anyone, and despite lots of experimenting, I found that I didn't have any special powers; just the weird dreams.

Now I'm all grown up, I can see that I've had many prophetic dreams, only they're all pretty much like that first one – mundane and pointless. Sometimes I realise that a particularly strange nonsense dream turned out to tell me something useful, but only after it's too late to do anything about it – like a crappy boyfriend, or a lame night out. But what's the use if you can only match the information with the event after it's happened? So now I write them down. A sort of dream diary, so I can check back and see if there's any odd matches going on.

It's like déjà vu. I never know when I have that feeling if it's because I dreamt it already or if I've done it before or I'm just having an odd brain moment.

So I write it all down, just in case.

I like writing anyway; it's made me much better at remembering. I still haven't told anyone, well except Becks, but she's not just anyone. I didn't even tell Nick and we were together for nearly three years. He wouldn't have understood. I think he secretly believes women are more than a little insane anyway.

I'm thinking about this now because of the dream I had last night. I haven't had time to write it down yet, so it's playing over and over in my head as I sit on the bus whizzing my way to my first call of the morning.

It did feel like one of *those* dreams; it was just too crazy.

I was at our old house; most of my dreams are set there even though we moved when I went to secondary. It was a great house, I still feel nostalgic when I pass it. A wooden modern eco-home, well before its time, set in its own small plot in Redland. Tall Victorian pale sandstone houses tower either side, throwing its narrow side gardens into permanent gloom. My dad was never one for gardening so those side corridors were slim forests of overgrown shrubs that I spent hours in, practising my recorder or communing with my Barbies.

In last night's dream, I'm standing at the front of the house looking into the gloom of the foliage in the side and I can feel something staring back at me. I'm scared, really scared, but I don't know why. I can smell something too, an intoxicating scent that wants to draw me in.

Then there's a low growl, a deep rumbling warning growl like from a very large dog.

I back away, edging my way to the door.

There's the snap and crackle of breaking branches as something heavy pushes its way towards me.

Turning fast I run. I can hear crashing and snarling behind me.

Leaping through our front door I slam it shut.

Holding it shut, breathing hard.

I'm expecting something to slam into the door, but it doesn't, nothing happens.

Then I hear it. Something big is sliding along the wooden side of the house. Following the sound with my gaze, I see the living room window – it's open.

I'm running for the window.

It's running too, but I'm quicker. I slam the window shut and stare out into the leafy gloom.

Nothing; just plants and twigs. There's nothing there but the fear in my throat that almost chokes me.

The musky smell of rot hits my eyes and nose. The living room walls are mottled with mould. Reaching out I find that they crumble under my fingers.

The growl of the beast just behind the dissolving wood shoves me onto my backside with a sharp shout of fear. The wood is pushing out, stretching into an animal open-mouthed muzzle like Freddy in *Elm Street*.

And that's when I woke up, gasping, heaving the air into my lungs. Had I been holding my breath? My heart was pounding, and my hearing on super alert. There was a sweet smell in the air, but it faded before I could identify it.

It's not dark in my sitting room. That's where I sleep since Becks moved in and took the bedroom. It's never fully dark in Bristol – too many street lamps. But I could still feel the shadows shifting and slithering. Was that breathing? I held my breath to hear better and felt the prickle of sweat on my neck, itching.

It got louder, a deep growling from behind the couch.

Huddling up into a ball I feel sick with fear, my heartbeat is pounding in my ears, but it doesn't block the animal sound.

Was it coming closer? I had to see.

Edging my head up, super slow, I peek over the top of the couch.

Empty. There's nothing there, and then I get it.

God, it's snoring from the bedroom. Relief floods through me. Who has my sleazy flatmate got in there now? Despite my tutting, I do admire her gall and sometimes wish I could do the same. But I can't, I'm just wired differently.

The adrenaline that filled my system stops me from sleeping, so when I finally do doze back off, I autopilot silence my alarm and end up being late for my first appointment.

I'm still thinking about the dream when I hop off the bus at the zoo. I've got a lady up in Clifton. Strictly speaking, as a walker – that's what they call us that don't drive – I should only be set appointments around my neck of the woods, South Bristol, Bedminster and the like. But they're such a ditsy company, I get sent off all over the place. Anyway, I like Clifton and I like this service user, that's what we have to call them, not clients but service users. It makes me feel like a vacuum cleaner or something. I'm a carer; undervalued, underpaid and – for my service users – an absolute necessity.

She lives in a lofty flat, accessed via a long winding staircase, on the side of a huge house, long ago carved up for profit. I think she's like Rapunzel, Mrs Percival, locked up in her tower by evil witches called Old Age and Infirmity.

Her flat is in part of a larger building set back down a quiet leafy lane. Most of the property is an upmarket dentist's practice; Mrs Percival's place is an odd tack-on affair at the topmost left of the building.

Crossing the expanse of the drive area set before the impressive stone-built Victorian property, I ignore the main front door and head for her private entrance, a black door to the left.

It's a solid panel wooden door – most likely original. A big brass knob, dulled with neglect, in its centre and a matching long rectangular letter box beneath it. To me it looks like an eyeless face, the mouth set with grim determination. I punch her combination number, 1131, into the key-safe box set mid-height beside the door. This is a mismatched chrome, like the round lock in the door. This stands out in comparison screaming its newness compared to the original brass door furniture.

Letting myself in, I put the key in my pocket and with some effort push the door shut behind me. The sound of its slam echoes in the white-painted hall space and stairwell around me. This side of the door is painted white to match the walls. It has so many layers of gloss that where it has flaked off in patches and been repainted over the general effect is of a topological map of the Antarctic. Two big bolts fitted top and bottom that had once probably been of black metal, have also been daubed with gloss. Painted stuck, I guess, as I doubt they are ever used now. I couldn't see Mrs P riding her stair-chair, which runs the length of her long stone spiral staircase, to bolt the door at bedtime. I doubt she's been out of the building in years. Her bit is sealed off from the rest. It's three flights up to her apartment. I imagine it was originally designed so that the servants could reach their sleeping quarters without ever having to disturb their masters. There must have been a door on the ground floor for access to the main house, but that was blocked off years ago. I start up the stone stairs knowing I'd be puffed out before I reach the top.

'Only me, Mrs Percival,' I call extra loud as I let myself into her flat via the flimsy glass and wood-panelled door. This is never locked, there's no need.

'Oh hello, Astrid love, you again this morning. Can you check Sir Lancelot? Be a darling and top up his bowl.'

Sir Lancelot is her extra furry extra lazy cat. Every room has a cat litter tray. It's the one thing she does manage to keep clean. I see the cat lengthened out across the end of her bed. He opens one eye, squinting at me before closing it again, dismissing me.

'Hello to you too,' I say to him as I remake the bed, careful not to dislodge him. Then I help Mrs Percival go to the bathroom for a wee and a wash, before dressing her in her choice of clothes for that day. That's about the only time she gets out of her chair; for the cat litter, the bathroom, to change clothes or to go to bed. It's a very narrow life.

I get Mrs Percival's breakfast and bring it to her on a tray, so she can eat it from the comfort of her armchair. Her chair is in the living room facing the TV and a high, wide window. There's a deep ledge outside, where a big seagull struts, stopping to eye us through the glass. He's Mrs Percival's other frequent visitor – at least she calls it he, I have no idea how to tell what sex a seagull is. I know that she will only eat about a third of any meal given to her before declaring it tasteless and insisting the leftovers are put out on the window ledge for the bird.

'Best fed seagull in Bristol,' she told me the first time we met.

I fetch her meds and put them on the tray with her breakfast before sitting down on the large brown sofa opposite to fill in her notes.

Meds – yes, breakfast – yes, mood – good. That's the type of thing we carers have to put in the service user's notes so everyone can be kept up-to-date on how our clients are doing. Then I ask if she wants a movie on. Mrs P has a whole stack of classic forties and fifties black-and-white DVDs. She must have seen them all a million times, but what else does she have to do? We usually have a chat, about whatever; well, she talks and I listen. But I'm late and in a rush today. I hold up a few selections until she says,

'*Casablanca*, lovely.' And I put that one on for her.

Fully absorbed she hardly registers when I shout bye, I'm dismissed just like with the cat. Grabbing my hat – the red pork-pie today to match my red cotton top – I trot down the spiral stairs as fast as the winding shape will allow, my footsteps echoing around me.

I walk fast past the Downs to my next appointment, and that's how my morning goes, until about ten-thirty when everyone is done till the lunchtime slot. That's the problem with this job; busy busy busy, with about an hour break between breakfast, lunch, and tea, where we carers are supposed to just hang loose and twiddle our thumbs. Given the chance, the company would want me available all night. I've found the only way is to stop answering their calls after about seven. If they get hold of me, I can never say no.

It keeps me fit, all this running about after people and I like the service users, well, most of them. They accept you into their lives and trust you, they have to. It surprises me that I like it so much. My previous job, before I got laid off, was just basic admin. I could stay hidden away behind my computer all day and hardly have to speak to anyone. Now I have to talk to people, I have to take charge and deal with them confidently or they wouldn't feel comfortable enough to trust me with really quite personal care. I mean, would you let an anxious, blushing person wipe your bum? So the shy side of me gets tucked away for the day, while I'm Astrid the confident carer.

In my own time, I'm quiet Azza – Azza, that's what most my friends call me. I was Astrid at primary school but for some reason, it was too much for everyone when I got to secondary. There's a whole stream of versions – Azzi, Az, Oz, A, Rida and Azza. When Becks and me became best mates it stuck at Azza because she liked it, and as we were always together we even got referred to jointly as Bazza. We were inseparable for years. It was only when she got together with Aaron that we drifted apart for a while. Never quite completely, but she was so caught up with him that I just slipped out of her thoughts for a time. Then I met Nick and I was all consumed too.

When both our relationships went tits up, coming together again seemed the most natural thing in the world. Sometimes I wish she were a bloke. We would be perfect together, she completely gets me. It's so hard, that whole bit when you first get to know someone. You're not really yourself, always speaking from behind a polite facade wondering how much you can let slip out. And since Nick and I split, and everything else that happened, I'm different; more vulnerable, more sceptical too. For now, Becks is about all the up close and personal I can cope with. And because she understands she doesn't push – well not too much – she just lets me be.

As usual, I've got my rucksack stuffed with my books with me so I'm going to pop into the library for a couple of hours, to read up on my coursework. I have to practise on myself so it can be pretty embarrassing sometimes.

I enter the library via the main doors and go up the curving marble staircase at the back of the entrance hall. These take me to the first-floor hallway that connects to various parts of the serene area of the serious reader's section. I'm after the bay window seat. I feel more relaxed just there because I can turn my chair to the stained glass windows and ignore everyone around me.

I'm in luck, there's a seat free with a small dark wood desk beside it.

Sitting comfortably, I dig my coursebook out of my rucksack. I know the set-up routine pretty well now, but I like to see the demonstration pictures as a reminder. Muttering to myself, I start tapping on the side of my hand.

'Even though I have this sadness I completely love and accept myself.'

I repeat this three times before moving to the side of my eyebrow and tap tap tap with the first three fingers on my right hand.

'I have this sadness.'

Feeling under scrutiny I glance over to my left. A man is staring at me. His stare is so penetrating; his eyes a startling, piercing, pale green intensified by dark eyelashes like that Afghan girl from the 1980s *National Geographic* magazine. The heat rises in my cheeks. He drops his gaze and seems absorbed with the book in front of him.

Looking away I continue with my mantra, but I can't concentrate and pretty soon I peek back over to the green-eyed man.

He dips his head.

I caught him, he was definitely watching me.

I can't carry on feeling exposed like this, so I pack up my books, decamp downstairs to the library shop and order a cappuccino – an expensive froth-topped treat. I'm not supposed to give in to these urges; I don't have money to waste, but the green-eyed man has unbalanced my morning and I need compensation. Still, not long now until my lunchtime appointments.

2

Hunting, sniffing, trapping

Too much noise; it's making his head feel wrong again as if a swarm of wasps have infested it.

Rubbing the back of his neck, he mutters a few lines to his co-worker and leaves; walking fast, head down, no eye contact – not caring where – just needing some space to calm him.

The streets are busy, people jostling for room on the pavement, some of them fixed on their mobiles, too preoccupied to see where they were going. A woman barrels into him, her perfume overwhelming him for a moment, filling his head with images of dark forests with exotic blooms moist and swelled with the heavy heat. His sharp intake of breath mirrors hers as they step away from each other. He has, in that short moment, a complete picture of her; short dreadlocks, dark clothing, pendulous red earrings that match plump lips, caramel skin, cheeks sprinkled with a surprising array of brown freckles, eyes so black his face is reflected back at him. It was his own features that frighten him out of the moment.

'Sorry,' he mumbles, ducking his head as they speed away from each other. No doubt she'd forget him in the time it took her to refill her lungs.

Taking care he weaves through the crowd, cautious, regarding each new face as they approach him. That woman had shocked the buzzing crawling out of his head and for that he thanks her, his lips moving in a sibilant litany. Now he caught more scents around him. He is alive and the city is his habitat.

He hasn't lived here that long, so everything is still surprising and new. This feeling is good, it makes him see more. And it keeps the scrabbling creatures in his mind at a lower more sustainable level, just as a deep guttural hum.

But the dreams disturb his sleep. Less sleep means more crawling.

Perhaps he needs a coffee? There's an out-door barista cart on a small paved square just at the edge of College Green. A short queue stands patiently waiting for their midmorning pep up. He's drinking more coffee than he should; when he has too much it makes his hands shake. He's seen people looking at his hands at work. They must see the shaking. Did they understand it was the caffeine, or did they sense a bigger problem?

The man in front of him stinks. It's the rancid smell of body odour. Peering at the back of the man's neck he can just see a dark stain along the inside of the white-collar.

Stepping back a little he tries to create enough distance to cut out the stench, only a woman has joined the line behind him, closing him in. He senses her move back away from him and hears her tut of annoyance. The buzz flares in his head and for a moment the world goes grey. Fighting the growl that rises in his chest he clears his throat with a harsh sound.

The man in front moves forward to order his drink, taking his obnoxious aura with him and making the space bearable again.

He inches forward and takes a deep breath, forcing down the crawling and catching the more agreeable scents around him. The city has so many aromas. Some were a colourful palette of pleasure, others fill him with red fury. Women in general smell fantastic. It's the perfumes of their hidden places that fascinate him. Those scents have the power to take him beyond himself and he knows all the areas to find them. Delicate perfume on the wrists just above the palm, the tiny cup inside of the elbow, vulnerable soft skin behind the knees and at the back of the neck – especially just behind the ear – are all pools of signature smells particular to that woman only. Only they cover their signatures with shop-bought perfume. This sometimes complements their personal scents, other times they clash like an orchestra of insanity. Actually, to him, the odours are colour. That's how he sees them, all these women, in colour and light. And some of them shine like angels with a golden aura of sun-bathed perfume.

When he catches the fragrance of a woman – that glowing brightness of perfume undulating as an ethereal opalescent scarf around her – he longs to bury his face into all her secret places and learn her like the blind reading Braille.

'Yes?'

He's caught unawares that it's his turn in the queue. Stepping forward into the comforting cloud of coffee he orders an Americano, black.

Taking his disposable cup of steaming pleasure he finds a spot in the manicured lawns of College Green to sit in the sun. The air is filled with a sweet aromatic scent of freshly cut grass and he sees the occasional clump of damp cut greenness that has escaped being picked up by the mower. He settles himself in the grass, his legs thrust out in front of him. Seeing as it wasn't yet midday the Green is quite empty of the usual huddles of teenagers and lolling office workers snacking on pots of salad or sandwiches. Many crows and seagulls fling themselves about scrounging for food. Their diminutive cousins, the pigeons, duck in and out trying to use speed to best the sheer size of the bigger birds. He hasn't yet got used to the seagulls. They're everywhere in Bristol, so noisy and demanding. They aren't afraid of confrontation either. A gull strides too close to check if he has any food and he sends it squawking and flapping away with a swift kick. He doesn't like their yellow eyes; they seem to inspect him with a cool knowledge beyond their species.

Drinking his coffee with small sips, as it's still very hot, he squints over the cup's rim at the buildings opposite. The cathedral, ornate and ancient, built from, he guesses, a local sandstone. Quite a lot of the older buildings in this, the more prestigious area of the city, appear to have been built from it. Other areas of Bristol are constructed from grey cement and scrawled over with bright graffiti. The city's authorities seem to have embraced the fly-by-night artists who're hunted like vermin in the other towns he has inhabited – and he has lived in so many, hunting for his lost love. He thinks the graffiti is good, he feels, it's an ever-evolving dressing to the otherwise grim parts of town. Also, he guesses it keeps these guerrilla artists from tagging the areas of real importance, like the buildings he looks at now; the Central Library for instance. Full of words on the inside, not a peep on the outside.

Screwing up his empty cup, he struggles to his feet. On impulse, he heads across the sun-soaked lawns towards the library.

Something catches his eye. It's black and silver, almost completely hidden in the grass. Picking it up, he finds a black rubber lead running from it with twin buds at the end. Headphones. Someone has dropped an iPod. He inserts the earbud and fiddles about with the iPod until music explodes in his head. Beautiful loud pulsing music.

How different this world feels with music filling it. It feels like this is totally his world, and not all ‘theirs’ at all.

With the music creating a barrier blocking the outside he carries on across the lawn to the library, his feet marching in time to ‘Radioactive’ by Imagine Dragons, his lips stretched across his teeth in intense joy.

3

'What do you think?'

Becks stands, arms out in a 'ta-da' pose. She's wearing white denim shorts, a semi see-through striped white top with a very visible turquoise bra underneath, and my white wedge sandals. Her toenails are painted neon orange (my nail polish too).

'Nice.'

'Is it too much?' She turns trying to peek at her own backside, pulling at the hemline of the shorts.

'You have a nice bum.'

'But does it look—'

'Big in this,' I finish for her. 'Becks, you have a big butt, you know it's one of your best features, so stop fishing.'

Satisfied, she stomps over to the fridge. I've been ready for ages, she must have changed at least three times. I'm not bothered though, we're on a girls' night out, guaranteed fun, and she always takes ages to feel just right. So I've been sipping at a bottle of Peroni while perched up on one of the barstools at the breakfast bar that separates the kitchen part of my flat from the sitting room.

'You look nice,' she says as she hooks out a can of gin and tonic. She hands it to me waving her neon fingernails under my nose by way of explanation. The can makes a secret agent 'Psst' sound as I pull back the ring.

'Charity shop.' I pull some of the neck round to the front so she can see the label. 'But it's Fat Face.'

'Nice find!'

I'm pleased; it *is* a nice top, but it's always good to have it confirmed by someone else.

'Nice colour, brings out your eyes,' she says.

'Does it?' I pull the petrol blue material out at the hem to take a closer look.

'Definitely fab.' She swigs her drink down. 'Ready?'

'Yep,' I say, slipping off the stool and grabbing up my hat, the black gaucho one this evening, and head for the door.

The noise hits as soon as we get through the second set of brushed metal and glass doors. High ceilings only accentuate the voices, all vying for sound space.

'Wow,' says Becks echoing my thoughts. 'Big crowd tonight.'

The huge bare red brick Tobacco Factory bar is always a popular venue, tonight being Thursday – the new Friday apparently – even more so, but the bar is at least four deep, it'd take forever to get a drink.

'Helen,' shouts Becks waving her arms above her head like someone drowning.

Becks has got one of those voices that carry in any crowd. I saw a slim arm protrude and wave above the sea of heads. Grabbing my wrist Becks pulls me after her in amongst the mainly male bodies. Watching their appreciative glances travel down her body as she slides past them I feel a wave of territorial protectiveness.

'Creeps,' I mutter, but no one notices.

Squealing, Helen grabs us both in a hug.

'Good timing, Harry's at the bar. What you both want?' she shouts into our faces.

'Half a lager.' 'G&T.' Becks and I say in unison and get a thumbs up from Helen before she taps Harry on the shoulder and relays our order.

'We've got a table at the far end,' Helen shouts. 'Only,' she makes a face of apology, 'Nick's there, with *her*.'

My gut clenches.

'We'll go somewhere else,' says Becks her wide-eyed gaze searching my face. I know she wants to be here, I could almost see the buzz emanating from her. And it makes me cross too, why did I have to run away because he's here? It's been over a year for God's sake, it's time to get over him.

'No,' I say, lifting my chin so she would know I mean it. 'I don't care if he's here, or her.'

'You sure?' She squeezes my hand.

'Sure.'

'Just say, won't you?'

I nod.

Harry turns, giving us a big grin and our drinks, shaking his shaggy head at our offered money.

'You can get the next,' he shouts.

He holds up a round metal tray with everyone else's drinks and we follow him as he bulldozes his way through the crowd.

Despite my bravado to Becks, my stomach is in knots. I feel sick – really, I might actually puke – and when I bring my glass up for a sip I see with horror that my hand is shaking. Bloody Nick, why did he still have the power to do this to me?

Taking a quick gulp of my drink I start to choke. And that is Nick's first view of me as I emerge from the crowd. Not the cool, controlled and ultra-beautiful appearance I had hoped for, but coughing, red-faced and eyes streaming.

Shit, even my body is betraying me.

'Hi,' say several people around the table, most of whom I know well. I take them all in with a glance as I struggle to regain the use of my lungs.

'Hhhh,' I cough, ducking my head in reply.

'Hi,' says Nick.

I look at him and the slim blonde, my nemesis, sitting across at the far end of the table. Great, now I would have to sit opposite him and hardly be able to avoid seeing them.

Becks pulls me down into my seat and gives me a look. Had I been standing there like a gorm? God. Ducking my head so the brim of my hat hides most my face, I take another sip of my drink.

I stay like that for the first twenty minutes or so. Not really making conversation with anyone, just sipping my lager and nodding at the others, listening to their animated chatter. Becks had got quite loud beside me talking to Sonia on her right. Helen saw someone she knew and bolted across the room, leaving me alone in my own void amid the hubbub. But that was okay; I duck my head and sip. Hats are good, they make a private space for you wherever you are.

'How're you doing?'

They also blinker you from what's happening right under your nose. Nick had taken Helen's chair and was leaning close to be heard, too close. I can't help jerking back away from him. I see his eyes widen in surprise and feel a spasm of guilt.

'You're growing a beard,' I say because I'm at a loss of anything more intelligent to say.

He strokes it. 'Getting there, it needs a bit more growth before I can cut it into a proper shape.'

Beards are all the rage at the moment, but just because something is fashionable doesn't mean it'll suit everyone. A beard doesn't suit Nick. He's ginger; nice red hair that he gels up at the front, and freckles in the summer – a real cheeky boy look. The beard has ruined that and now he just looks like a slightly battered red panda and not even a cute one.

'You don't like it.' It was a statement, he'd read my expression.

Screwing up my face I shrug. 'You looked better before.'

And that says it all – 'better before' you cheated on me, 'better before' you left me to cope jobless with a crippling mortgage, *our* mortgage, 'better before' you left me pregnant and alone.

'Hey, come to the bar,' says Becks hauling me out of my seat and off towards the bar.

'Sorry,' she says. 'I saw online that if you spend more than seven minutes talking to a man you're in danger of falling for him.'

I laugh, grateful, she was always saving me at the moment. 'I just want to pour a pint over his bimbo girlfriend's head,' I say. I want to, desperately, but who am I kidding.

'You should,' she says over her shoulder as she manoeuvres through all the huddling clusters of drinkers.

I knew I couldn't though, it wasn't me to do something like that. It's just that I itch to.

As we got close to the bar, an area near the far end that had thinned a bit, a very tall man hit on Becks.

'Hi gorgeous,' he says.

'High yourself,' she says looking him up and down.

He laughs. 'Funny and beautiful. Let me buy you a drink and see what else you've got to offer.'

I wince at the terrible pick-up line, but it seemed to have worked on Becks.

'G&T and my friend here will have half a lager.' She gives me a wink. She was dragging me into a chat up. Oh well, she was probably right, it might make me feel better about myself, or worse as they all fuss over her. And it might just remind Nick what he'd lost. I lift up my head and smile at Goliath.

'Whoa,' he says. 'So much light under that bushel.'

I frown, not sure if he was taking the piss or really means it. Men usually save their compliments for girls like Becks.

The man beside him steps into view and we both widen our eyes. It was him, from the library, those eyes. He looks confused for a moment.

'I… Er. Hi,' he says.

Goliath gazes from one to the other of us. 'You two already know each other? What've you been keeping from me, Mark?'

Becks laughs, her deep warm chocolatey chuckle drawing all of us back to her in an instant. 'Well I for one would like to know,' she says.

'I… we were in the library. I saw her there,' says Mark, and he looks sheepish.

I nod, not sure what to say.

'Love over literature,' says the giant.

'Oh, we didn't…' 'She wasn't…' Mark and I say in unison before we both fall silent.

'Okay, obviously awkward, how about those drinks? I'm Greg, this is Mark, and who're you two?'

'Becks,' she says placing her manicured hand on her chest ensuring eye contact with just some of her crown jewels. 'And Azza,' she says indicating me.

'Azza,' says Mark. 'That's unusual.'

He really is gorgeous, why hadn't I noticed in the library? All I'd seen were those amazing piercing eyes.

'Short for Astrid,' says Becks. I shoot her a look and a grin spreads across her face. 'But she can explain it herself.' She takes Greg's arm. 'Let's see about those drinks shall we.'

'Okay,' Greg says with a broad smile.

Mark steps closer to me as the other two went to the bar.

'What were you doing?' he says tipping his head a little to peek under the brim of my hat. That felt too close and intimate, I want to take it off and create some distance, or fan my face. It's too hot in here all of a sudden.

'What?' I say. 'When?'

'In the library, you were…' He stops for a moment and taps his head and then his face.

'Oh.' Some clarity brought relief, but only a little as perhaps I now have to explain. 'EFT,' I say.

He squints at me, sort of screwing up one side of his face. It's unbelievably attractive, I want him to do it again. God, I'm staring. I glance away across the crowd of people catching Nick's eye. He's staring at me. Turning back to Mark I give him a big warm smile.

'EFT, Emotional Freedom Technique.'

'What does that do, I mean, what's it for?' he asks.

I start to explain, the short abbreviated version, how voiced set-up lines followed by tapping on pressure points on the meridian lines on the human body can release trapped emotions.

'And trapped emotions can lead to sickness and psychological problems,' I finish up. I hate explaining it because I can usually see the scepticism in people's eyes, 'more hippy shit' they're thinking.

But he doesn't have that look, he's nodding and seems interested.

'So is that your job?' he asks.

'Not yet, I'm a carer for now, but once I've passed and got my certificate…' I let the rest hang.

'Is it a long training?'

So many questions, but I'm enjoying the attention. Most men I meet just want to talk about themselves, but to be fair that was probably a reaction to my shyness.

‘I’m near the end now, I just need one more case study,’ I say.

He makes that adorable expression again, which I now know meant ‘what?’

‘I’m doing some real-life case studies, working on a couple of people, to help release their issues and then write it up for the EFT panel as part of passing my certification,’ I say.

‘And you need another guinea-pig?’

I nod and thank Greg who has just returned with my drink. I take a big gulp, I feel like I need it.

‘It’s okay,’ Becks is saying to Greg. He gazes at her, smiles and nods.

‘I find the workload too much sometimes, but once I’ve got enough practical hours under my belt I can work anywhere in the world.’

Greg nods. ‘Everyone always needs nursing.’

‘Especially you,’ says Mark and they both laugh. Was that some kind of private joke?

‘What about you?’ I say looking from one to the other of them.

‘Engineers,’ says Greg. ‘We work together.’

I didn’t know what to say, I have no idea about engineering, it was a generic word that seem to cover a lot of things.

‘Hard or soft?’ says Becks lifting an eyebrow.

Please, did she have to!

Greg chuckles, ‘Soft, embedded.’

Whoa, too many innuendos going on here. I feel a flush creeping up my face. Next, he would be asking her about her bedside manner.

‘Actually,’ says Mark. ‘We’re with a big crowd.’ He waves to a table with a large group of blokes sitting around it, a cheer went up and most of them do a thumbs-up at us.

My face burns.

'I'd invite you over but they're a bit…' he trails off.

Are we being dismissed? I feel cringing embarrassment and stare at my toes. *Ground, please open up and swallow me.*

'But,' he says touching my arm and regaining eye contact. 'If you need another case study, I'd be up for it.'

I stare at him, not quite believing.

'Or if you'd rather not?' he says. 'Only…' Now he looks embarrassed, ducking his head and glancing at me through his dark flopping fringe.

'No, that's great. You'll be helping me as much as I'd, hopefully, be helping you.' Am I really doing this? I don't know him from Adam for God's sake. Where could I say we'd meet, I don't have a practice space?

'We could meet at the library,' he says, seeming to read my mind.

'Oh, okay, great.'

'So, can I have your number?'

I must've looked confused because then he adds, 'So we can text and arrange a time that works for both of us.'

He's all business all of a sudden. That helps me feel less flustered somehow. I dig my phone out of my bag.

'Give me yours, I'll text you,' I say. *Good move, Astrid, take back control.* I can make the decision whether to text him or not when I'm sober.

4

Dream

I'm in the forest, moonlight strobing through the branches. I'm worried about someone, I have to hurry, quickly now before it's too late.

There's something familiar about this place, I've seen it before. Then I know, it's a scene from a modern fairy tale movie, one where all the stories are mashed together. The trees are grey, the branches bunched tight and covered in giant razor blade thorns. The air around me is cold and dank, the smell is of rot. I'm wearing my alpaca hat. I take it off and use it like a glove to sweep the thorn filled branches aside. There's blood dripping from them and soft things under my feet, but I can hear crying so I don't stop to investigate, just push on until I get to the base of a tower.

I call up to the dark window high above me, 'Mrs Percival, Mrs Percival, let me come in.'

The thin crying sound of a very old woman floats down to me from the tower.

'Mrs Percival. Are you alright? It's me, Astrid, I've come to feed the gull and help you choose a movie.'

The crying gets louder and I start to edge around the tower looking for a door in its cool damp sides.

Then I hear the howling of wolves deep in the forest and the crashing of branches as they hurtle towards me.

Panic lurches over me. I can see no escape except up the sides of the impossibly steep tower.

Using the long ties on my hat I swing it up, lassoing it on an overhanging rock and pull myself up. I crouch on a ledge as two dark wolves, their green eyes bright in the moonlight, jump and snap at my feet.

I can barely keep my grip and the ledge seems to be shrinking back into the rock face of the tower. Any moment now I will fall.

I shout for Mrs Percival just as I feel my grip giving way and the sharp pain of fangs sinking into my foot, pulling me down.

Down off the couch onto the floor. I wake, shocked and bemused, Mrs Percival's name on my lips.

5

Today is Friday and it's my day off, time to just laze around with a cup of coffee and clear my head from last night's boozing. But I can't stop worrying about Mrs Percival, because my dream's still lurking in my thoughts. Fishing my notebook out from under the couch, I write it down with the date and a few sketches of particular features, like the tower and the razor thorns. I'm quite good at drawing and the simple act of it usually fills me with calm, like a physical meditation.

But not today. Mrs Percival won't stop nagging my thoughts.

Should I pop round and check on her? If anyone from work was already there, they would think that very strange, even suspicious maybe. Mrs Percival wouldn't mind, though. I chew on a ragged bit of nail. Indecision is gonna get you, I hear Nick's voice in my head. He was always ragging me for my lack of decisiveness. Why are you always so embarrassed about everything, he would say, what's the worst that could happen?

Loads, I have a good imagination too.

Sighing, I ring the office to see who is scheduled for Mrs P's morning visit. As usual, it takes an age for someone to answer before I get Chanelle, and then she's unsure who, if anyone, has been. I can see Chanelle in my mind's eye standing behind her desk supporting her back from the weight of her swollen belly. Not long now, everyone keeps saying, not long now. There's a lot of office chatter going on back and forth before it's confirmed, Mrs Percival's visit this morning hasn't happened as the person pencilled in was a no show. There's a begging tone in Chanelle's voice; someone has to go.

'Please, Astrid, I know it's your day off but…'

How can I say no? I agree because I'd had it in the back of my mind for a walk on the Downs anyway, I'll hop on the bus and be there in twenty. And I would take my alpaca hat too, just in case.

Running up the stairs two at a time, I'm out of breath by the time I get to the top. She's not in her chair. I go from room to room calling her name and then I see Sir Lancelot sitting outside the bathroom door. He stares at me, meows and looks back at the door.

Knocking, I call her name before putting my ear to the door. I can hear crying.

'Mrs Percival. Are you alright? It's me, Astrid.'

The crying gets a little louder so I try the door but I can't get it open, there's something blocking it. I push slow and steady at the door.

'Noooooo,' cries out Mrs Percival and I realise she's right behind the door, blocking it.

Squatting down with my mouth close to the wood I ask, 'What's the matter?'

'Fell.' Her voice is querulous, almost a squeak.

'I can't get the door open. Do you think you could wriggle over a bit?' I say.

There's scuffling and a loud cry of 'Hurts!'

Pushing on the door I find she must have moved a bit because now I can open it a sliver. The acrid smell of urine hits me. Squeezing my body side on through the crack, I can see her now, lying close by the door. Climbing all the way in I find that Sir Lancelot has followed me. Purring loud motor sounds he rubs his head on his mistress's cheek.

Kneeling beside her I try to assess the damage. 'Where does it hurt?'

'Hip, oh everywhere,' she says managing to stroke her cat's head with a fluttering hand.

'I'll have to call an ambulance. Do you know how long you've been here?'

'All morning. No one came. I was desperate for the lavatory.' These last words break up with tears.

'I'm so sorry.' I squeeze her hand.

Putting one of her big soft pink towels over her, I hope it will help her feel a little less exposed lying there in her wet nightie. Then I call for an ambulance before I sit down on the floor beside her, holding her hand.

Poor Mrs Percival had a suspected broken hip. It was a real bother getting her down all those stairs on a stretcher. She made me promise to come every day to feed Sir Lancelot.

'And don't forget the bird,' were her parting words before they took off to the BRI.

After cleaning up the bathroom and feeding the cat and gull, I lock up and start walking home, stopping to look in a few charity shops on the way. My head's buzzing and I need some distraction, even though it's a beautiful day with a light wind that brings fresh summer scents to Bristol's usual city brew of cars and dank dust. Most people have a smile for me, but I can't shake the feeling of horror lurking at the edges of my thoughts. So it had been one of those dreams, but what about the forest and wolves? I could still feel those teeth sinking into my foot.

And seeing Nick last night was bothering me too.

Generally, it had been a good night. Becks had swapped numbers with Greg so no doubt he would turn up at some point. But he was so tall, I can't imagine how he would fit in my, now Beck's, bed.

And meeting Mark.

I don't know what to think of him. He's attractive, but am I ready to get involved with anyone right now? I'm still licking my wounds. It would probably be a really bad idea.

Something has caught my eye; I'm in Whiteladies Road ambling round a shop of useless pretty things – a shop that I don't even remember deciding to come into when this tiny house just shines out of the shelf at me. Picking it up, I turn it over and over, examining it from every angle.

Then I slip it into my jacket pocket and leave.

After another forty minutes' walk, I'm home.

Making myself a cup of coffee, I sit down at the breakfast bar and take the miniature house and stand it on the counter in front of me. It's a tiny thatched cottage with wooden steps and a crooked silver chimney. It looks like the kind of house a fairy might live in. I glow. From experience, I know this feeling will last for a few days.

I put the little house up on the shelf under the kitchen unit along with the other shining things. Gazing at it fills me with equal measures of pleasure and pain.

The doorbell buzzes making me jump. Did someone see me take the fairy house?

Answering the intercom, I hear Nick's voice asking to come up.

My stomach tightens into a hard painful knot, but I press the door release button before I can stop myself. Although I'm standing right by my closed front door and can hear every tread of his progress up the stairs, I still shudder when he knocks.

'Hi,' he says, ready with a smile when I open the door.

We stand for a moment, awkward in the doorway.

'Can I come in?'

'Oh.' I step back and he enters, glancing about him. He hasn't been here since we split, so I guess it all looks different.

'Looks nice,' he says and sits down on the couch.

Bristling, I offer him a coffee in my coldest tone.

'Sugar?' I ask, I know he has sugar but he's different now under *her* influence, so maybe he doesn't anymore.

'Please.' He stands beside me at the counter. 'What are these ugly things?' he asks, poking at my fairy house with its brethren.

'Don't.' My voice is sharp and he holds his hands up in surrender.

Giving him his coffee, I retreat to a bar stool with my own hot drink.

'I just wanted to see you. I hope that's okay?' he asks.

I sip my coffee and glare at him over the rim.

'It was good to see you last night. I'm so glad we can be friends.'

Friends! What a joke. If he could see in my head right now.

'There's stuff we need to talk about, stuff which needs sorting,' he says.

When I don't answer he makes an impatient sound in his throat. 'Please talk to me, Azza.'

'You're thinking about the flat,' I say, the words almost spat out.

'And us.'

'Us, there is no us!'

At least he has the good grace to look ashamed, ducking his head. When he looks up his eyes are shining. He always was emotional; quick to anger, even crying at movies, but I'm thrown by this. What's he playing at?

'I wanted to tell you,' his voice hitches. 'I want to tell you how sorry I am, that I wasn't there for you when you lost the baby.'

‘Our baby.’

He winces.

‘Why should you be sorry, you didn’t want it? Losing it must’ve been a weight off your mind.’

‘It wasn’t like that.’ His tone’s more defensive now, eyes dry already, I see.

‘Oh really, please tell, just what was it like?’

‘I was confused.’

‘You were confused!’ I snort, disgusted with him.

‘I wasn’t ready, it was a shock when you told me,’ he says, his expression pleading. I want to punch it off his face.

‘That’s the lamest excuse in the book!’ I shout, jumping to my feet my arms rigid at my sides, fists clenched.

‘I didn’t want you to lose the baby. I could see how happy it made you.’

‘But you went, leaving me to deal with,’ I lift my arms indicating everything around us, ‘all of it, baby, mortgage, jobless. And what hurts the most, you already had someone else. How long had that been going on?’

He looks deflated. ‘I can see you’re not ready.’

‘Don’t turn this on me!’

‘We do need to sort stuff out, this flat’s still half mine.’

‘Just get out!’ I scream this at him. I’m not a shouter and he’s shocked.

‘Azza, please.’

‘Get out, get out, get out!’

And he does. Slamming the door behind him.

I sit down on the floor, bracing my back against it, and cry.

I’m still upset when Becks gets home. She looks tired and overheated, but she knows as soon as she sees me.

‘Hey?’ She comes over and sits next to me, where I am now, huddled on the couch, putting her arm around my shoulders.

‘Nick.’ I start crying again.

‘What’s that shit done now?’

‘He came round.’

‘What the hell!’ she says, indignation widening her eyes.

‘He was on about us needing to talk. Said he was sorry he wasn’t there for me when I miscarried.’

Becks snorts.

‘And about the flat.’ I look into her eyes, ‘It *is* half his.’

‘For fuck’s sake!’

‘I don’t know what to do.’

‘Hope you didn’t agree to anything,’ she says.

‘I couldn’t think, I just shouted at him, told him to get out.’

‘Good for you,’ she says squeezing me hard.

‘But it doesn’t solve anything. This flat is half his,’ I say.

‘But you’ve been paying the mortgage.’

‘So the sooner we sort it out the better. I can’t afford a legal wrangle and I can’t bear to think he’ll benefit from my hard work,’ I say, the bitter taste in my heart twisting my lips.

‘Could you buy him out?’

I make a face; Becks knows my financial situation better than anyone. I would have lost the flat by now if she hadn’t rented my bedroom.

‘What about your dad?’

‘He’s hopeless, used up the last of his savings ages ago,’ I say.

‘Your mum?’

It was my turn to snort.

'Oh babes, I wish I knew how to help, you know my finances are crap. I'd give you my liver if you needed it, you know that don't you?'

I laugh. 'Your liver would do me more harm than good. No, I'm going to have to talk to him, come to some arrangement. At least until I'm qualified with the EFT and maybe earning a bit more.'

'You close?'

I wrinkle my nose. 'Both case studies are well underway, so I'm a lot more confident now. I think I just need one more, preferably someone younger, as my others are both over sixty.'

Becks pats her chest and raises her eyebrows.

'I need something a bit more complex than an incurable need for shopping and new boyfriends, but thanks all the same.'

'What about that bloke, Mark was it? Greg's friend at the Tobacco Factory. He seemed keen?'

'That's what I don't need,' I say.

'But he was really cute, and he definitely liked you.'

'Exactly.'

'Oh come on, Azza, time for someone new in your life.'

'No thanks.' And when I see her expression, I add, 'No, really, Becks, I'm still getting over Nick. A new relationship is the last thing I need.'

'You do need a cup of tea though, and so do I,' she says getting up and busying herself in the kitchen, the last of the day's sun streaming through the window, turning her bleached hair – held up in an untidy lopsided bun – to spun gold.

I go to the bathroom and stare at my face in the mirror. Pale skin blotched red, swollen eyes, spiked eyelashes and red nose – lovely. Getting some tissue, I blow my nose before washing my face.

Feeling a bit stronger, I go back to join Becks in the kitchen. She's stuffing the contents of my handbag back into its confined space. There's an art to this because I loathe big swampy bags where everything lumps together at the bottom. So I have a tiny red bag and slot the items one beside the other, necessities only; purse, mobile, small work diary, keys, and pen. Becks is flustered because she had been caught red-handed – the biggest unwritten sin in the world, going through a woman's handbag.

'Sorry, I knocked it off and everything just…' she says bending up the diary pages as she tries to force the catch shut.

Taking it from her I put everything in as it should be.

'Sorry,' she says pushing a floral mug towards me. 'You feeling any better now?'

Smiling I nod and sip my tea.

'I have a date with Greg later,' she says. 'Will you be okay?'

'That was quick.'

'We have a lot in common.'

'Sex.'

'Well, hopefully.'

I laugh, then add, 'I've got an early tomorrow.'

'Don't worry, I'll be as quiet as a mouse,' she says marching her fingers across the counter.

'A little mouse with clogs on,' I sing at her.

Becks gets ready for her date and I vet her outfits until we were both happy that she's looking as good as it gets. As usual half the stuff is mine but she always looks better in them than I do so I don't begrudge her – much.

We leave the flat together, her to meet Greg and me to an EFT session with one of my service users, Lil Robbins. She lives quite close so it was just a convenient quick trot across town. I have some new plans for Lil that I'm keen to try.

6

Hunting, sniffing, trapping

He'd agreed to go out with some work colleagues, not because he liked them – he didn't – but in order to get drunk. If he got very drunk he would sleep tonight, a deep dreamless sleep.

The bar they went to was heaving, with a sea of sweating jostling people, so noisy he can't understand what anyone says to him. So he just drinks and nods. He doesn't need to speak, they were so keen to tell him all about their lives.

The man beside him is telling a joke. Everyone leans forward to hear, their red faces and stinking breath crowding in on him, the obscene stickiness of the thick orange varnish on their table further adding to his sense of claustrophobia. His breath comes out in a rush as everyone leans back for the belly laugh of the punch line. He joins in with false high laughter; he doesn't want to stand out as the one not participating in the ritual. His gaze wanders even as he nods and pretends to listen. There are women everywhere. Barely covered, flushed faced women. He goes to the toilets, pushing up close to some of them, their soft skin brushing his arms, the stirrings of an erection pushing against his jeans. When he heads back, some of the men are up near the bar flirting with girls. He joins in; it's expected by the group. It makes his head feel hot and light. It's easy; they only need him to say a few words. He got to lean close to be heard above the noise, to press his face in their hair and drink deep from their aromas. And they laugh and laugh, thinking it's all one long big happy joke.

When time is called he stumbles out into the street with the others, slapping each other's backs in congratulations, before going their separate ways. Even though it's late the air was warm. A heatwave, someone had said. It makes people looser, wilder; drinking more and talking more. He doesn't want to go home just yet. He still feels hot and elated.

Walking the streets, stumbling a little, he begins to get his senses more under control with every step. Everything is becoming sharper with a bright edge to it. It's a feeling he recognises, he didn't think he would want to tonight, but the women in the bar, one in particular, had brought the feeling on – the urge to hunt.

Hunting; just thinking about it makes him giggle, an oddly childlike sound even to his ears. Yes, he was going to do this. He hadn't hunted here in this city, in these busy streets, and he has a hunch it would be easy. The women took such risks, they acted like they owned the place; wearing next to nothing, tottering in ridiculous heels. Who could run in those? Quickening his pace, he scans the streets for the dark shaded places where he can duck inside and take his time. He wants only the right girls. The ones that shone the brightest.

It's never dark here, there's always some light. Yellow electric light flooding everything with its putrid sickness. Standing in a dark doorway he knows he is invisible to the people walking past. They come in groups, some pressed together, noisy as geese. Others in pairs, quieter, heads pushed close together talking, breathing in each other's stink. Everyone talks here, he finds it hard to imagine they really have that much to say. Just loose hot air. Vacuous chatter, lies and deceits, all trying to look bigger than they are. Sickening unreal people, they make him want to laugh, only they're not worth the effort.

When it suits him, he leans out to snatch a view up and down the street, to see if he can spot a straggler. When one passes he pushes forward, inhaling until he catches the scent of one of the bright ones. Those he might choose to follow, for as long as he can, drinking them in.

A girl passes his darkness. Leaning forward he breathes in her essence.

She's so bright that he almost falters, but his instinct takes over and he steals out of the dark to follow her.

Her scent is intoxicating, he has to get closer. Breathing her in, washing her pure light over him until he glows too, a silent inner glow like the white-hot coals in the fire.

Now he can feel the beast within welling up to fill him. It will have most of the pleasure, and some will be his too. The beast is his compass; it makes the final choices.

There were girls before, where he used to live. He tried the other way, the way they all seem to do it, with all that talking. But the girls always changed, shrinking back from his touch, and then it was too late. He would have liked to get to know one of them. Get close and make it last longer, have a chance to feel more intimate. Only they all expected so much, he didn't know what they wanted. They would whine and complain, telling him that he just didn't understand, didn't he love them? He tried saying it, *I love you*, only it sounded all wrong and it hurt him inside. Maybe they could tell by his face because the words only made it worse and they would shout until some darker part of him rose up and silenced them. So now he kept to himself, except when one of the bright ones crossed his path when he is hunting, and then he couldn't resist.

This one is idling, stopping to look at her reflection in shop windows. She makes it too easy for him to step close and drink in her intoxicating perfume.

But she turns, confronting him.

'Are you following me?'

He doesn't know what to say so he nods.

'Fucking creep,' she says. 'Stay away from me.' Pulling her phone out of her pocket she points it at him like a knife. 'I'll call the police. Now fuck off.'

The beast growls displaying its status and she shows the whites of her eyes. She's not so brave now that she has heard the power within him. She's just a child compared to this greatness. It rose up filling the whole of him until he shrank back behind its shadow, engulfed by the pulse of its fury. *I am just a child too*, he thinks, *powerless to the rush of blood pounding in my ears.* The feeling is so good that no drug, no amount of alcohol, has ever taken him this high. The deafening pulse of the beast's heartbeat, fast and strong, filled the world with its heat.

Pulling her into the dark of a shop entrance and the deep unlit sleeve of the corridor beyond, the beast covers her mouth, biting into her ear just enough to hold her still. A deep rumbling growl swells in its throat. He and the beast are as one. This girl is theirs to do with as they please.

But she does not submit.

She's squealing and squirming. So she will learn.

Biting into her cheek, soft and sweet, its juice fills their mouth and they swallow the bitter nectar.

The beast will bite and bite until she submits. It's the pain that'll hold her still, bringing calm to her thrashing limbs.

It is the way.

7

Lil Robbins is a lovely woman. Overweight and homebound. The two problems exacerbate each other. If she got out more she might not be so fat. If she wasn't so fat she might not feel so scared of going out.

Lil is agoraphobic, she's been like that for at least thirty-five years. She hasn't left the house at all for about twenty-five years. We're working together with EFT to see if we can find the trigger that started off her fear.

On the surface, she's a perfectly nice, sociable person with lots of hobbies and interests. Obviously underneath there are underlying problems. I first met Lil when I was sent round for her care work. Being so overweight has created some secondary problems, including diabetes, and she can't get up her stairs anymore. A nurse visits every week too, but she was one of my regulars and I pop round a couple of days a week to see how she's doing. I don't think she holds out much hope that I'll be up to helping her, though I know she enjoys the extra company and conversation.

Letting myself into her little red brick council house after getting the key from the key-safe, I try and stop her little dogs from scratching my legs to shreds. As it's a hot evening, I'm still in my denim shorts: bad choice. Lil's dogs are some of the ugliest I've ever seen. They look like they've been created with a child's flipbook; head of a pug, tail of a baboon. She loves them to bits.

They follow me into her cramped sitting room; the air is suffused with body odours, and every surface boasts some of her unusual craftwork.

'Oooo, hello, Astrid.' Lil is flushed and sweating with just a T-shirt and a large pair of knickers on.

It can be a shock the first time you meet her, but with her size and overheated body temperature, it's the only way she can get comfortable, especially in this weather.

Her two abominations jump up on the couch with her as I'm enfolded in a warm damp hug. She feels soft and welcoming like a big feather duvet.

'You okay?' I ask.

'All the better for seeing you. Awful news today,' she says with glee.

Lil is a fan of any news programmes, she has Sky and there's a ticker-tape that runs a constant stream of text along the bottom of her telly screen.

'I haven't seen any TV,' I say sitting down beside her.

'Fighting abroad, some poor fool blew themselves up for the sake of religion. And a nasty attack on a girl, right here in Bristol.' She purses her lips and shakes her head, sucking on a sweet morsel of other people's miseries.

Half the battle with Lil is to get her thinking about the positive and not the negative. 'What are you making today?' I ask peering into her lap.

She holds up a fine piece of needlepoint depicting a pair of children who might be Hansel and Gretel skipping hand in hand through a meadow of flowers and butterflies in glowing iridescent colours.

'I don't know how you do it.'

She grins. 'Keeps me fingers busy.'

'You could sell some of it on eBay or Etsy,' I say. 'You're very clever with your artwork, I bet people would snap it up.'

'Oh, I don't know.' Her face clouds.

Stupid me, she was worried now about how to get to the post office. 'Not to worry, I like seeing them. Shall we get started?'

She nods and I get each of us a glass of water before sitting down and opening up my notes.

'Any aches and pains?' I ask.

Considering for a moment she says, 'Nothing more than the usual, but I haven't been sleeping well. Not in this hot weather.'

'Has that come up since our last session, the sleeping I mean?' I ask.

Lil nods. 'I think so.'

'Good, that shows we are definitely getting somewhere.'

As Lil's on a lot of medication, I worry that our work together isn't getting through to her subconscious. It's like pushing through damp blankets, especially the antidepressants. We do her checklist, twenty set questions that tell me where she was emotionally and physically at the moment. As always, Lil's scores are low because of her constant anxiety. Finished, I tuck the list away for next time.

'Last week we talked about your mother. Would you like to work further on that?' I ask.

Lil's mother was very controlling from how she comes across, but only out of the need to bring up four children on a horribly tight budget. I get the impression Lil was frightened of her. From what she's told me, I think she was a sensitive child who always tried to hide out of the way.

'Can you describe your feelings for your mother when you were little?'

Turning her head, Lil looks out the back window. It's not quite dark yet and I follow her gaze at her overgrown garden. It could be such a nice garden, but even that's a step too far for her now.

Her voice small, Lil says, 'Mum said I was a nasty dirty little girl.'

'Why was that?'

'I'd been digging in the garden, hunting for bugs. I took my shoes off before I came in the house, but my hands were muddy, I got it on the taps.'

'You were trying to wash them, trying to be clean?' I ask, making a quick note on my pad.

'But I still made a mess. She didn't seem to like me much.' Lil says this last, peering round at me, her eyes sad.

'I'm sure your mum loved you.' *She was very busy and didn't want any mess though – poor things, both of you.* 'Shall we work on that then? Even though I have this sadness when I made a mess and Mum got cross, that's alright.'

It should be, "I deeply and completely love and accept myself," but Lil can't say that just yet so I have got her to say "that's alright" instead. My teachers have said for some people it takes a lot of work to get to the point of saying that they love and accept themselves; that makes me so sad. But having been through the process myself, I know that just saying that bit can be difficult at first. I wasn't feeling exactly lovable when I first found EFT, thanks to Nick and my mother, and – despite his best efforts – Dad too. We've all been through it, somewhere down the line.

We work through the phrases together, Lil mirroring my tapping actions. It sounds simplistic, but we're working on the child in Lil, the one that got hurt and the emotions that got trapped in her body. Those trapped hurts can cause all kinds of problems for the adult Lil. It's easier to get at the adult problems once you've released the child's ones.

‘Okay, I think we’ve done brilliantly. Now I’d like to try something a little deeper. It’s called Matrix Re-imprinting,’ I say, digging in my bag for one of my books. I show her the front cover and she makes a face. ‘What we’re going to do is take one of your memories, maybe the one we’ve been working on today, and change it for a nice memory. What do you think?’

‘Don’t see how you can do that,’ she says.

‘It’s pretty much the same as we have been doing with the tapping, but I want you to imagine that you’re talking to yourself as a little girl when your mum got cross. You’ll have your eyes closed and I’ll tap on you. While I tap I want you to imagine you’re tapping on yourself as a little girl, but we’ll both say the set-up line. You want to give it a try?’

‘Not sure I understand, but I’ll give it a go.’

‘Okay, shut your eyes and imagine you can see you, as a little girl, coming in from the garden all muddy. Can you see yourself, Lil?’ Lil had shut her eyes and I held her hand, ready to start the first phase of the tapping.

Lil nods. ‘Got my yellow trousers on and my red sandals. I can see my white ankle socks, only they’re not white anymore.’

‘That’s great, Lil, can you see the garden?’

‘Yes, it’s a lovely sunny day full of butterflies and I’ve been digging. Mum’ll be ever so cross. Oh, I’m feeling all scaredy now,’ says Lil. I feel her hand tremble.

‘That’s okay, because you’re here, grown-up Lil, to help little Lil. Can you speak to her, that muddy little girl?’

‘Oh I don’t know, I feel a bit silly.’

‘Don’t mind me, talk to the little girl. Ask why she’s scared.’

‘Alright then. What’s the matter, sweetie, why are you frightened?’ Lil still has her eyes tightly closed and I see her nod. ‘She says she’s scared of Mummy.’

‘Okay, great. Now we’re going to tap on that little girl. I’ll tap on you, and you imagine you are tapping on her. We’ll use a slightly different set-up line. You just copy what I say.’

And that’s what we do. I tap on Lil as I speak, ‘Even though I got muddy digging in the garden and made Mummy cross, that’s completely alright,’ and Lil copied my words. Even when I change it slightly to ‘I completely accept myself,’ she’s able to say that too.

‘That’s brilliant, Lil. Now we can change the memory a bit. How about something lovely like you go and wash your hands and then you and your mummy do some baking together.’ I see a slight smile light Lil’s face. ‘Did you ever do baking with your mum?’

‘Sometimes. She made a lovely Victoria sponge.’

And so we tap the new memory onto Lil’s little self. With prompts from Lil, we invent a new memory, of a loving mother who was happy to make a cake with her little girl.

When we’ve finished, I hand Lil her water and see that she’s smiling.

‘How did that feel?’ I ask.

‘Really, really nice,’ she says. ‘Much better to remember her like that. She could be a lovely mum when she could spare us the time.’

‘And what happens when you think about digging in the garden?’

Putting her head on one side Lil considers for a moment. Then she looks surprised. ‘I can smell cake.’

One of her little dogs starts barking and scratching at the back door.

‘Oh dear, poor thing must be desperate,’ she says heaving herself up off the couch. She took a few heavy steps to the door, once white, now yellowed and deeply scratched down near the bottom by her pets’ small claws. As soon as she opens it, both little mutts dash past her legs and out into the garden. Lil gazes after them. She glances back at me, then steps over the threshold and out of view.

By the time I get home, the sun is completely gone and the moon is large, halfway up on the horizon with a star shining brightly beside it. It's going to be a clear glittering night. I'm still on a high after the success with Lil and humming under my breath. Looking at the hallway letter boxes, I see there's something posted in my slot that I hadn't noticed earlier. One of the items is a card telling me I have a parcel to collect. Damn, now I'll have to get up even earlier to be able to get my parcel before my first client. And there's a letter from the bank. My heart sinks.

I take my mail up to the flat and open the letter once I'm sitting at the breakfast bar. It's an overdraft notice and more, explaining that they didn't pay my direct debit for the mortgage, again. The letter alone cost thirty-four quid, just to add salt to the wound.

With my throat tight and eyes stinging, misery runs through me. I just don't have enough money, even with Becks' rent. Nick's right, we need to talk. Maybe I should face facts, I can't afford this place. But, if we sell, I'll never raise another mortgage on my salary. And with current house prices at a low, I'd probably lose my deposit money. Not just any old money, but what Nan left me in her will, an amazing fifteen grand. It doesn't sound like a lot to most people, but I know how hard it must have been for her to save up that money for me, so I could have a start in life. I don't think she had a lot of faith in Dad being able to help me. If just for Nan's sake, I need to hang in there if I can.

My mobile starts ringing, it's Dad. 'Hi,' I say trying to keep the sadness out of my voice.

'Hey baby, how's it going?'

I burst into tears, a useless but natural reaction to parental kindness.

'That good!' he says.

'I'm behind on the mortgage,' I wail.

'Sell up, come live with me.'

That's the last place I want to be. I make a derogatory sound.

'And I love you too.' His voice has a smile in it, but I can hear the hurt too.

'Sorry, Dad, but twenty-five and living at home, no thanks.'

'Boomerang kids. Everyone's doing it.'

'Maybe, just not this one.'

'Come over and play some tunes. Have dinner with me, knock back some beer. You know you want to.'

Thinking about me on my tenor recorder and him on his guitar makes me smile. I miss those sorts of times. They were good, just not that frequent.

'Another day maybe,' I say.

'Always so busy. Look, I'm sure I can scrape something together,' he says.

'No, Dad, it's okay. I'll ring them, I'm a big girl now.'

'You'll always be my baby.'

'Night, Dad.'

He'd phoned at the right time. I feel gloomy now, but not at my wit's end anymore. I'm twenty-five, for fuck's sake, I could make a phone call and sort this out.

That's what I promised myself, after I'd come out of all the pain – after everything – that I'd be grown-up now, take charge of my life, and look after number one.

8

Dream

It's dark, but a nice comforting dark. I'm curled up in a lap – Mum's maybe – and she's humming a tune I don't think I recognise. Only in the way of dreams, I know the words and start to sing along.

'Sweet sweet pretty dreamer,
Love and hold me; rock, rock cry,
We sing, we cry, we die, we fly,
Hush, hush cry.'

My voice sounds light and lovely so that I'm startled when a hand clamps over my mouth.

'Hush hush, child,' the woman says close to my ear and I breathe in her scent of spices, and something floral, overpowering in its sweetness. I can taste the nectar in my mouth.

She's putting something sweet in my mouth, silencing my song with honey.

9

My alarm is horribly early. I still feel warm and loved after my dream; my tongue roves around my mouth hunting for the sweet honey taste that just about lingers there. What weird words. I sing them through in a whisper. They'd sounded so perfect last night whereas now they're just odd. I make a few quick notes in my dream book. I'll write it up fully later, no time now. Note to self: not getting things done is becoming a bit of a habit.

Tiptoeing around, being careful not to wake Becks, I have a quick cup of tea. Not sure why I'm being so considerate because I'm pretty sure I didn't hear her come home last night. Putting on my beanie hat, the grey and navy broad striped one, I stuff the reminder card from the post office in my pocket, grab up my rucksack and shoulder bag and set out for the day.

Because it's Saturday the queue for the post office is long, trailing up along the pavement before even getting inside the tiny outer collection office. I stand there fighting down my impatience, chewing on my nail and double-checking the time on my phone. I really don't have time for this. There's an eighties song stuck in my brain by Kajagoogoo. Probably a spin-off from the dream. I keep muttering, 'Hush hush,' and I'm conscious of other people's glances. Just great.

When I eventually get to the desk the packet is tiny. I'm pretty sure it would fit through the letter box. Slipping it into my jacket pocket, I speed walk to the bus stop. I'm going to drop by Mrs P's first.

After I've fed Sir Lancelot and the gull, I sit down on the sofa and open my parcel. A small glass bottle of what I guess is perfume oil in a pretty baby blue box decorated with white star-like flowers and foreign writing. There was also a letter:

"My darling Astrid,

We are in Bucharest! Quite charming, old and rundown. Peter has been transferred temporarily as the British Ambassador is unwell and sent home to London for an operation. So this is a sort of promotion until he's back on his feet.

I thought you might like this perfume. It's a local product made from a blend of Romanian flowers, one of which is edelweiss. When you wear it think of us singing along together to the Sound of Music when you were small.

Please fly out and stay with us, the boys would love to see you.

Your always loving,

Mother"

My gut cringes at the word fly. I'd had a particularly vivid dream about being on a crashing aeroplane in my teens and I've dreaded flying ever since. I've never set foot in a plane, and so far, no amount of EFT has changed that. Although I've explained this to my mother countless times, she just sees it as another excuse to stay away from her, her husband Peter and my two half-brothers, Stephan and Dane. I know her and her family better through Facebook than real life, for God's sake. My feelings towards my brothers are mixed. They are so much younger than me, both in their early teens. I would have liked to have known them. What only child doesn't fantasise about siblings? But they also represented the solid form of my mother's abandonment.

Her letter is a pleasure that also brought pain. Especially how she signed off – 'your always loving Mother' – don't make me laugh! Mother is new too; she wanted to be called by her first name, Mette, before she met Peter and had the boys. She used to think that being called Mummy sounded old. Perhaps she likes being old now?

Opening the perfume, I sniff. The aroma is like mountain air, fresh, light, with a delicate floral edge. I really like it, she's got something right for once. I dab a bit on my wrists and behind my ears before popping the bottle back in my pocket and heading off for my first appointment.

'Hi, Astrid.'

It's Shanna. We're doing a double this morning to wash and dress Audrey. Audrey's daughter, Sarah, hovers nearby pretending to straighten up an already perfect room. She appreciates the help, but she's so used to caring for her elderly mother, she can't quite hand over the reins just yet.

Shanna and I wear thin latex gloves like surgeons; we talk to Audrey as we work, explaining what we are about to do. She doesn't respond other than to shrink in fear when we roll her on her side. Audrey is beyond conversation, her reactions now are pure animal instinct. We talk to each other too as we wash, dry and change her.

'Cody's got a job,' says Shanna.

'Oh,' I say glancing up to meet her heavily lashed eyes. I've got to know the ins and outs of Cody in the short once or twice a week job slots with Shanna.

'It's with a firm out at Avonmouth. Bit of a trek, but not too bad.'

'That's good,' I say trying to scratch my nose with my wrist.

'It's just factory production line stuff, boring really, but he's been so down, not being able to find anything,' says Shanna combing through Audrey's sparse candyfloss hair.

I button up Audrey's cardigan, beige again today. Everything in this room is beige or brown. It adds to the general feeling of old and tired. 'Day or nights?'

'Half an' half. That'll be the difficult bit when he's on the nights. Makes me wonder if we'll see each other at all. We'll be like ships passing in the night,' she says.

'It's a start.'

'True. He says most of the people he saw working there are foreign, Polish and Romanian and the like. Makes you wonder, doesn't it, and he's been out of work almost two years now,' says Shanna removing her rubber gloves with care not to damage her long acrylic nails.

We chat like that for the next ten minutes as we finish tidying up around Audrey, then I block out Shanna's chatter while I fill the service user's notes.

We say goodbye to Sarah and Audrey, and then head off to our appointments in different directions. I've got Pauline next.

Pauline's house is yellow. A soft yellow bungalow with a sunny butter yellow door. Number nine. The number gets caught in my mind like a CD glitch, endlessly repeating itself. I know it's from something Dad used to play, I just can't remember which.

Her door is always bright and clean, the colour complemented by the polished brass fittings. I stab her code into the key-safe box, get the key and let myself in. The hall is yellow iris patterned wallpaper and the carpet is mustard lit to a golden glow by the sunlight streaming in through the hall window.

I always feel warm here.

'Pauline, it's Astrid,' I call, hanging my jacket and hat on one of the coat hooks. Opening her bedroom door I check she's awake as it's still early, only just after eight. Pauline is propped up in bed, her toothless mouth open in a cavernous snore. I leave her and go make her breakfast. She's on a liquid diet, high protein drinks mixed with milk. I don't know why and have never asked. Taking it through to the bedroom I find her awake with her teeth in.

Pauline is also one of my EFT testers. She gets a frozen shoulder and she finds tapping on the pain very helpful.

'How are you this morning?' I ask as I struggle to find a clear spot amongst the clutter on her bedside table for her breakfast drink.

'Sore,' she says wincing as she struggles to pull herself up on her pillows. 'My shoulder was aching so bad last night I had to sleep propped up like this.'

'Shall I get you an Ibuprofen?'

'Be a love.'

I get the painkiller with her other morning meds and watch as she pops them on her pale fur-coated tongue, knocking them back with a gulp of breakfast drink.

'Shall we tap on it?'

Pauline nods and I sit on the edge of the bed. She repeats along with me a set-up line while mirroring my tapping motions as I run through all the meridian points.

'Even though I have this pain in my shoulder I completely love and accept myself.'

We repeat this until the pain has diminished to a dull ache and we can adapt the set-up line along with it. 'Even though I have this small ache in my shoulder I completely love and accept myself.'

'You know,' I say, drawing back the yellow floral curtains revealing a small paved area outside the back with a cat-sized grey statue of Puss-in-Boots forever held in mid-march across the centre. 'We could try getting rid of it completely if we did some work to find the root of your pains.'

I'd talked about this with her before, but she won't budge. She's old-fashioned and doesn't like to talk about 'personal' stuff.

'So you said. The tapping does the trick for me, but thank you, dear, for offering.'

I don't push it. It was hard enough for her to get her head around the idea that just tapping and talking could reduce pain.

When she's finished her breakfast I help her get up and into her bathroom. She sits on a plastic chair while I wash her, then we get her dressed before I help her out to her sunny sitting-room with the aid of her Zimmer frame. Her daughter is coming by later to take her out, so I leave her happy and full of expectations for the rest of her day.

I fast walk to my next two appointments, Mr Ali and Mike. They live quite close to each other so that saves me some time. Mr Ali is Turkish, he lives alone, has mild dementia that causes some complications that need to be kept track of; like cleanliness and has he remembered to eat. Sometimes his English just blows away with the wind. Confused and bewildered, he tries to communicate in Turkish – which I don't speak, so we have to resort to hand signals. He's a nice gentleman who moves with the speed of a tortoise. Actually, he reminds me of a nappy wearing giant sloth, covered in reddish-brown hair with small surprised black eyes. I make him breakfast, administer his meds and fill in the diary sheet and I do a bit of washing-up – although we're not supposed to clean – and then hurry off to Mike's house.

Mike's an alcoholic. He's cheerful and tiny. It's as if all the years of cheap cider have sucked the sap out of him, shrinking him to a wrinkled brittle shell. He looks like he's in his seventies when he's actually only forty-six.

Mike's an easy visit, the agency just sends one of us round to check he's still alive, see if he needs anything like help getting more of his two-litre bottles of alcohol back from the supermarket or, God forbid, some food. I've never seen him drunk. He just continually tops himself up from his bottle of Thunderbird and rolls another cig.

After Mike, I've got some time, so I head off towards the library. On the way, something catches my eye. A collection of snow globes.

They shine with a light all of their own.

I go inside the shop and mooch around, trailing my fingers over the top of the display items until my feet bring me to *their* display. Ten little snow globes. Each containing a tiny log cabin with seven tiny elflike characters set around it employed at various tasks.

When I leave there are only nine.

Settling myself into my usual spot at the library, I get my book out of my rucksack. It's the one Carey got for me on Matrix Re-imprinting. Carey's my mentor, she's also the one who got me started on EFT and all this. I found her on a Google search when my world was falling apart and the only thing I could do coherently was cry. My mother said I should go to the doctor and get some antidepressants. Having seen what they've done to Dad, they were the last thing I wanted. Trawling the therapy pages and YouTube demonstrations I'd come across EFT. Fascinated, I searched for a practitioner working close to me and found Carey. I'd wanted to see a woman too, as men were not my favourite species at that moment. Only Carey turned out to be a bonus because she wasn't just EFT, she was into Matrix Re-imprinting too.

I open my book and get stuck in.

'Hi.'

Looking up, I feel a jolt of surprise. 'You!'

‘Sorry, I didn’t mean to give you a fright,’ says Mark and he looks at his watch. ‘This is the right time? You said eleven?’ He seems acutely embarrassed; glancing around as if he expects an audience, even though we’re both keeping our voices low, mindful that this is a reading area, not meant for social chitchat.

‘Sorry?’ What was he on about?

‘For our session.’

‘Session?’ I’m sounding like an idiot to my own ears. ‘Look, Mark, sorry you’ve lost me here.’

Pulling his mobile out of his pocket he scrolls through his screen and nods to himself before turning it for me to see – ‘hi Mark, tomorrow 11 at Bristol Central Library. I would love you to be one of my test subjects, thanks a million. Astrid.’

Blinking I stare up into his expectant bright eyes. Bloody Becks, that’s what she had been doing with my bag.

‘Look, Mark.’

‘Actually, it’s Marku,’ he says smiling.

‘What?’

‘My name, it’s Romanian. It’s really Marku, people just tend to shorten it.’

‘You don’t have an accent,’ I say.

‘I was adopted. I’ve been in England since I was about seven.’

Intrigued, I point to the chair next to me and he sits down, never taking his gaze off my face.

‘So is that why you want EFT, because of…’ I search for the right words. ‘Issues from having been adopted?’

‘No, my parents were great, really good people. From what I read on the web they rescued me from a lot of pain.’

‘So?’

‘I’m not sleeping.’

I carefully study his face. He looks great to me. Better than great, but I could see there were dark circles under those black lashed eyes. 'How long?' I ask.

'Weeks now. Sometimes I have a couple of good nights and then it starts again. I wake up about two or three in the morning and then I can't go back for hours. It's exhausting.' He twitches and shifts around in his chair as if his body needs to show me just how uncomfortable his insomnia had made him.

'Much stress at work?'

'Only the usual, nothing to stay awake over.'

'Do you drink a lot of coffee?'

'I didn't used to, but just lately…' he trails off.

I put my head on one side, considering. 'Are you okay if we do a checklist?'

He makes that funny expression I'd seen him do in the pub and my stomach flips, he's just too cute.

'I'm going to ask you some questions and make some notes. See if we can't work out what set off your insomnia,' I say rubbing my palms down my thighs as they seem hot and sweaty all of a sudden. Seeing his gaze drop to my lap I quickly search my bag for a notebook.

'Alright,' he says but I think his face shows discomfort. Awkward in fact; he really is shy; he must be suffering if he was prepared to put himself through this.

'They aren't anything too personal. Just scores from one to ten on how you're feeling right now,' I say. I head a page with his name. 'Mark?'

'Osbourne.'

'Marku Osbourne,' I say as I write it.

'Just Mark is fine.'

'Okay.' I cross out the 'u'.

I start with the usual lists, how he feels, grading himself from one to ten. His scores are okay, not great, middling, but if he hasn't been sleeping that's to be expected.

'Any changes in your life lately, since the sleeplessness started?'

'No. Not that I can think of. Except the building work,' he says, frowning.

'What's that?'

'The office next to ours has a massive refurb going on. Builders everywhere. I can hear them shouting at each other all day long, even above the air con. It's irritating because I can't understand them, I think they're all Eastern European or something.'

'I can imagine. Anything else?'

'No.'

'And what wakes you in the middle of the night, what are your first thoughts when you wake?'

'Dreams, nightmares really. I wake up scared, but I can't remember what they were about,' he says squirming in his seat, his hands clasped in his lap, fingers knotting and un-knotting.

Ah, now we are getting somewhere. 'What do you remember of the orphanage?' I say pinning him still with a searching look. He smiles a little at me before his expression shifts back to business.

'Nothing. Before my parents brought me to England it's a blank.'

Nodding to myself I scribble some notes, I feel him leaning close trying to decipher my spider crawl and shut the book with a snap, that sits him up straight again.

'Okay. I think we should start by tapping on the dreams that wake you up, maybe make them less strong so they won't have such an impact on you. Does that sound okay?'

He nods.

'I'll tap with my fingers like this,' I say demonstrating. 'And you copy what I'm doing.' I run through the routine to show him which areas we would be tapping on. 'It takes a few rounds to get used to it.'

He nods, his face drawn in concentration. I fight the urge to peek around me. People must wonder just what the hell we're doing. We're both talking in low murmurs so as not to annoy other library users, but they must be intrigued. A grin is threatening to spread itself across my face and I cough in my hand as a cover to quashing it. Thankfully Mark is engrossed in what we're doing and doesn't notice.

'Repeat after me,' I say. 'Even though I wake up in the night with these scary nightmares, I completely love and accept myself.'

He'd been murmuring the lines along with me but now he stops speaking and pulls a new facial expression I hadn't seen yet, one that I guess expresses deep embarrassment.

'Can you say "I completely love and accept myself"?' I ask.

He shakes his head and looks pained.

'That's fine, we can work on that another time. Lots of people can't. We'll use "I'm alright" instead.'

I start another round. He stumbles a bit over the words at first, and we're still talking in whispers, even so, I can feel the prickle of curious glances. I decided to up the pace a bit by changing the set-up line to, 'Even though I have these horrible scary dreams that frighten me awake in the night, that's alright.' His eyes widen but he still follows my words and actions through the routine. 'Even though these terrifying dreams wake me in the night and stop me from sleeping, that's alright.'

'Even though I have these dreams,' I say, tapping next to my eyebrow.

'Even though I have these dreams,' he repeats copying my tapping on his own face.

'These terrible dreams that wake me up,' I say tapping my cheekbone just below my eye.

'These terrible dreams that wake me up,' he repeats.

‘And I can’t sleep because I’m so afraid.’

‘And I… I can’t sleep because I… I… I am so… so afraid.’

His voice begins to quiver and his body shakes. His eyes fill with tears and his teeth are chattering so hard he can’t say the words properly.

Leaning forward I push his hands down into his lap and then, peering into his wide streaming eyes, I tap on his meridian points for him. ‘Even though I feel this strong emotion that’s shaking my body I am safe and everything is completely and utterly alright,’ I say over and over as I tap all the points, in turn, shortening to just, ‘I am safe and everything is alright.’ As I run through this a couple of times his body begins to calm, the shaking stops and he closes his eyes. Then to my surprise, he wraps his arms around me, buries his face in my neck and sobs.

I hug him back, it seems the only human thing to do. His grip is strong and he smells of musky man; a good smell, one I now realise how much I miss.

Coughing he straightens and lets go of me.

Sitting back in my seat I look at him but he avoids my eyes.

‘Sorry,’ he says, so low I almost miss it.

‘No Mark, that was good, really good. You tapped into something, quite literally.’

He risks a glance at me. ‘I don’t usually…’

All of my practice people had been women and they sometimes cried. They did get a bit embarrassed by their emotions, but my heart goes out to him. I guess this was a first for both of us.

‘Let’s just round off with some exercises to get back into a good place,’ I say and start tapping with a new set-up line. I nod at him and he mirrors my actions mumbling the words under his breath. ‘I feel alright because I’m in a good and safe place.’

The words sink in after a few rounds and he draws a deep breath, wipes his face and sits up straighter in his chair. When I feel he's back to his old self I stop and rootle in my rucksack for my water bottle.

'Here,' I say. 'Drink this.'

He looks surprised but takes it from me anyway.

'Water helps after a session otherwise you might get a headache,' I say as I watch him drink.

Giving the bottle back, he says, 'I hadn't expected anything like that.'

'People react in different ways. It shows there is definitely something going on with those dreams of yours. Your subconscious knows, we just need to bring it to the surface so we can unravel and clear it.'

He's nodding but looking confused.

'When are you free to meet again?' Despite my earlier reservations, I'm hooked. He's fascinating.

'Can it be somewhere more private?' he says, glancing around us for emphasis.

I think for a moment. 'You could come to my flat?'

'Okay.'

I write down my address on a bit of spare paper and we fix a date for the day after tomorrow.

'I must get back to work now,' I say sticking out my hand.

Clasping it in a strong grip, he pulls me into a hug.

'You smell amazing,' he says into my hair.

I laugh. 'It's Romanian perfume my mother sent me. Maybe your subconscious recognised it.'

'Who knows,' he says, smiling.

'Your subconscious knows everything,' I say.

10

Hunting, sniffing, trapping

He comes out of the cool shadows of the building and turns his face to the strong heat of the midday sun. With his eyes closed, he can see it as a blood-red ball blazing against his eyelids. A bubble of happiness fills him up so completely, he thinks he might rise up like an untethered helium balloon. This place, this city, it is the best of all places – and he knows, he has roamed through so many. He let his thoughts fly in a multitude of joy.

He has found her, the perfect one.

She shines out and calls him to her; he knows her by her scent, that intoxicating perfume, the same wonderful fragrance that belonged to his only one, his dear one. As these thoughts fill his head he almost skips across the soft grass of College Green and playfully chases into the air a strutting group of pigeons.

All the others are dust in comparison; he spits their dirty dust from his mouth. A woman turns her face away as he spat an ugly blob at her feet, and he laughs at her scuttling back. Then his pace slows as graver thoughts seep through.

But he knows he must go slow and careful because she requires the greatest of care. She is like a delicate piece of the finest porcelain; nothing must disturb her on that pedestal he views her on, no grubby fingerprints from low-life kinds, and no dirty ideas to blemish her, his queen.

He shakes his head as he mutters his thoughts aloud. *He won't risk losing her, not this time, not like the others. They had enraged the thing within and been sucked down into the dark, taking their lovely light with them.*

Nodding to himself, because now the path is becoming clear in his mind, he increases his pace across the lawns towards the pavement. He turns left and walks up Park Street, seeing nothing of those around him, his thoughts alive in his mind. *So he must hide her from it until he has her somewhere safe from interruption. He mustn't risk it being near her, not until she understands. And she will understand because she is good and clever, he can tell. Then all will be well, just like it was before when the world made sense. He can rest and she will soothe him. He so needs to rest, but the beast within wouldn't permit it. It hungers for the hunt. It demands the shining ones. It wants what he wants, all of them together again, their special family. He has looked for so long now, searching for his lost love ones. Only then will there be peace.*

Now he had found her he will follow, careful, careful not to be seen. He'll get to know all there is to learn about her. He'll know her inside and out. Her light and her dark, her soft and her hard. She can only be his. Her brightness will shine just for him. And then for it, it will not be denied.

But he will not let it taste until he is sure, completely sure, that after all this time, all the wasted hunts, that he has found her. His one, his only one.

His heart swells with the joy of it, so impossibly big, surely his heart will burst and he will bleed out right here in the centre of Bristol.

Only she can understand, and become one with him. They could be whole, he knew, as it was before. He would bring his family together again.

Where there is pain there is light.

Where there is light there can only be love.

But for now, he will stay quiet and go unnoticed. He could be invisible when he wanted. Like the wolf, he was silent and swift as the wind.

No one knew his purpose.

No one suspected.

Putting in the earbuds of the iPod his feet march in rhythm as the music engulfs him. The sweet heavy beat of 'Monster' by Imagine Dragons is so clear, the band could be playing right beside him. Their words are him. It's as if someone has looked inside his head and written down what they saw there. *Could there be others, like him?* Impossible. He knows that an elite few are called to the hunt, just as he is, but he's unique, they all are. He was made, hand-crafted by the love of Felicia, to be what he is. Pain at the thought of her – his one, his love – shoots through him as a burning shaft. Mother, teacher, playmate, and lover – she was all. Thoughts of his childhood came like a spliced movie scene. Hunting with Felicia. Their special secret meetings in the dark empty corridors at the top of their home. Treats she kept just for them, her chosen ones. Sweet treats of honey, sometimes dipped in hard dry cheese, sometimes on the tip of her finger. Those small extra morsels were what kept her special pets above the others, those small malnourished forgotten creatures. They were only good for one thing – prey. Prey for Felicia and her cubs. That's what she had called them, her cubs. They were a pack, a family, just like wolves. They cared for one another and they hunted for one another. Felicia sent them off, her cubs, to corner their next plaything. It was usually one of the smaller, weakest children. They herded it along the corridors with kicks and pinches as it scuttled – snivelling, desperate to get away – up the stairs onto the forgotten corridors of their domain.

Then Felicia would show them all the faces of love. Bitter-sweet love. Where to bite, to hold them still, and which places on those little bodies held the richest perfumes. Those dark unspoken pleasures that only they could know. He always got to choose Felicia's treats. She said he was a natural at picking off the very best for her to tame. But woe betide them if they came back empty-handed.

Those had been the golden days of his childhood. Felicia was the light that shone in a dark grim world of the unwanted forgotten children.

Then one day she had gone and taken her light with her. First, they had stolen his little cub brother, and then his mother. Something inside him had torn apart and the beast rose up to fill the hole she had left. He still played the game, with himself as the leader, but it hadn't been the same without her. It was all he knew and it gave him some measure of comfort.

Only now, after all this time, he has found another who shone with her brightness. He won't lose her again, he won't go back into that world of loneliness.

11

It seems that my subconscious is with Mark for the rest of the day – I just can't get him out of my head – he's so intriguing. He seems shy, and yet warm and affectionate too. I love his floppy dark hair and those eyes! They're to die for. And when he hugged me: I liked it, much more than I'd like to admit. I've got an appointment with Carey later. I'll talk some of it through with her.

My lunch and teatime work visits pass quick enough and then by five I'm at Carey's dusk rose-pink door. We try to meet up at least once a month, so I can work on myself and discuss where I am with my course, ask questions and be assessed. Mark is still in the forefront of my mind and the first thing off my lips as I enter her pretty sitting room, painted in a calming pale duck-egg blue, which doubles as the consulting room.

'I met this man,' I say before I can even get my rucksack off.

Carey smiles, her large grey eyes crinkling at the corners. 'That sounds positive.'

Taking off my hat, I rub my hand through my hair, airing it. 'Not like that, at least I don't want it to be like that. A new client. He has sleep issues.'

Pushing some stray blonde hair from her almost perfect bob back behind her ear, Carey points at her grey Ikea sofa, the sort that takes over a whole corner and has a sticking out bed bit at one end. Maybe some of her clients like to lie down, or perhaps it's just nice to watch telly that way. I'm tempted for a second to try it out, only she passes me a glass of water so I take it, sitting down to sip for a moment, thinking.

'He had a really strong reaction. It was only our first session, and he cried,' I say putting down my drink on her small square glass-topped coffee table.

'I expect his concern is very close to the surface, we all know when we're ready to be helped,' says Carey.

'I'm not sure, I think it shocked us both.'

'What're you worried about?' Carey comes and sits next to me on the sofa, her trim body hardly stirring the cushion beneath me, and peers into my eyes, a deep searching look so that I have to glance away before I can answer.

'I think he likes me, I'm not ready for anything just yet. I want to help him though,' I say turning to meet Carey's calm gaze and searching her soul for answers. 'But, I don't want to give the wrong impression. Mostly I'm…'

Carey slow nods encouragement, never taking her scrutiny off my face.

My words come out in a rush, 'I don't want to do more harm than good, there's something… Something so strong there. What if I don't know enough to help him?'

'All you are doing is helping him lessen his pain and fears. You say his problem is sleep related? You've discussed with him ways he can help himself – cut back on coffee, hot baths, and all that kind of thing?'

I nod.

‘I think if you work with just EFT to start with, define the base of the problem, working upwards and out from there. He sounds interesting.’

Nodding I open my mouth, but she waves a fine-boned hand. ‘Let’s not get too bogged down with this one. Tell me how your existing people are doing?’

I feel a niggle of disappointment. I want to talk about Mark, I want Carey to see him like I do, only I respect that she doesn’t have a lot of time to give and this is the end of the day. She’ll be keen to get supper on the go before her family gets back. So I tell her about Lil. She’s thrilled for me.

‘Brilliant; so, with the re-imprinting, build up some more created happy memories. Did she bring anyone into the visualisation to help, someone from her past?’

‘No we didn’t do that.’

‘Next time ask her to imagine a helper, someone she feels confident about. I think that a person with Lil’s kind of issues, someone she trusted as a child to stand beside her would really help.’

We discuss how I was doing with my other case and then finally on to me.

‘I had a bit of a wobble at the weekend because Nick came round,’ I say.

‘Oh?’ She tips her head to one side.

‘I still don’t know how I feel about him. He has the power to throw me completely off balance.’

‘You need to forgive yourself, you have a lot of history with him.’

‘But I thought I dealt with all that.’

‘Some things run deeper than you can imagine. Would you like to work on that now?’

We do a few set-up lines together about Nick and my feelings for him. We turn them from a negative to a positive. Carey is a great believer in positives; she says it’s all a matter of outlook and forgiveness. I know where she's coming from; only, some things are harder to forgive than others.

'When you're ready to let it all go, all will be right,' says Carey, seeming to read my mind as usual. She can't be more than forty, but she seems to have all of life sorted. I hope I can feel like that one day.

I smile and nod but there's a lunatic scream lurking in my mind. I've got such a lot to feel angry about from my mother upwards. I'm just not quite ready to let them all off that easily.

'Yes you can,' says Carey and I open my mouth in surprise. Laughing, she pulls me into a warm hug.

As I hug her back, I know she's right, but just forgiving them feels like they got one over on me somehow.

I do feel lighter when I leave though. Carey has that effect like she's lifted a shroud from around my head and shoulders. Because I'm feeling so good, on impulse I jump on a bus and head up to Totterdown to visit my dad.

Letting myself in, I shout a greeting. The house is a jumbled mess as usual. He isn't in sight so I follow the sounds of '80s music to his den. At first he looks asleep with his head tilted back in his old brown leather swivel chair. I'm standing watching when his eyes flick open, pale washed-out grey, unfocused. He blinks a few times, sees me, and sits up, swinging the chair round to face me.

'Hello.' He beams, his face creasing into the impossible folds of a much-loved landscape. 'I didn't hear you come in.'

'Not much you could hear above this din.' I'm aware that I'm shouting louder than necessary to make the point. It annoys me, always has, putting his music up so high and shutting out the world. Leaning over his desk he turns it down. Relief floods me and I give him a hug and kiss.

'That's nice,' he says.

He has a few friends, mainly music business buddies from the past. Most of his time is spent like this, alone, bathed in music. On the wall above his desk is a poster of his band in its heyday. Banned Substance; the one-album-wonder from the early '80s. My father, spiked hair and eyeliner, is grinning out of it centre-stage with his band grouped around him. They're so young, younger than I am now. So sure of their future success, the lack of which has drained the whole of his life and, to some extent, all of those around him. My gaze is caught by a framed picture of Mum, which he's hung below it. She has pushed her face up close to the camera: grinning impish cute face, dark hair, dark elfin eyes, and snow pale flawless skin. Although the photo is in black and white, I know those eyes are deepest blue slate like the winter waters just off the Norwegian shores where she was born. I know too because I see those eyes every time I look in the mirror. She looks young and happy. That's from when they first met. She'd come over to work in the music industry and met Dad, the latest comet feted by all. To be fair, she stuck around long after the stardust had left his shoulders and he had withdrawn into a shadow of disappointed maybes. But when she went to find the success she craved, she forgot to pack me along with her chic charity shop gear. I was just more baggage associated with her failed life, the one she brushed neatly under the carpet along with most of her other associations with Dad.

'Tea?' says Dad.

'Great,' I say, straightening my mood along with my back. Carey's voice chirps in my ear, 'Positivity, Astrid, negatives take seed only if we let them.'

I follow him out to the faded kitchen. 'Yuck, Dad, don't you ever clean?'

Picking up a grimy dish sponge I wash it out and start wiping down the surfaces.

'So, have you sorted out the bank?' he says pushing cereal boxes aside to make space for our mugs by the kettle.

'Give me those,' I say snatching the mugs and rinsing them before letting him make tea. Their insides were stained a dark tannin brown. 'No, I should be doing that now only I had this crazy notion that it might be nice to come and see you.'

He laughs. It wasn't supposed to be funny, but I suppose too much '80s music can do that to you.

'What exciting plans have you got for the weekend then?' I ask.

'Oh, the usual. Off to Buckingham Palace to get my MBE. Hang with Phil, swap a few vibes, while Liz boogies with the corgis. Then I might ride a Harley the wrong way down all those one-way streets of Clifton before jamming it up with the crew on College Green.'

'Sounds good,' I say with mock gravitas.

'Actually, I do have an event. Do you remember Beanie?'

Beanie was the drummer from Banned Substance. My mind pulls up a faded memory of a scruffy man sheathed in scuffed leather who looked a bit like the Rumple character from the Netflix series *Once Upon a Time*. I learnt from Beanie that leather collects body odours. 'Mmm,' I say into my tea.

'We're meeting up tonight, at the Duke.'

'That beardy weirdy pub?'

'The very one,' he says, his eyes gleaming.

'I thought he lived in France, or somewhere?'

'Portugal. He's over for a few weeks, so we thought we'd catch up.'

‘That’s great, Dad.’ I hope it is. In the past, meeting up with people associated with that glorious part of his life tended to bring on deep pits of gloom for weeks afterwards. ‘Dad, you know I do this EFT thing. How would you like a session?’ I’d asked before, but I think we both knew that dealing with his depression might bring on my own.

‘Thanks, but no.’

I sigh. I would just have to visit more for the next few weeks, to keep an eye on him.

‘Stop that. Come and sit down, it will only get dirty again,’ says Dad tugging at my arm.

‘That’s not the point,’ I say, but I put down the sponge and follow him into the TV room. ‘Mum sent me some perfume.’ I settle myself into my favourite small battered armchair. It pongs a bit, but it’s a welcoming stink of the familiar.

‘That’s nice of her.’

It’s been long enough now that he can talk about her without any of the old acid creeping in.

‘I like it actually. It’s got Edelweiss in it and some other stuff. From Romania.’

‘Eh?’

‘That’s where they are at the moment,’ I say, omitting anything about Peter and his promotion; there *are* limits.

‘Interesting,’ he says. He sits in his chair facing me like a shop mannequin – arms out on the armrests, feet a sensible distance apart; it’s his listening pose.

‘She’s asking me to visit them.’

‘You should.’

‘She doesn’t get it.’ I feel grumpy all of a sudden. His faded maroon and brown wallpaper is scratching at my nerves. Time to push into the positive. ‘So tell me more about Beanie?’

He beams. It’s a cheap mood-lifting shot, but my dad is as easy as Pavlov’s dogs if you know which bell to ring.

‘He’s still drumming. Everyone always needs a drummer.’

‘And everyone plays lead guitar.’

Laughing he nods his head. ‘I should have been a drummer.’

‘You don’t have the temperament,’ I say.

‘Fancy a jam?’ He glances over to the corner where he keeps a collection of instruments. This was the only tidy well-organised bit of the house.

‘Okay.’

He gets his acoustic and gives me a long wooden flute. It’s an American Indian replica. It plays just like a recorder with beautiful bass tones. We shuffle about a bit, musically speaking, and then get into our stride. These are the best moments with my dad. Where we are truly together and run from the same song sheet. Love flows with that music, it’s unsaid, but felt bone-deep.

By the time I get home, I’m still riding on a wave of melodic calm. All is right with the world and I’m smiling, even the orange evening sun smiles with me.

‘You look happy.’

I can’t help a gasp of shock. I was so deep in my mood bubble I didn’t even notice Nick walking towards me. I just stand there with my arm outstretched, key pointing at the lock.

‘Are you going to use that?’ He’s grinning because he knows the effect he’s having.

Emotions flood like a tsunami. My hand shakes and I can’t get the key in the lock.

‘Here.’ He steps forward, putting his hand around mine, and unlocks the door.

I’m bereft when he releases my hand, so I squash that feeling under a lid of determination. He follows me into the hall and upstairs to the flat. We’re both silent; I couldn’t speak if I wanted to, not coherently anyway.

Entering the flat together, he makes himself at home on the couch. I feel like I need a strong drink all of a sudden. There's only beer, though, so it'll have to do.

'Beer?' I say, having positioned myself almost inside the fridge, its coldness bringing me a little closer to earth.

'Please.'

Uncapping them I join him on the couch. We drink in silence, then I have to ask. 'Where's Kate? Does she know you're here?'

He looks away. 'No.'

'Why *are* you here?' I wait, feeling impatient. I want to hit him, and pick at the label on my bottle – little rips, tiny screwed up balls, flicked towards the kitchen. They make me angry too.

'I…' He's looking at me, his eyes filled with pain.

'Nick!'

'I'm so confused,' he says staring down into his lap.

Not just me then. 'Why?' I ask him.

He looks up now and takes hold of my hand. I try to pull away but he holds firm. 'Yesterday, seeing you, I…'

I don't know what he's trying to say. My mind is going crazy.

'It's all such a mess, Azza. I've been such an idiot. And when I saw you, I just knew, I had to come and see you, to see, if there was…'

'For fuck's sake, Nick, just tell me.'

'I need to know, do you still feel anything for me? Because I think I've made a horrible mistake.'

'I… Oh.' I can't finish, my words are locked in my throat and my eyes fill with tears.

His arms are around me and he's holding me tight. His body quivers, tiny tremors passing up and down his spine. 'I miss you so much,' he says into my hair. 'I can't stand it.'

I rub his back and then his fingers are in my hair, massaging my scalp and neck. An electric surge passes through me. Somehow we're face-to-face and we just breathe, heavy and fast.

Then he's kissing me.

I have missed this so much, the surge of desire is painful. The scratch of his beard unfamiliar, yet sexy. Before I know what I'm doing I am sucking his breath into my lungs and digging my nails into his back, his thin T-shirt, little protection.

Giving a guttural sound deep in his throat he pushes me back onto the couch, my bed for so many weeks.

My legs wrap with the ease of memory around his hips. We're pushing against each other like teenagers, urgent. His hands slide inside my shirt, pushing up my bra. When he holds my breast I bite the firm flesh of his shoulder. Sucking in his breath he pushes up my top to softly bite my breast.

Gasping, my back arches.

I need him so much, all rational thought is gone.

Almost.

'Nick, stop, Nick.' Putting my hands on his chest I push him away. Struggling, he strains forward towards my body, and then stops himself and sits up.

I pull my shirt down, fighting to get my bra back over my breasts. They're damp from his mouth and the flesh protests. My body protests; it wants him, all of him. My mind is fighting with itself. 'I can't do this.' That's the rational part of my brain. I know I'm right. I spent too many months getting over him to put myself back there again. Only the need fills me; it's frightening, animal, and primeval.

He takes my hand. 'We both feel it. I'm scared too.'

Is he?

'What have you got to be scared of?' I say, pulling my hand free. I can hear the raw edge in my voice.

'We never talked, we couldn't after I left. It hurt, going, I missed you all the time,' he says. His gaze searches mine.

'But you had her!' He's making it about him again – just unbelievable, I can feel the anger and indignation bubbling up.

'You miss the point. I didn't leave you for her, I left because I was frightened about the baby. I was frightened of what it meant.' He lifts his shoulders and opens his hands in a helpless gesture. 'All of it, it would mean so many changes. Kate was just there at the right time.'

I make a face. Kate wasn't a car or a new job.

'She's not a bad person,' he says.

But I wasn't quite ready to hear that and got up to get another beer.

He follows me to the fridge. 'I never stopped loving you.'

I snort.

'Kate is a kind sweet person, but she's not you. Being away from you, it's made me understand just how much you mean to me.'

I flick the lid off my beer and throw the opener at the sink, just past his head. He flinches. I take a big swallow of my drink, hoping it'll push down some of my boiling emotions. So many conflicting emotions. And my body still craving the sex I had just denied it.

'Nick.'

His eyes are pleading like an abandoned puppy.

'I don't know how I feel. What is it you want?' I say, my voice flat.

'You, us. I want us again like it was.'

Part of me had yearned to hear this from him. I had imagined this very scene so often that now it was actually happening I was lost for words.

'Say something. Please,' he says, trying to take hold of my hand again.

I flap his groping hand away. 'Nick, I'm confused. How can I know what to say?'

'Say you want me back. Say we can go back to how it was.'

'I don't think that's possible.' And I don't, however sad he looks. Things have changed. I have changed.

'Please don't say that. We can try again.'

'I wanted my baby, you didn't – end of story.'

'I… I *do* want children, I just want to plan it, choose when, together. It was thrown at me, I wasn't ready.'

'You weren't there when I needed you most. I didn't plan to get pregnant, it was as much a shock to me as to you. *I* wasn't ready, but I was ready to cope as best I could. And I expected you to be there beside me.' That was a bit of a speech. I take a big swig of beer to recover from it. The alcohol is buzzing in my head now, and I haven't eaten properly all day.

My phone starts ringing from inside my bag. Putting down my drink on the counter I go to answer it.

'Leave it, this is important,' says Nick.

'No, my life is important.' I open my bag and slip out my phone. It's work. I'm not going to answer it, they probably need a stopgap to fill in for one of their missed appointments. Drunk I was no use to anyone. Putting down the phone, I go to investigate the fridge. Not much in there as usual. Turning back to Nick I fumble for my beer. Another sip and I feel a little sick. 'I need to eat,' I say.

'Come on.' He grabs my bag from the counter and jacket off the hook and heads towards the door.

I hesitate for a moment and then follow him.

We go to the new burger bar that recently opened in North Street, just ten minutes from my house. Nick is urgent, kind and even manages to slip in the odd joke or two. I enjoy it. And I feel better now I'm eating, more able to cope with the situation. It's incredibly good having him want me; I need to bask in it as long as I can. We have a couple more beers and I let him do most of the talking. A lot has happened to him since we have been apart; a promotion at work, his sister has got engaged. I struggle to remember what her boyfriend looks like. I'd only met him once, just before Nick and I split, so all I have is a vague impression of a smile and dark clothing. Nick is very careful to keep Kate out of the conversation, and I'm glad of that. Only I know that if we are going to go anywhere with this, I'll need to know everything about her and their relationship. And that was going to hurt. When we finish this pleasant evening together he'll be going back to her. Where would he tell her he'd been? More lies. Would they have sex? Perhaps they would have sex and he would imagine she was me? The tables are turned, all the things I had imagined when he first left me would be happening to her. There's pleasure in these thoughts that I don't want to admit to. Part of me wants to get back together with him just so I can hurt Kate as much as she has hurt me.

'Did she know I was pregnant?'

'Sorry?' He's confused, he'd just been talking about a work colleague and what a dick they were.

'When you left me, did Kate know I was pregnant?'

He stares down at his plate, empty but for a few pieces of salad.

'She didn't. You didn't tell her because it would have made you look shitty.' In my gut, I know this. He won't look at me. 'Nick, you want to get back together, but there's stuff I'll need to know.'

The waitress is clearing the table next to ours. She seems to be taking longer than necessary to pick up a few items. I lean across towards him and lower my voice, 'I need you to be honest with me.'

'Do we have to?' His glance flicks from me to the waitress and back again; furtive and nervous.

Then I know this is going to take some time and a lot of thought. It would be hard for both of us. Did I really want the relationship that bad? It was so hard when he left; all I wanted in the world was him back again. Maybe some things can never be mended; trust is one of those. Forgiveness was what Carey always went on about. If you want to get well you had to forgive. Could I forgive Nick? Or Kate?

'I'll need some time to think about all of this,' I say.

He reaches across the table and takes hold of my hand. 'So you could get back with me?'

'I need to think, okay?'

He walks me home and is disappointed when I won't let him in. He tries to kiss me but I turn my head and get a peck on the cheek instead. We hug, a long meaning-laden clinch and then I shut the door on him and run up the stairs to my flat, my feelings flinging from one extreme to the other. It's going to take forever to get to sleep tonight.

12

Dream

I'm walking with Nick in rich green rolling fields. There's bright sunshine, birds are singing and there are beautiful white flowers everywhere. They're like stars peppering the bright green grass. When I step on them they make a light fluting sound. Amazed, I jump from flower to flower to see if I can make a tune. Nick has gone, I've lost Nick. Calling his name I search for him. The grass has grown impossibly long so that it's as if I'm tiny, like a mouse. I'm Thumbelina and the white flowers tower above me, their lovely music muffled by the dense foliage.

Pushing and forcing my way through the thick undergrowth, I hear crying. It sounds like a baby. I squeeze through the grass following the sound until I find it, a small baby lying on a dirty blanket by a dark rotten door. The poor thing wears only an old-style towelling nappy and when I pick it up I find it's wet through. The stench of urine makes me gag but I hold it close, trying to warm its chilled damp flesh. Rocking it in my arms, I knock on the door. When no one answers I push it open. Who would leave a baby like this? The thought brings an anger rising in my chest. Stepping into the building I find I'm in a maze of dark grey corridors that reek of a mixture of chlorine and piss. The baby has stopped crying. It's busy nuzzling my neck, I can hear it snuffling just below my ear with wet sniffing sounds. Most likely starving, I think, and now I'm searching for a kitchen. With all these corridors and the many rooms opening off them there has to be one somewhere. Only the rooms are all empty with dark barred windows. Ahead there's a closed door. Hurrying up I find it locked so I knock on it, light raps at first and then angry blows with my fist.

'Shhh,' says the baby. 'They're coming.'

'Who?' I ask, but the baby only starts crying again.

Worried, I hurry up the corridor finding that every door I come to is locked. The baby has become so heavy I have to put it down, only now it is a boy of about four years old. He's very thin and dirty with huge watery eyes that dominate his skull-like face.

Grabbing at my hands, he pleads, 'They're coming, they're coming.'

Glancing behind me, I see a pair of luminous animal eyes and I hear the clink, clink of claws on stone flooring.

Grasping the boy's hand, I tell him to run. We race down the corridor; I'm practically dragging him behind me.

Hearing a cry I look back to see it's Mark whose hand I'm holding, and he's being dragged back by his feet.

I try and hold on to him. For a moment there's a tug of war between me and whatever it is that has his legs.

Then he's gone, pulled with lightning speed back down into the gloom of the corridor, his wide frightened eyes and outstretched arms beseeching me to save him.

13

The first thing I see in the morning is a text from Nick saying how good it was to see me, and when can we talk again. My instant thought is – *I bet he wipes that from his phone before Kate sees it*, and then I know, that's how it was just before he left me. The tables are turned and I'm 'the other woman', potentially that is.

I hadn't heard Becks come back last night. I don't think she's on nights this week so maybe she stayed at Greg's? I really want to talk to her about Nick and how it had been with Mark at the library, so I send her a text asking when she'll be back, adding, 'need to talk,' with a confused face emoji. I hope she gets back to me soon. I hate waiting for replies; it makes me constantly check my phone. I also need to go on Facebook but have no time now. My dream book was suffering too. I'm not likely to forget last night's dream; it was so vivid. Not surprising after all that's happened.

My phone buzzes and I snatch it up.

A message from Mark, 'Still on for later?'

'Looking forward to it,' I text back and add a smiley emoji.

I am looking forward to seeing him, but I'm nervous too.

Glancing around the flat I'm dismayed at how messy it is. Okay; shower and dress super quick, a bit of a tidy, dab of the new Romanian perfume, put on my pork pie hat and then off to my first appointment.

My morning whizzes by. I visit three people; get them washed, dressed and fed. Dole out meds, write up notes, chat and find out how they're doing. Everything is just routine today. My mind is plagued here and there with thoughts of Nick, Kate, and Mark. I pop into the library for coffee and write up some of my notes about Mark, which helps me think about what direction I want our session to take tonight. Noticing one of the computers is free, I decided to check Facebook, but what I actually do is horrify myself with Google images of Ceausescu's Romanian orphans. Fragments from my dream and the grey corridors flicker in my mind. Mark came from that! No wonder he doesn't sleep at night. He says he doesn't remember anything before coming to England, he must be blocking some of it?

My phone's ringtone pulls me out of my thoughts. It's Becks.

Avoiding the hostile stares of the other library users I hurry out of the building to take the call in the external stairwell alleyway at the side of the building.

'Hi,' I say.

'Got your text, what's up?'

'Loads.' Glancing around me I see the hunched shape of a man in a grey hoodie standing with his back to me on the pavement. I start to walk towards College Green. 'Nick came round last night. Where were you by the way?'

'Greg's. What's he up to? Same stuff about the flat?'

'No, he wants to get back together.'

'Never!' She sounds shocked. 'Do you?'

'I don't know,' I say, but I'm grinning.

'Azza.' That's her teacher voice, all foreboding.

'I missed him so much,' I say making a quick hop sidestep to avoid being run over by a skateboarder wearing a Disney princess T-shirt featuring the Little Mermaid as a zombie.

'I know you did.'

'I just don't know. I'm scared, I couldn't go through all of that again.'

'No reason why you should,' says Becks.

'Only…' I swivel round, taking in the bright green lawns, the dark of the Goths bunched together in groups like crows – *they must be so overheated in all that black.*

'Don't!' Her sudden shout pulls me back sharpish.

I know what she means. I start cajoling and wheedling about how much history there is between Nick and me. He's a good bloke; he just panicked when I got pregnant. Becks cut me off.

'Just listen to yourself, you sound like him. I went through this breakup too, you know. I heard your pain and held the tissue box. I, personally, don't want to be going through that again. Tell me you didn't have sex with him?' There's a moment's silence before she adds, 'You didn't!'

'No… nearly, we… It was close but I stopped him.'

'God!'

'I know. I don't know. What do I do, Becks, tell me, what do I do?'

'Nothing, don't be doing anything with that little shit. But what about Mark? I thought—'

'Ah, about Mark. Funnily enough, he thought I'd made an appointment with him to meet at the library for an EFT session.'

'Oh.' There's a guilty tone in her voice, but curiosity wins hands down. 'Did you meet up? How did it go?'

'Yes, we did. What did you think you were doing?' I hear her splutter of laughter. 'I had no idea what he was on about, it was embarrassing.' More laughter. I'm smiling now. 'Honestly, Becks, you're the pits.'

'So is he your new patient?'

'Doctor-patient confidentiality,' I tease.

'Is he?'

'He's interesting.'

'Brilliant. This is what you need, someone new in your life, a challenge. Not Nick messing with your head again. And… what about Kate?'

'What about Kate?' I bristle, my smile slipping off my cheeks.

'He's doing it again. Have you thought of that? What's he running away from now?'

Frowning I sit on the bench and hopeful pigeons gather around my feet. I don't know what to say. I want to believe Nick loves and misses me, not that I'm a convenient escape hatch.

'I think you should go very careful with Nick. Don't let him back into your life unless you're absolutely positive he's being upfront. When's your next meeting with Mark?'

'Tonight.'

'Wow, where?'

'He's coming round the flat. Are you home tonight?' I hadn't thought about it before but I don't really know Mark and although I don't want her listening in I'm keen to know that Becks will be around at some point, just to make sure everything is okay.

'Briefly, then I'm meeting up with Greg.'

'That's going good?'

'Soooo good.' She pulls out the so into a long sighing sound.

I giggle and feel myself blushing. 'Rebecca!'

'Oh, it is. He's just great. We should go out on a double date, you, me, Greg and Mark. There's this new place near Millennium Square where you can play golf against a screen simulator thing. We could all go there first. It'd be a laugh. And somewhere to eat after.'

'Don't.' I manage to cut in when she draws breath.

'Why not?'

'I don't know yet. He's coming over for an EFT session, not a date.'

'Oh yeah.'

'No really.'

'He likes you, it's obvious. The EFT's just his excuse to see more of you.'

'I don't know, he really does have a problem.'

'Really?' Her voice lights up with curiosity.

Cross with myself, I kick at a pigeon. It flaps back out of my way and then advances strutting and tutting.

'Forget it, it's just a sleep problem,' I say.

'See, he's into you.'

She's like a dog with a bone.

'Look, if he's there when you get back, try to be as unobtrusive as possible, okay? He might feel embarrassed if someone else is watching and flapping their big ears.'

'I never flap.'

'You're not exactly unobtrusive either.'

'No, I wasn't designed to go unnoticed.'

'You said it.'

We're both laughing, so I'm sad but happy when she says she's got to go.

'Catch you later,' she says and rings off.

Checking the time on my phone, I realise I've got to get to my next appointment, like, five minutes ago. Jumping up, I walk fast down Park Street to catch a bus at the centre back towards Bedminster, home and my next clutch of service users.

At lunchtime, I pop into the office. Even though it's Sunday they are open, no rest from the needy. I want more latex gloves and some timesheets. I chat with

Chanelle, busy at the desk, phone permanently in hand. She stands and her enormous belly looms into view. You'd never guess while her stomach is hidden behind the desk. She's not your typical mum-to-be either. She has interesting pink and turquoise hair for starters and fancy painted acrylic talons that could scar a newborn for life.

'Wow,' I breathe. 'You grew so quick. Not long now.'

'So they tell me. I've just about had it, I'm that hot. No one said it was this uncomfortable,' Chanelle squeezed out from behind her solid brown desk. 'Mind the phone, Azza; me babber, I need to pee so bad me bladders fit to bust.' And she hobbles off in the direction of the bathroom.

That could've been me, I think before I can stop myself. The baby would have been born mid-March, just over five months back if it had gone full term. I wonder about her often. Would she have had Nick's red hair? I decided it was a girl as soon as I knew I was pregnant. My little girl.

I open up the supply cupboard where they keep the stock and rootle about for the things I need. A burst of women's laughter seeps from the room next door. Probably another training session, new eager recruits. Most of them won't last long. They're keen at first, but the job just wears people down. It's depressing for some I suppose; old people get sick and need to be cared for, and they don't generally get better. It's just a matter of making them as comfortable as possible. One odd thing I've noticed since I've worked here is that most of the staff, the ones that have been here for a while, have July birthdays. It must be something about July people that draws them to the caring professions. Not that I fit that bill. I'm a December baby, Christmas and birthday in one almost.

Some people said it was a blessing that I lost her; stuck as I was, jobless and alone. Not to me; I never saw it as a blessing. They were trying to be kind, I think. Trying to find a positive to help ease my pain. Really, they couldn't have said anything crueller.

'Find what you need?' says Chanelle wobbling back to her desk. 'I'll be glad when it's just me again.' She sounds breathless like she's been on a run.

'Have you bought all the gear?' I ask struggling to close the cupboard with my arms full of boxes and slippery packets.

'Stu has bought out most of Mothercare, and we're supposed to be saving.'

'Nice stuff?' I dump all the things on her desk and open up the stock book. I have to sign off everything I'm taking so they know where it's gone and what to re-order.

'All a bit too yellow for me. Poor bugger's going to look like a banana,' she says and grins at my snort of laughter. 'He's just being careful, like, 'cause we don't know what we got till it's here.'

I smile and nod. 'Baby shower?'

Her smile broadens to show teeth that would rival a wolf's. 'My sister organised it. Loads of people gave us lovely stuff. Mum doesn't hold with it mind, says it's American.'

'Like Halloween.'

'Right. I don't care. Thought it was lush being given all that nice stuff. Sets you up, don't it?

We jump when the phone rings. Chanelle snatches it up, 'Your Home Care?'

I mouth, 'Bye' and she waves me off, busy already with what sounds like a new enquiry, judging by her scrabbling about her desk for a pen.

Arms full, I set off for home, only a ten-minute walk from here. My thoughts are filled with Mark, should I get some biscuits or something, when I'm hit by a tiny highchair in a charity shop window.

Stopping dead in my tracks I stare. It's small and perfect; made of pine with a tiny teddy, with a gingham bib, set on the seat with what looks like a mini bowl of porridge and weeny silver spoon placed on the tray in front of him.

It shines.

Entering, I walk around the shop eyeing up the shelves searching for minuscule high chairs, but the one in the window is the only one, and because it's in the window I can't get to it unnoticed.

With careful nonchalance I circle the shop once more, glancing over my shoulder at the window, from time to time, assessing. Everything is set out on open shelf displays so I could just dart my arm through.

I do another circuit of the shop. There's hardly anyone in here; only one assistant at the till, an elderly woman busying herself pricing up a box full of crusty old jewellery. I cruise back towards the window, and with all the Your Home Care stuff held tight to my chest with one hand, I reach through the shelves and snatch up the high chair. As I pull back my fist catches something china and shoves it to the floor to smash in a loud expensive way.

I stand shocked.

'Oh dear.' The elderly woman is beside me in seconds.

'I'm so sorry,' I say, attempting to pick up the bits of broken china. Only I've got my ill-gotten gains hidden in one hand and all the care things in the other. Plastic wrapped timesheets and boxes of gloves spill from my arms and I struggle to trap them, without much success, against my legs. I push the thieved item into my jacket pocket before shrugging off my backpack and scooping the timesheets into it. The glove boxes are too big, but everything is more manageable now. Relieved I help pick up bits of what I can now see was once quite a nice teapot.

‘I’ll pay for it,’ I say.

The woman smiles, ‘I’ll see if I can find the bit with the ticket on it, just a mo.’

She goes to the back of the shop and comes back with a dustpan and a carrier bag. As she scoops up china I find a ticket with £5.99 written on it.

‘Next time just ask, dear. These window displays can be tricky,’ she says as she rings up my money and gives me my change. ‘We’ve got other teapots?’

I say no thank you and head off out of the shop.

When I get home the rumbling of my stomach takes me over to the fridge. Not much there, there never is. Funny how two women can live together with every available beauty product swarming the shelves in other parts of the flat, but the pantry is always bare. Toast again then.

I have my afternoon visits, then I’ll tidy up. Biscuits, I’ll get some of those on my way home.

14

Hunting, sniffing, trapping

He doesn't think she's seen him, not this time, but he needs to be more careful in the future.

Ducking his head low he pretends to fiddle with his iPod as he watches to see where she went before following at a safe distance. Her delicious scent still lingers in the air leaving a bright trail behind her. *Could anyone else see it or was it only him?* How could they not notice her brightness, the white glow of her like an angel, his angel?

She's too busy on her phone to really notice anything. She has a lovely face, natural and fresh with clear cream coloured skin, no make-up that he can see. He likes that; it means she's real, not one of those made up fake pretties. He wonders who she's talking to. Whoever it is, they make her smile and he doesn't like that.

Suddenly she's up and walking fast towards the street. He runs towards the big building to his right, a smart hotel, and then up along the side of it to the pavement so he can watch her unobserved. She crosses the centre and stops by the bus stop. When her bus came, could he get on with her unnoticed?

He waits where he is until he sees her absorbed in fiddling with her phone again, then he walks up and joins the end of the queue, lounging around the back end of the bus shelter so she can't get a clear view of him. With his headphones on, the music closes his world off from those around him as he snatches quick glances at her, drinking in all her loveliness. If he loses her that will be fine; he's seen her at the library enough times now to have built up a picture of some of her habits.

A bus comes, but she ignores it. Then another, number seventy-five, and she shuffles forward with a small crowd to mount the step. Following, while keeping behind some others, he sees that she went and sat near the back. It's too risky to stay downstairs because she'll notice him. Sprinting to the top deck he takes a seat right at the front where he can have a clear view over the front of the bus and pavement either side of the road. Every time the bus stops he carefully watches everyone who disembarks. They must have been travelling for about half an hour when he sees her; narrow shoulders and funny red hat, moving fast up the road. He bolts down the stairs but he's too late; the bus is already moving off.

The next stop took ages to get to, due to idiots who don't know how to drive and some road works. By the time he's jogged back up the street, she's nowhere to be found.

Slowing to a walk he starts to take in his surroundings. This is unfamiliar territory. The people here made his skin crawl, and he can feel their glances and stares. Despite the heat, he keeps his hood up and rounds his shoulders, forcing himself to disappear. He's good at that, being invisible, it's easy. Plain dull colours, nothing striking in his clothes or hairstyle, eyes downcast and just like that, he's invisible. He turns to a street on his right and begins to search every shop for a sign of her. It's important to be thorough, not to miss something just because of a stupid lack of concentration. Felicia had taught him this. Watch everything, take nothing for granted. That's how he got to pick out the weakest ones to bring back to her. The ones that didn't tell, not that anyone would have listened, they were all too busy just getting by. He continues like this all the way up the street, and the next until he comes to a roundabout noisy with traffic, then he turns back and retraces his steps from the other side of the road. He wasn't going to find her, he knows that now. He has to get back to the city centre and his job. However absorbing she is, he still needs to eat. He'd be back later. The excitement gnaws at his gut, and he whistles a flat tune through his teeth, tapping his fingers on his leg in beat to the iPod's music as he waits in line at the bus stop.

15

By six I've almost finished everything I set out to do when I remember the biscuits and find a plate for them. Chocolate digestives, always everyone's favourite. All the same, I jump when the door buzzer goes.

'Hi?' I say into the entry phone.

'Hi Astrid, it's Mark.' His voice sounds cracked and robotic, cut about by the electronics.

'Come up.' I press the buzzer and open my flat door, waiting and listening for his tread on the stairs.

He's running up. Keen! His smile is wide as his head comes into view.

'Hi,' he says with no hint of breathlessness.

'Hi.' I usher him in and direct him to the couch. 'Tea?'

'Please.'

Feeling jittery with butterflies I scold myself for being such an idiot; he's just a bloke, and my client, no need to be worked up.

I bring over tea for us both and the biscuits. Mark thanks me and takes one. I'm too nervous to eat so I put the plate on the floor.

'So how have you been doing with the insomnia?'

'Worse,' he says, his smile apologetic.

‘Oh.’ I feel a moment of guilty responsibility before I ask myself what Carey would say. ‘That’s good,’ I say nodding.

He makes that funny half-smile and my stomach flips.

‘It’s good,’ I explain, ‘because we must have opened something up at your first session. Tell me, how is it worse?’

‘I go to sleep for a couple of hours, but then wake up from a nightmare. I can’t get back to sleep after that, just small naps.’

‘Ah.’ Thinking for a moment I make some notes. ‘Okay, let’s start with a wellbeing status count.’

His face twitches.

‘It’s just to measure how you are at the beginning of the session compared to the end, same as we did at the library.’

He nods and I get out one of my worksheets.

‘Right, on a basis of one to ten how would you rate yourself on the following?’

I go through my questions, noting down his answers. His scores aren’t good as his anxiety is way too high, but I don’t tell him this, I just say ‘that’s great thanks’ and slip the list away in my folder.

‘Can you tell me about your dreams?’ I ask.

‘Yes. They’re really clear like I’m living them. They’re horrible, terrible.’

‘Can you describe one for me?’ I ask.

‘Okay. Last night, I was in this building. It was cold, I was shivering and my teeth were chattering. I could actually hear them. It was grey cement everywhere, dark and dirty and water underfoot so my feet were particularly cold.’

‘Mmm.’ I nod encouraging him on.

‘I was so afraid because she was angry with me.’

‘She?’

‘I’m not sure, only I knew it was a woman. I was trying to find somewhere to hide from her, but everything was so bare, nothing to hide in or behind. I heard someone calling my name and there was this boy. I felt so happy and relieved to see him. He was standing in a doorway so I went to him. He pulled me into a really tall cupboard, there were things… rags and bits under my feet. I tried to talk to him, but he just put his hand over my mouth to silence me. We stood close together holding hands and then I heard it.’ He stops speaking and sips his tea.

I notice his hand is shaking so that ripples disturb the surface of his drink. ‘What did you hear?’

‘Growling.’

I felt the hairs stand up on the back of my neck.

‘There was some big animal brushing up against the cupboard, it was growling and scratching at the door. I was terrified, we both were, we were both shaking and his hand was holding mine so tight it hurt. It still hurt when I woke up.’ He held his hand up in front of his eyes flexing the fingers.

‘Were your other dreams like this?’

‘Some have been similar. The same dark grey place and the same sense of fear, but no growling beast or the boy. It’s odd because I’m sure it was a wolf, but I like wolves. I’ve made a study of them, about their habits. I’ve been fascinated by them for as long as I can remember. I even have a tattoo.’

I raise my eyebrows and he unbuttons the top of his shirt. He pulls it open to show me a smallish tattoo across his heart of a wolf running under a full moon.

‘Nice,’ I say.

Smiling a little, he buttons up his shirt, stopping me from asking if I could touch it, which I almost did.

‘So, I like wolves. I understand them and I don’t think of them as something to be frightened of.’

'Things are different in dreams – their meaning – the wolf is just a metaphor,' I say.

'I know what you're saying, but this seemed real. It was a really, really big wolf. And, it felt like something I had done before. It felt familiar.'

'Do they have wolves in Romania?'

'Yes, but only high up in the forests. They generally stay away from people. They're not stupid,' he adds.

'Could you have actually experienced this as a child in the orphanage?' I ask.

'A wolf in the building?' He shook his head. 'It would never happen, especially not a busy people infested place.'

Infested, odd choice of word. 'What about the boy who pulled you into the cupboard?' I ask.

'I knew him in my dream, but have no idea who he was.'

'A friend at the orphanage? The grey cement building sounds like an orphanage. I looked some up online, they were pretty grim places. Bare, cement corridors and rooms full of cots. There wasn't much for the children and hardly any staff to care for them,' I say, thinking of the online images I had seen at the library.

He nods, giving me a searching look.

'From what I read you had a lucky escape. They were horrible places, definitely not for children.'

He stares down into his tea. 'I think I was one of the lucky ones.' Glancing up again, he strikes me with the sadness in his eyes. 'Makes you wonder about those left behind.'

'Do you think that's what's worrying you, in your dreams, the friends left behind with a wolf at the door, so to speak?'

He tilts his head, thinking so that his dark fringe falls across one eye. 'Could be? I hadn't thought of that. I don't remember anyone in particular. I don't remember anyone, full stop.'

'But you feel afraid in your dream?'

'Terrified, yes.'

I can see Carey's disapproving expression in my mind's eye when I open my mouth to say, 'There's another technique we could try called Matrix Re-imprinting. Would you like to give that a go?'

'Sounds like science fiction,' he says with a grin.

'It's better than that because it's not fiction,' I say with a returning smile. 'Here, have another biscuit and then we'll begin.' I hold up the plate for him to take one.

'Right, sit around a bit and face me. That's it. Now you just sit with your eyes closed and imagine that you, as your current self, are talking to you as a child in that grey corridor. I'm going to tap on you. With each tap you feel, imagine you are tapping on your child self. Talk to that child out loud and tell me his answers,' I say with more confidence than I feel.

Mark puts the rest of the biscuit in his mouth and sits still, eyes closed, his hands resting on his lap. I'm now free to have a proper look at him. A bit of dark chest hair is visible where the top couple of buttons are open on his pale grey shirt. On his chin is a dark shadow of stubble, most noticeably around the moustache line, that went down the sides like a cartoon bandit. His mouth is generous like a girl's, and his nose is long and straight. Thick dark lashes brush down on his high Slavic cheekbones. Broad bony shoulders and a visible collarbone. He looks like he needs feeding, hungry and lean. I see his eyelashes flicker.

'No peeking,' I say, and feel a wave of heat flush my face. Have I been caught staring? 'Okay, I want you to imagine yourself in the dark corridor from your dream. Can you see yourself there?'

Mark nods and swallows so that I see his Adam's apple rise and fall.

‘Can you see you, little Marku, in the corridor?’ *That was inspired, remembering his Romanian name.*

‘Yes,’ he says, his voice hoarse with the first crack of emotion seeping through.

‘Can you talk to him?’

‘Hello,’ says Mark. ‘I feel a bit foolish, Astrid.’

‘Don’t worry, just go with it. I promise you it’s a very powerful technique, and you hardly notice the camera.’

He flinches and I laugh.

‘I’m trusting you here,’ he says but he’s smiling.

‘Okay, talk to Marku. Find out how he’s feeling,’ I say.

‘Hello,’ he says again and then smiles a little. ‘What’s the matter?’ He leans towards me and says, ‘He says he’s scared.’

‘Who’s he scared of?’ I say as I lean forward to tap lightly on the top of his head.

‘Felicia,’ says Mark.

‘His mother?’

Mark tilts his head as if to catch a whisper, ‘Felicia is everyone’s mother.’

‘Why is Marku scared of Felicia?’

‘She’s angry, Marku wasn’t doing what he was told.’

‘How old is Marku?’

‘He says he doesn’t know. Oh, he’s really scared now.’

I’m tapping gently with just two fingers on Mark’s face. ‘Okay, ask him to stop right there. Stop, we’re going to freeze everything as it is, like magic, so no one can hurt him. Is Marku okay with that?’

‘He’s still scared.’

‘Explain that nothing can hurt him because you are with him and you’re going to protect him. What does it feel like in your body, Mark, right now, when you think about where Marku is?’

‘I’m… He’s… just frightened. So scared, and very, very cold. I feel cold.’

'Tell him you're going to make everything okay. You're making it warm. Does he feel warmer?'

Mark nods.

'Okay, you tap on him in your head just where I tap you and tell him, 'Even though I feel so scared everything is completely and utterly alright.'

We go through a round of all the meridian points, me tapping on Mark and him sitting, eyes closed, repeating my words under his breath. Then I ask if Marku is still feeling scared.

'He says a little and can he have a hug.'

I can hear the surprise in Mark's voice, it's amazing how deep some people get relating to their younger selves. 'You must give him a hug then.'

'Alright, a mental one,' says Mark.

I guess this role-playing is embarrassing him, but I feel proud of him for going along with it.

'Is Marku ready to start the scene moving again?' I ask.

Mark nods.

'Ask Marku if the boy is there, the one in your dream?'

Mark's nodding, and shivering a little I notice.

'Are you cold, Mark?'

'It's freezing here.'

'Remember you're in charge, you can make it warmer.'

He nods.

'What's the boy's name?' I ask as I tap just below his collarbone.

I can see Mark's mouth working but can't quite catch the words. 'Say that again.'

'Dragos.' His voice is a child's whisper.

'Dragos?' I repeat the foreign name, hearing it stumble on my tongue.

Mark nods. 'He wants us to come.'

'Do you want to go with him?'

'I must.'

‘Mark, stop, freeze the scene again.’ Taking hold of his hand to tap on his wrist I feel shocked how cold his skin is. ‘Talk to Marku. Ask him about Dragos, who is he?’

‘Dragos is… Marku has to go with him. She’s coming. Felicia is coming.’

Mark’s shaking, his teeth bared and his eyes flash open wide, rolling in fear like an animal.

At a slam of the front door downstairs, Mark jumps to his feet.

‘Mark!’ I say jumping up beside him and kicking the plate of biscuits in my haste. It skids across the floorboards shedding chocolate digestives in its wake.

Mark leaps sideways, half falling onto the couch, grabbing my arm as he goes, pulling me down on top of him. His arms wrap around me, holding me in a tight bear hug. We’re both breathing hard. His eyes are wild and his face drained to a corpse’s pale moon glow.

‘Oops, sorry!’

I glance up to see Becks standing smirking in the doorway.

Struggling out from Mark’s tight grip, I hustle Becks into the bedroom, leaving Mark huddled on the end of the couch.

‘That was quick,’ she says in a loud whisper.

I flap my hands. ‘I said to be discreet, and it wasn’t what you thought.’

‘No,’ she makes an arch expression that makes me want to giggle and slap her at the same time.

‘No, we were right in the middle of a session.’

‘I’ll say!’

‘Not that kind of session.’ I sigh. ‘He was deep in a memory. You slamming the front door shocked him.’

‘Oh, I’ll be out of your hair in a jiffy and you can get right back to it.’

'It doesn't work like that. I have to bring him down to a happy place, but he won't be comfortable to work with me until you're gone.'

'It'll be as if I was never here,' she says pulling off her uniform and wriggling into one of my tunic tops.

'That's just a top, you'll need some leggings or shorts with it,' I say seeing how much leg is on display and nearly most of her underwear with it.

'*You* do,' she says grabbing up some silver sandals.

'You might get cold.' God, now I sound like her mother.

'Na,' she says, lifting my jacket off the coat hook and straight onto her shoulders. 'I'll be just cosy.' I follow her back into the sitting room. 'Cute,' she adds, dumping something into the palm of my hand. Looking down I see it's the tiny highchair, I forgot it was in the pocket. 'See ya, Mark.'

'Are you alright?' I ask him. He's standing by the sink staring out of the window.

He turns and gives me a stiff smile. 'What's that?' He indicates the little chair in my hand.

'Oh, nothing.' I put it on the shelf with the other pilfered pieces.

He comes over to me and we both stare at them in silence for a heartbeat.

'It was so real,' he says.

I nod. To be honest, I'm shocked myself. I haven't heard of anyone reacting that strongly before. 'How do you feel?'

'Exhausted, like I've been on a ten-mile run.'

'Sit down again, we'll talk it through,' I say showing him back to the couch. I get the dustpan and brush and squat down to clean up the broken biscuits. 'Tell me how you felt.'

'It was…'

I look up at him, his face seems aged somehow.

'I was cold and scared. I felt the same fear as in the dream.'

'Do you know who Dragos is?'

'He was one of the bigger boys at the orphanage. I'd forgotten him. I could see him so clearly, how could I have forgotten him?'

I shake my head as I couldn't explain it. 'What about Felicia?'

He shivers. 'Someone I was scared of, but I can't remember why.'

'I think we should go through a tapping session to get you back on an even keel.'

We go through a few runs of 'even though I felt so afraid…' until he says he feels more normal again.

The sun has lowered and a soft orange light tinges the kitchen lighting up my pine wood flooring.

'God, I'm hungry. Are there any places around here we can go and get food?' he asks.

'Quite a few. What do you feel like eating?'

'Let's just walk about a bit and see what appeals when we find it.'

As Becks has pinched my jacket I go and find a big colourful wrap and wind it about my shoulders and put on my brown bowler. When I come out of the bedroom he smiles.

'You look Peruvian,' he says.

'Is that good or bad? Are you allergic to llamas or something?'

'It suits you, brings out your exotic side.'

'Hardly exotic. My mum was Norwegian.'

'Ah, now I can see the Björk resemblance.'

'She's Icelandic!'

'One of those frozen northern countries anyway,' he says with a grin.

Romanian, English, and Norwegian. We'd have interesting looking children, not that I should be indulging in these thoughts.

'Do you wonder about your family in Romania? Have you ever tried to contact them?'

I open the door and he follows me out to the landing standing close while I made sure I've pulled it properly shut.

'No I haven't, but I think about it all the time,' he says.

I catch the wistful tone in his voice. 'Aren't there agencies to help with that kind of thing?'

'There are, but at the time when I was adopted, paperwork was pretty lax, on the Romanian side that is. The agency I spoke to have protocols. They contact the mother and have to get her consent before I can have any details. I've tried to create some dialogue with agencies in Romania, without much success. Also, there's always the danger of corruption in some areas, especially during the Ceausescu era. I can't be sure the person I'm told is my mother really will be. My adoptive parents are amazing loving people and I owe them everything. I'm not sure how they might feel?'

'You haven't discussed it with them?'

'A bit. It's… It's not straightforward.'

We walk down the stairs side-by-side, caught for a moment in our thoughts. I have so many questions, but I can sense his tension. He's been through a lot this evening. I need to give him time and let him relax a bit.

'What do you fancy?' I say as a way to get his thoughts away from our previous conversation.

'Hmm?' He searches my face, one eyebrow raised.

'To eat,' I add quickly a heat creeping up my neck. 'What have you got an urge for? There's plenty to choose from in North Street.'

'How about the Tobacco Factory. I remember they had a good selection on the menu.'

'Okay.'

Thinking about food, my stomach tightens. I haven't really eaten today, an occupational hazard of the job. The Tobacco Factory's only about five minutes from my flat and we walk fast, chatting as we go. He pulls open the door for me and I sweep in, the grin falling from my face as my gaze meets Nick's.

He's with her.

Now my gut clench isn't out of hunger. Why am I feeling guilty? Mark cannons into the back of me.

'Sorry,' he says. 'I didn't realise you'd… What's the matter?'

'Nothing,' I say and hurry over to the bar. 'Half a lager,' I tell the barman and look at Mark. 'You?'

'Pint of ale.' He points at a pump further down the bar. 'Can we have a tab?' he says to the barman as he collects a couple of menus from a roughhewn log that serves as a menu stand.

We take our drinks to one of the small round tables. The side of my head itches with what I presume is Nick's scrutiny.

'I like it in here,' says Mark. 'When I bumped into you that night with Greg, it was my first time.'

I grin.

'What?'

'Now you're supposed to say do you come here often?'

He returns my smile. 'Well, do you?'

'It *is* my local, so I guess so.'

'And do all your mates come here too?'

The urge to point out Nick is feverish. I swing my head around taking a slow sweep of the room, Nick's leaning towards *her*, but his gaze is fixed on me. 'There's a few familiar faces but no one in particular,' I say with a shrug.

'No disgruntled boyfriends demanding to know why you're with me.'

I laugh a bit louder than I meant to. 'No, you're quite safe.' And now I need to know. 'What about you? I hardly know you. You might be married with three kids and mortgaged up to your eyebrows.'

He smiles into his drink before glancing up with those bright green eyes. 'No wife, or kids. A mortgage, yes, and a lodger. No significant others.'

'Oh.' I feel exposed; the blush is creeping up my neck.

'Are you hot? You look flushed,' he says.

I take off my hat and run my fingers through my hair before fanning my face with it.

'Hi.' Nick's standing by our table.

'Hi,' I squeak.

'Aren't you going to introduce me?' says Nick.

'Ah, Nick this is Mark, he's…' I don't know what to say he is. They're both staring at me expectantly. 'He's a new friend,' I say as bright and cheerful as I can manage.

Mark raises his eyebrows, then holds his hand out to Nick. 'Mark,' he says.

'Nick,' says Nick.

And they shake hands, and this simple friendly gesture has never looked so filled with menace. There's a moment of awkward silence.

'I just thought I would say hello,' says Nick. 'As you were here, it would be strange to ignore you.'

'Yes.' I glance over at his table, it was empty. 'Kate?'

'Popped to the ladies.'

'Ah,' I say with a slow nod.

Mark looks from one to the other of us, his expression perplexed. Catching Nick's gaze flick over towards the toilets, I turn and see Kate start her long manoeuvre between the tables back to her seat.

'I'd better…' says Nick.

'Yes,' I say, and he goes.

'None of my business, but what was that about?'

'My ex.'

'Ah.' He leans back in his seat for a moment before coming forward across the table to whisper in a conspiratorial tone, 'Am I safe, he looked none too happy?'

'That's his girlfriend he's with so you should be completely safe.'

'I sensed a certain atmosphere?'

'He's…' I don't want to explain any of it, not yet, all too messy. 'He's confused.'

'Were you together for a long time?'

'Three years.'

'And you've been split for a while?'

I nod and sipped my drink.

He stands up. I feel a pang of panic. Is he leaving?

'Come on, let's go somewhere less crowded.'

'But…'

'Give me a sec to settle up at the bar.' He strolls off and I knock back my drink. He's right, I can't relax with Nick across the room. I want to be able to concentrate on Mark without Nick's constant interference. I stand and Mark's beside me in an instant.

'Come on, you,' he says smiling and wraps my scarf over my shoulders. 'Let's try that place across the road, it looks good.'

He puts his arm around my shoulders and we leave like two close friends already intimately comfortable with each other.

Nick's fierce gaze burns into the back of my head.

It feels brilliant.

We're lucky and manage to get a table in the hugely popular mezze place opposite. It's noisy so we're forced to huddle close to hear each other's words. The closeness feels good, he smells nice in a bloke kind of way, a bit musky with a hint of spice. I keep finding reasons to lean in and take a deep breath of him. I hadn't realised he could be so funny. In minutes he has me wiping tears from the corners of my eyes. It feels good, I needed this.

'How long have you worked there?' I ask between mouthfuls of vine leaf-wrapped parcels of rice and herbs.

'Just over six months now. It's good, a great crowd in an open-plan office, and let's not forget Greg,' he says laughing.

'Heaven forbid I should forget him.'

'Who?'

I laugh and we both make a grab for the last breadcrumb-coated fish ball. Actually, I couldn't eat it if I wanted to, but fighting over the food has become a bit of a game. Our forks clash and the little golden ball shoots across the plate, pine table and off out of sight under the next-door table. Glancing up we encounter disapproving glances from our neighbours.

'Oops,' says Mark and neither of us can stifle our laughter.

Actually, I'm a bit drunk. This is becoming a habit; maybe I should be worried, only not now because I'm having too much fun.

The waiter starts to clear our plates. 'Pudding?' he asks.

Mark looks at me and I shake my head. 'Don't let me stop you,' I say.

He shakes his head. 'Coffee would be good though?'

'Okay,' I say, but coffee at this time a night will probably lead to broken sleep, only I'm just not ready to end the night just yet.

Our waiter brings two tiny black coffees and some chocolate-coated coffee beans. We sip. It's harsh, bitter and delicious coffee. Crunching the chocolate bean I marvel at its horrible yet addictive taste. Some of the tables have been cleared and what had been a bright and noisy atmosphere has dulled down to lowered murmurs.

Our mood is dropping to match. Mark is still leaning close although he no longer needs to. His hand touches mine and I feel a flash of heat run up my arm. Brushing my cheek with his fingertips he asks if I'm okay. I can't speak; a sudden rush of electric desire is cutting off my throat. His gaze locks onto mine and he takes hold of my hand. We sit like that, not speaking, just silent communication.

'Bill?'

It's our waiter. He breaks the moment so that Mark releases my hand. 'Yes please,' he says.

I'm silent as he pays and we leave the intense light of the mezze restaurant for the darker street outside.

As we walk slowly down the pavement he again takes hold of my hand. Such warmth and pleasure from such an everyday gesture. We walk like that, in silence till we turn off to the much darker street just before my flat.

'Astrid.'

We both stop and gaze at one another. His face is bending towards mine and I don't realise that I've been holding my breath until his mouth is on mine. Our kiss is a soft careful caress that at first is just lips pushing together, like children in the playground. Then his arms are around me pulling our bodies into each other and my mouth opens before I'm conscious of it. His tongue in my mouth is a shock that reaches through to all the baser parts of me. Groaning I tug his head closer, kissing him back hard enough to feel the grind of his teeth on my lip. He draws back with a murmur of apology and kisses my bruised top lip before our mouths are hungry for each other again.

'Sorry.'

We're blocking the pavement and a passer-by carefully circles us. I just catch a smirk and he's gone up the road with noisy booted steps that echo intrusively round the moon-drenched street. The world is tinged in silver night dust.

Breaking apart, Mark takes hold of my hand and we carry on towards my flat. My mind is spinning. I want him, that much is easy, but what are the consequences? Mark is supposed to be my client; will we still be able to work together if I sleep with him? Is this a one-night stand; do I want that if it is? And what about Nick?

By the time we reach my door I have cooled enough to stop him coming in with me.

'Look, Mark I…'

'Hey!' Leaning forward he gives me a gentle soft kiss. 'Don't fret. I hope you'll agree to see me again though?'

I nod and we stand a moment holding hands before he wraps his arms around my shoulders and pulls me into his chest. Hugging like this I can hear the fast beat of his heart like a bird caught in a cardboard box. I breathe in the male scent of him. Then we are kissing again, for a long moment in the dark of the doorway, before he disentangles from my arms.

'I'll ring you,' he says, a soft smile crinkling his eyes.

Nodding, as I don't know what to say, I push open the front door and stay in the doorway watching as he walks off down the road to his car. Only once he's inside it and started up the engine do I go into the hall of my building and push shut the front door behind me.

16

Dream

Mark holds me in his arms. We're kissing and desire slides like a snake up through my belly. I want him so bad. But there are too many other things in here. We're huddled together in a wardrobe, wrapped in each other's arms. I can hear someone banging about outside, I think it might be Becks.

I giggle and Mark puts a finger to my lips.

'Shhh,' he says. 'She mustn't find us.'

'Let's find somewhere else.' I try to open the cupboard but Mark stops me.

'Listen,' he whispers. 'She'll be so angry if she catches us.'

I can hear it now, a low growling as something circles the wardrobe.

'When it's round the back we can run,' he whispers.

'I'm scared.'

'Ready?' He's getting ready to jump.

'Don't leave me.'

But he's gone, leaping through the door and then I hear his shouts as it slams shut behind him. He's calling my name, his voice getting fainter as he runs further and further away.

And the thing is still circling the wardrobe.

I'll jump out once it gets near the back.

Pushing open the door, I leap, but the ground is soft like I'm running on damp mattresses.

I'm too slow, I can hear the thing behind me gaining fast. I spring up into the air, flying. If I concentrate really hard, I can fly just enough to stay out of reach of its snapping jaws. My window is open and I bound out of it, flying like Wendy in the Peter Pan cartoon into the lovely blue night, a trail of fairy dust lighting the air behind me.

I fly across the street to land on a lamp post. Clinging to its hard cool surface, I look back.

A huge grey wolf leans half out of the window, the light of the full moon shining in its eyes.

17

Waking disorientated from a bunch of confused dreams, I reach for my laptop and log into Facebook. There's a load of messages from Mum and my brothers. I haven't watched TV lately or read any newspapers, but apparently, Bristol is locked into a crisis of fear due to some psycho stalking the streets. Mum wants to know if I'm being careful. My brothers want to know if I've seen or heard anything. I don't know why I bother. I'm tempted to tell them to stop scaremongering when a headline posted by one of my Bristol friends catches my eye.

The latest attack was last night in Bedminster.

A chill runs through me. I bring up Google and type in Bedminster Bristol attack. There's an alarmingly long list of choices. I choose one near the top.

"Bemmy girl latest victim. Local girl reports that she faced the Bristol Beast and escaped unscathed."

Bristol Beast? The hairs on the back of my neck rise.

"Coming home late from a night out, the petite Bristolian nurse explained how a shadowy figure stalked her up East Street. 'He got really close and I could hear him breathing,' said the plucky blonde. 'He seemed to be sniffing my hair like an animal, and then he suddenly grabbed hold of me and pulled me into a doorway. I shouted and he started growling. It was so weird.' The courageous young woman struggled with her attacker, managing to rip his shirt. She didn't get a chance to see his face, but described a tattoo on his chest of some kind of animal – possibly a wolf or dog."

I sit back and stare at my ceiling. Wolf tattoo. I felt sick. But it couldn't be Mark, I'd seen him go off in his car, a car he shouldn't have been driving because we both had a lot to drink. A blonde nurse. Oh God, I hope that wasn't Becks.

Shouting her name I run to the bedroom. It's empty.

Then I remember, she saw Greg last night, so it can't be her. Only I need to check.

Grabbing up my phone I call her, she answers after a couple of rings.

'Becks?'

'Oh Azza, have you seen the news? I'm at Greg's, but I'm okay.'

'So it *was* you.'

'Yeah.' Then she's silent.

'Talk to me. What happened? It says in this article that a man grabbed you into a doorway. That he had an animal tattoo. What did it look like?'

'It was weird. Greg and me argued and I stormed off. A silly argument. We're okay now. I took the bus. Stupid. I don't know why I didn't take a taxi. I got off at the stop opposite Asda, you know the one, and started walking. It's really spooky and empty there at night, I haven't really walked there so late before otherwise I would have never…'

She trails off so I make an encouraging noise to get her going again.

'I wasn't aware of him at first, so I guess he must have been hiding in a doorway or something. Then suddenly I notice, there's someone else in the street and he's walking really fast. Cos I was a bit drunk and riled up after my fight with Greg, I didn't feel that scared. I thought, just let him try, the fucker. Then he's right up behind me, and get this, Azza, he's sniffing me!' Becks' voice is outraged. 'Sniffing my hair and shoulders, creep. I try to turn round, to give him a piece of my mind, only he grabs me and pushes me into a shop doorway. I'm shouting like anything and he bites my shoulder, only he just gets a mouthful of jacket, lucky, but there's a bruise so he must have pinched a bit of skin, and listen to this, he's growling and shaking his head like a mad terrier, you know, like that little dog that Sasha had, from school, we used to let it bite our sweatshirts.'

I can hear a little shake of laughter in her voice only I'm not finding the image funny.

'I'm scared shitless, but I'm furious too. Who does he think he is? So I'm struggling, batshit crazy trying to turn around, cos I want to kick him in the goolies or scratch his eyes out or something. He's still got a load of my jacket in his teeth, so I'm able to wriggle out of it, but I rip his shirt in the fight. Funny how you notice these things. I've got a mad growling werewolf trying to eat my clothes and all I clock is a tatt on his chest.'

'What was it?'

'A wolf; crazy fucker had a wolf tattooed on his chest. It was a full moon last night, did you see it? I did, and the werewolf that came with it.'

Becks is saying something about staying at Greg's for a while but I'm not really listening. 'What kind of wolf?' I say loudly to cut through her chatter.

'What?'

'His tattoo, what kind of wolf, what did it look like?'

'I don't fucking know, a big hairy kind. For fuck's sake, Azza, I get attacked by a werewolf and you want to know his shoe size!'

'Sorry.' I am really; I'm not being a good friend. 'Are you okay, did he hurt you?'

'Lucky I had that jacket on, or it would have been my flesh he was biting. Have you seen the reports on him? There was a girl attacked a couple of nights back. Google it. God, I don't know what planet you're on sometimes. No, I'm okay really, shaken up, a bit bruised is all. But don't think I'll be walking the streets alone for quite a while, or at least until he's caught. You shouldn't either.'

'And you didn't see his face?'

'No, couldn't. Mostly he was behind me or had his face buried in the jacket. Your jacket actually; sorry, he still has it. I legged it and left him to it, shaking it like a dog with a rag.'

'God!'

'Crazy animal. I was lucky, though. The other girl he bit all over her face and chest before he raped her. She was incredibly hurt, scarred for life, most likely. The police say I was really lucky.'

'I didn't know, I haven't heard.'

'You must have, it's been in the news. It's all anyone talks about on Facebook.'

'But where did you go, when you ran from him? You didn't come home.'

'Round to the nearest pub, lots of people and noise. I got them to ring the police while I rang Greg. He was brilliant, came straight away.'

'You didn't ring me.'

Becks' tone becomes a little sheepish. 'I knew you were busy, and Greg and me had some making up to do.'

'Oh!'

'I felt so shaken, still do, I needed some stiff drinks. The police were asking questions till really late and I didn't get to bed till after two.'

I hear the rumble of a man's voice in the background.

‘Thanks, babe. So we’re both going to take a day off work. I’ve got to go to the police station in a bit. I expect they want me to try and do a photo-fit or talk to one of them special artists.’

‘But you didn’t see his face?’

‘No, but they’re hoping I might remember something.’ I hear her slurping on a drink and imagine her, a small vulnerable tousled girl-woman sitting on a bed in an over-sized man’s shirt clutching a giant mug of tea. ‘God I needed that,’ she says with a sigh in her voice. ‘There’s nothing like tea in the morning, is there?’

‘Can I see you? Oh, Becks, I’m so worried about you,’ I say.

‘Don’t be, I’m in good hands. Anyway, you haven’t told me, how did last night go?’

‘Great,’ I shudder with pleasure and embarrassment at the thought of Mark kissing me in the street. Then a cold finger runs down my spine, possibly kissing him at the same time as Becks was all alone just streets away fighting off some crazy man. No, the wolf tattoo is just a mad coincidence, I feel certain of that. ‘I’ll tell you more when I see you. Can we meet up? When will the police be finished with you?’

‘What time is it now?’ she says.

I can hear Greg saying nearly nine and I realise I’m going to be late for work again.

‘Okay, I’ve got to be at the station by ten. Should be done by twelve I’d have thought? It’s the one where the old family courts were, you know the giant graffiti and that club, the one we went to for New Year’s?’

‘Uh-huh,’ I say nodding even though she can’t see me.

‘I’ll meet you in the Costa on the corner of Union Street about twelve thirty. Can you be there then?’

I say I could, I’d have to shuffle some of my appointments, but I can work it. I’d meant to do Mrs P’s flat first thing, but I'd have to go there later instead. Right now I need to shower and to be gone as soon as possible.

Forty minutes later I'm letting myself in for my first appointment, profuse with apologies at my tardiness. I speed like this through all my visits; late breakfasts and early lunches. I'm safely seated, coffee steaming on the counter in front of me, by twelve forty at one of the window tables so I can easily see Becks, and she me.

I wait, sipping and checking my phone. I'd had a message from Mark earlier in the day, only I'd been too busy to properly absorb it. I return to that now.

-'Hi, great evening last night'- My stomach flips. -'Need another dose of EFT asap. Give me a date?!'-

Did he mean a date as in a day in the week or going out on a date? I chew on a nail. I want to see him asap too for too many reasons. I stare out the window scanning the faces of passers-by, trying to pick out Becks. Where is she? I check my phone again, ten to one now. People flood past, probably rushing to fit stuff into their lunch break. My eyes lock on the curves of a round, ready to burst, pregnant belly. The owner of the belly is flushed. Must be the summer heat. I'd read that your body produces much more blood when you're pregnant, to pump all those nutrients around where they're most needed. I'd been really sick in the beginning. In fact, I'd been sick and miserable through most of it, but that didn't stop me feeling even worse when I lost her.

My phone rings, making me jump.

'Mark,' I say in a squeak. Seeing his name on my phone's screen somehow restricts my throat.

'Hi. How are you?' His voice sounds warm.

I feel a flush run up my neck and onto my cheeks. 'Okay.' I really couldn't say more than that.

'Where are you? I went to the library, just, you know…' He sounds a little embarrassed. So, he was looking for me. A smile parts my lips.

'I'm in town, waiting for Becks.'

He's silent so I feel compelled to speak. 'She was attacked last night.'

'What!'

'She's okay, luckily, only she had to go to the police station near here to file a statement, and probably shown some pictures, to find a match, I expect. I won't know till I see her.'

'Where did it happen?'

'Bedminster.'

He swore. I'd never heard him swear before and it sends a tingle up my spine.

'She's okay,' I repeat. 'The guy jumped her from behind, but she managed to get away.'

'But that's near you.'

'Yeah.'

'Astrid, how late do you come home from your caring appointments?'

'Late sometimes, but I generally do earlies, morning to early evening.'

'Please promise me you'll take a taxi if you have to travel late.'

I smile. 'Thanks. I'm pretty sure I won't be taking too many risks after what happened to Becks.'

'If it's related to the attacks I've seen on the news the guy sounds totally crazy. The newspapers are calling him the Bristol Beast.'

'Is that because of the growling?' I ask.

'And the biting.'

I shudder. I can't think of anything worse than the pain of being bitten. Horrible. I want to change the subject.

‘You said in your text that you needed some EFT. Bad night?’ I ask.

‘Wonderful night.’ I feel a rush of pleasure at these words. ‘Only followed up with some terrible dreams. I couldn’t sleep from about three. The moon was so bright even with the curtains drawn. It kept me awake.’

‘You free tonight?’

‘That sounds great. What time? Same as yesterday?’

I explain about having to go to Mrs P’s in Clifton after my last appointment, to feed her cat and everything, so we fix for him to come round to my flat at eight. In a moment of what could only be insanity, I offer to make some supper. Realising the rashness of this after he’s hung up, I become so absorbed in what I might make, and if I could remember there being any food in the cupboards at home, that I don’t notice Becks come into Costa until she was standing right next to me. I give a little shout and leap up to wrap her in a hug.

‘Are you sure you’re okay?’ I say pushing her away from me so I can look her up and down, searching for signs of trauma.

‘Shaken, not stirred,’ says Becks as pulls a chair close to sit next to me.

‘You were at the station for ages. What did they want?’

‘Last night they combed my hair and picked under my nails for any DNA. Today they wanted a full description of everything that happened. They asked so many questions, I think it drove me insane.’

‘Do you want coffee?’

‘No thanks, I’ve had enough hot drinks to fill a bath. It was boring if anything, nothing like the movies.’

‘Did you do a photo-fit or anything?’

‘No point. I didn’t see his face, did I? It was dark in the doorway. To be honest, it all happened so fast, and I was so shocked that he could have been anyone. Tom Hardy and I wouldn’t have noticed.’

'Oh, I think you would have noticed him.'

'Well maybe if he'd spoken, and if it was Tom Hardy, he would have been the one running for his life!'

We both laugh, but it's a nervous uncomfortable sound.

Becks pulls down the side of her T-shirt to show four clear fingerprint-shaped purple bruises on the top of her arm. 'It's the same the other side, from where he grabbed me.' She cranes her neck round to peer at her shoulder where a small crescent black bruise stands out clearly – a new moon in negative. 'And that's where he caught my skin when he tried to bite me.'

'Oh, Becks!'

'It's okay, it's not much compared to his other victim,' she says.

'He bit and raped her.'

She nods. 'Just like a werewolf. They wanted to know if he did anything sexual. I said he didn't get a chance. They think he's playing out some kind of erotic fantasy. He's trying to have sex with his victims only they don't do what he wants so he hurts them. Who knows? Crazy bastard.'

'So you didn't see anything – not his hands, face, clothes, only a tattoo?'

'Well yes, I saw his clothes. Jeans, buttoned-up shirt and trainers, I think. But nothing else. I ripped the buttons off his shirt. It could have been any colour because everything looked grey in the moonlight. There're no street lights on in East Street, how mad is that? I saw the tatt for just a short time, I had only the briefest impressions of a wolf. I'm not even sure about that now, it could have been a dog or a bear, anything really. His chest was hairy but no more than most men. The police had me look at hundreds of pictures of dog and wolf tattoos. I think that confused me even more. Now my head is so full of possible images.'

'I'm just so glad you're alright.'

'It really shook me up though. We get all these pamphlets and lectures at the hospital, about being careful, awareness and all that. You know how nurses are the favourite targets for the loops, I just never thought it would happen to me.'

I shake my head. None of us ever think it'll happen to us; it's always some other poor person.

'I tell you, Azza, it's changed my perspective. I'm going to be a lot more careful from now on, take some self-defence classes. You should too.'

I nod and pull her into another hug so it's particularly loud when she says into my ear,

'Especially while I'm away, you'll be careful won't you?'

Pulling back, I scan her face.

'Greg bought tickets to Lanzarote, on that last-minute website. We're going on a holiday because he's worried in case the attacker is targeting me. He feels that if he takes me away for a bit he can keep a proper eye on me. Is that sweet or creepy?'

She laughs, but I feel the sting of loss.

'That's really kind of him,' I say, but it isn't what I was feeling. It *is* kind of him, but I want to keep an eye on her too.

'It is, isn't it?' she says her voice bright with enthusiasm. 'Work has said I can have some time off to get over the trauma. To be honest, I do need a break, and it'll be brilliant to go away with Greg. Although we haven't been together that long I feel so good with him already. You'll be okay, won't you? Things are going good with you and Mark?'

I tell her about last night and she squeals and claps her hands.

'And you're seeing him again tonight? See, I told you he liked you.'

I scowl at her.

'Oh, come on, you like him. Don't pretend you don't. You deserve this, someone kind and caring, and gorgeous.' She punches my arm. 'Someone to make a fuss of you.'

'I don't know if I'm ready.'

'Shut up!' she says, loud enough to silence the other customers in our immediate vicinity. 'Don't talk crap. You like each other, he's hot, end of. Stop beating yourself up over the past and live in the now.'

'Is that you or Greg talking?'

She mock smacks my hand. 'It makes sense. When we get back, we can go on that double date.'

'Ergh!' I stick my finger in my mouth miming inducing vomiting and she laughs.

'Babes, I'll miss you. Now.' Jumping up, she grabs me into a hug. 'I've got to dash. Time to pack and nip to Asda for any last-minute necessities.'

'When's your flight?'

'Early tomorrow so I'll stay at Greg's tonight. Get Mark to stay with you.' She points at me, adding in her teacher voice, 'No walking about after dark on your own. Promise?'

I promise to be extra careful. We hug once more before she's gone, off with a flounce of blonde hair and a new fragrance, leaving a trail of sexiness behind her. At least it isn't one of mine, for once.

18

Hunting, sniffing, trapping

He had her, he was so sure of it, then she'd tricked him at the last moment. Tricked him by turning into someone else.

He'd gone back to the street where he'd lost her earlier in the day. He wasn't sure why, just following an impulse. His brain was addled from too much drink so he shouldn't have risked it; he should have just gone straight home. But the moon, it was so big, so bright he just needed to be there, on *her* streets. So he'd gone walking in the quiet deserted places, enjoying the moonlight and the solitude, when she'd walked by him. It was her perfume, he was sure of it. It left a light trail behind her.

He tried to hold back. To keep himself in the shadows and follow at a distance. After all, he'd promised himself to take this slowly, get to know her, to gain her trust. Only instinct had taken over. The thing within him had risen up and taken control. That was something he couldn't risk happening again, not when he was with her, his bright one.

The thing within had taken over all his mind and it had driven him to attack. And then it wasn't her after all, it was some other girl. He'd seen that as soon as she'd escaped him. He'd been able to watch from inside the beast as it bit and shook the girl's coat, he'd seen this blonde girl running from him, fast as lightning up the street. He'd given chase but then the girl had run into a busy pub, with smokers hanging around outside, fogging the air with their stench.

So he had slunk back into the shadows.

He still has the coat, a blue denim one that smells of her, his angel. He took it home with him and laid it across his pillow. All night his dreams were filled with her, and with Felicia. In his dreams, she and Felicia became one, and she held him in her arms. She had rocked him, singing softly and putting the honeyed taste in his mouth. Then she had given him the sweet love that he had not known for so long now, the love of the rare and mighty. When he woke his cheek was wet with tears and the dank musk of sex clung to the sheets.

He would find her again. He would follow, and if he could, this time he would catch her and make her his.

19

What I love about summer is that the days are so long. It means that even after work I feel like I'm enjoying some sun. It's a bit chillier in the evenings now though and when the sun went behind a cloud, the baking pleasure went with it. The wind is up this evening too and since Becks has lost my favourite jacket to the Bristol Beast, I feel the cold as I walk up Blackboy Hill in Clifton and then head towards the zoo, the expanse of the green lawns of the Downs doing nothing to halt the wind. There are plenty of people here and there enjoying the parklands: jogging and dog walking most of them. I veer to my left, making room for a man in a bulky grey hoodie who's leaning against a wall. It isn't that cold that he needs a hood covering so much of his face. He seems for a moment when I pass him, to lean towards me and I shrink away from him, ducking my head behind the brim of my gaucho hat.

I hear his intake of breath. Did he just sniff me?

Quickening my pace, I move fast up the road risking a brief glance back. He's still leaning against the wall, but his head's turned my way, his hood shadowing his features.

Taking a few more steps I look back again. I see him straighten, turning his body fully towards me.

Feeling a pang of fear in my chest I quicken my pace, walking fast towards the leafy tree-lined road that leads to Mrs P's building.

As I turn into her road, I risk a speedy peek back at the way I have come and experience a stab of alarm when I see him following me.

Half running now, I hurry up the road, the rattle and swoosh of the wind-filled trees killing all sound of my stalker from my perceptions. Turning into the large driveway in front of Mrs P's I see that the car park is completely empty because the dentist's practice is closed for the day.

I'm halfway across before risking another glance behind me.

A grey-clad figure stands in the gateway entrance. He seems to be staring directly at me, but with his face in shadow, it's hard to tell.

Running to the front door I tap in the entrance code for the key-safe box.

It won't open

'Fuck, fuck, fuck.' Hearing the fear in my voice I try again while impulsively looking over my shoulder.

He's walking across the driveway.

I yank open the box and pull out the key.

Key in the lock.

Fumbling, I drop it at my feet.

'Fuck.' Grabbing it up, I can hear running footsteps behind me.

Key in lock.

Door open.

Jump through.

Slamming the door shut just as his body crashes into it, making it bounce and shake in its frame.

Hearing a scream; I know it came from me.

Looking around the doorframe, my frantic search catches a metal bolt high in the frame. Reaching up on tiptoe, I try to shove it closed.

The body slams against the door again and I shout in fright and frustration.

I try to force the bolt across. It won't budge, so I hammer at it, karate chopping with the side of my fist.

Pain shoots through my hand, but my fear gives me a strange strength, keeping me at it till I feel it give a little. Then I wriggle and force it screeching across and home.

Only now do I feel safe enough to run up Mrs P's spiral staircase, clutching my hat which keeps slipping down over my eyes. I'll ring the police from there and see if I can get a glimpse of him out of the window. Maybe I can even take a photo of him on my phone.

Racing up the stairs I nearly fall over Sir Lancelot as I rush through the flat's front door. Running to the kitchen window I open it and lean out as far as I can, but I can't see down into the doorway area. Dialling 999 I hold the phone to my ear as I scan the ground below.

'Which service?'

'Police.'

It seems an eternity before a female voice asks what my difficulty is.

As I explain I know how crazy it sounds. Basically, I'm stuck up in the tower because a hooded man chased me. A man who seemed to sniff me as I walked past him, so I was scared in case he was the Bristol Beast.

'Is he still outside?' says the voice of calm.

'I don't know. I can't see him.'

'Okay. There's a car on its way to you. Stay on the line with me until they arrive. Have you got a view of where the vehicle will come in?'

'Yes.'

'Are all the doors locked?'

‘Downstairs, yes,’ I say, hurrying over to lock Mrs P’s flat door with the small chrome bolt. It’s a flimsy glass panelled door that wouldn’t hold back a hungry cat let alone an insane sexual predator, but it might buy me thirty seconds. There’s a lot I could do in thirty seconds, I hope.

‘What’s your name?’

‘Astrid.’

She makes small talk, in an effort to keep me calm I guess. I try to answer, but all my senses are on hyper-alert, distracting me, so I don’t think my conversation would have won many prizes.

A sudden bang from behind makes me scream.

‘Astrid, are you still there? What happened?’

‘Stupid seagull,’ I mutter.

‘What?’

‘Nothing, just a bird pecking at the window.’ I glare at Mrs P’s gull as he struts up and down his window ledge calling for food. Bloody bird has frightened me half out of my wits. Sir Lancelot is threading himself around my legs and making loud demands.

‘Is that your cat I can hear?’ she asks.

I explain about caring for Mrs P’s creatures when a police car turns into view and drives slowly across the car park, halting me midsentence.

‘They’re here,’ I say my heart lifting in joy.

‘Alright, Astrid. Can you go downstairs? Don’t open the door until you’re sure it’s them.’

Trotting downstairs with the cat at my heels I slow to a creeping tiptoe as I reach the bottom, and steal over to press my ear to the door. I can hear a man and a woman talking, and the squawk of a radio. Even so, I jump when they hammer on the door.

I work hard at the top bolt to get it open again before opening the door. I shout a warning as the cat shoots between my ankles and out across the tarmac.

'Sir Lancelot!' My shout is greeted by a confused WPC.

'Your cat, miss?'

'No, yes, no. I'm looking after him for someone.' Peering around her I can see her partner scouting round along the front of the building. I can't see the man in the grey hoodie anywhere. 'He's gone,' I say. I don't know if this fact made me feel good or bad.

The WPC stays with me on the doorstep while her partner checks all around the outside of the building and along the road. He comes back after a good twenty minutes of searching having found no signs whatsoever that someone has been there.

The WPC walks with me as I skirt the same area calling for the cat. We don't find him. I'm close to tears.

'Can we come in and just take some details, have a chat about what happened?' says the WPC. She's about the same age as me; sensible, kind, her brown hair in a bun tucked underneath her cap. I bet she doesn't have to kip on her living room sofa or cry herself to sleep at night.

As I take them up, both panting by the time they reach the top, my mobile rings. It's Nick.

I try to explain that I can't talk, because of the police, and that I'd lost Mrs P's cat when I burst into tears.

'Text me the address, I'm coming to get you,' he says.

I never wanted to hear something so much. 'Okay, thank you,' I manage to say through my sniffling.

The two constables sit looking awkward on Mrs P's old living room furniture while I pace the room and explain what happened; about Becks and how I thought it must be him, the Bristol Beast because I thought he had sniffed me as I walked past him.

'And he chased you?' says the WPC.

'Yes. At least I think so. I saw him in the driveway, then I heard him running. I felt him bash into the door.'

‘Did you see his face at all? Could you give a description? Did he make any distinctive sounds?’ she says, notepad and pencil in hand, her clean, sensibly arranged face giving nothing away.

With genuine disappointment, I shake my head. ‘He was wearing a hoodie so his face was covered. I think he was white? His hands were white, I think, but I couldn’t see his face. He didn’t growl if that’s what you mean.’

‘Did he say anything?’

I shake my head. My phone rings making me jump. It’s Nick saying he’s parked outside. I say I’ll be done in a minute and ask the police if it’s okay if I go now. They say I can but I should come down to the station tomorrow and give a statement.

‘Most likely just someone being an idiot, miss, but if it were more than that, anything you remember could be helpful to us,’ says WPC Sensible.

They escort me downstairs and help me get into Nick’s car.

‘Go to the central station in town and ask for Detective Inspector Reid. He’s heading the investigation regarding these attacks, and he or one of his colleagues will take your statement.’

I say goodnight and thank them both profusely before climbing into the passenger seat of Nick’s car. He pulls me into a hug and my tears come again, unchecked down my cheeks.

‘Oh God, Nick, I’ve never been so scared, ever.’

‘You’re okay, I’m here now. I won’t let anything happen to you,’ he says and I breathe in his comfortingly familiar aroma and feel some of the shock sliding off me.

‘I think it was him, the Bristol Beast. He tried to get in. What if he comes back?’

‘It doesn’t matter. This isn’t your house,’ says Nick.

‘But I lost her cat!’ I say, my voice is a loud howl choked off by my tears.

'It's just a cat,' he says rubbing my shoulders. 'It'll come home when it's hungry.'

'You don't understand. No one's there to let him in. I can't abandon him; he's all she's got, apart from that stupid bird.'

Nick must feel confused because he stops trying to persuade me to calm down with back rubs and just hugs me tight.

A sound outside startles me. I sit up straight with such suddenness that I catch Nick under the chin with my head. I hit him hard enough to make his jaw clack with an audible snap.

'What's that? Is your door locked?' I say looking around his sporty two-seater in panic.

'Hey!' He reaches out, presses a button on the dashboard and to my relief I hear the click of the central locking system. 'See, you're safe. Come on, let's get out of here.'

'But Sir Lancelot?'

'We can't sit here all evening. I'm hungry, how about you?'

I remember Mark. 'I need to get home.'

'Okay.' He starts the engine and as he pulls away I look around me, scanning the dark corners and hedges for any sign of the hooded man or Mrs P's cat. However scared I feel now, I know I'll have to come back and find her cat. But not tonight, tonight it could damn well slum it in the bushes with the rest of the wildlife.

I'm silent as Nick drives me home. After the first ten minutes or so he gives up trying to coax some conversation out of me and just concentrates on his driving. He has a nice car and is a good, if a little too fast, driver. I think his car is one of the most important things in his life and he keeps it in pristine condition. Two comfortable slippery bucket seats. There never was room for a baby carrier in here.

He parks outside the flat and turns to me, his expression unreadable. 'Can I come up?'

I shake my head.

'I just want to talk,' he says.

'I'm expecting a friend.'

'The same friend I saw you with yesterday?' There's an edge to his voice. Good.

'Actually yes.'

We're silent for a moment, the car's cooling engine ticks, measuring out our thoughts.

'I thought we were going to give "us" a try?'

'That doesn't mean I can't have friends,' I say omitting the obvious, that he's living with his "special" friend.

'So is he just a friend then?'

'At the moment, yes.'

'What's that supposed to mean?' Colour flushes into Nick's face making it all too much of a redness. Somehow his emotions make me angry.

'He's not my boyfriend, but neither are you,' I say.

'I thought…'

'You're still with Kate aren't you.' It's a statement, not a question.

'Yes, but…'

'So you're not free to be with me, are you?'

'No, but…'

I open the door cutting him off and turn to get out. He leans across me and yanks it shut.

'Hey!' I shout.

'I haven't finished,' he says.

'I think you have!' I say struggling with him to open the door. When he won't let go and knowing that we're about to be reduced to scrapping like children, I give up and turn round to face him. 'I'm listening,' I say, all the anger from the evening's frightening experience building up to a thumping pain in my head. Tears sting my eyes. Why did anger make me cry? Why did it fog my brain so all the brilliant sarcasm got locked away to come bubbling to the surface hours after when it was too late?

'Azza, I love you.'

'So?'

He looks genuinely shocked. I think his profession of love is supposed to knock me flat, but right this second it's probably the last thing I want to hear.

'Doesn't that mean anything to you?' he says. There's the glint of tears in his eyes.

I glare at him, so angry now that my jaw's locked.

'Don't you believe me?' His pleading tone sickens me so much that I slap his face. Now we're both shocked.

'Nick,' I say.

He holds his hand to his cheek, his eyes wide.

'I'm so sorry,' I say reaching out to touch his face. The huge anger of just a moment ago has drained out of me. 'I shouldn't have done that. Are you okay? God, I'm sorry, it's just been such a fucking awful night. I do care about you.'

His expression moves through a fluid mix of emotions, but his mouth stays pressed into a thin line.

'I do know that I don't want to do to Kate what she did to me,' I say.

He opens his mouth, but I hold up my hand.

'Even if she wasn't aware of my pain, I *am* aware and I'm not prepared to be "the other woman". If you're serious about us you need to be free for us to make a go of it.'

'So if I split with Kate we can get back together?'

'It's not quite that simple, I don't think I'm ready yet for you to move back in.'

'So, I have to be living somewhere else without Kate and then you'll consider getting back together?' he asks and I'm pretty sure I detect sarcasm in his tone.

'Why's that a problem? If you and I don't work out do you still want Kate to fall back on? That's sick!'

‘No, you don’t get it. I do completely want you – us. I can’t just move out. I need somewhere to live and this flat *is* half mine.’

‘God Nick, we’re not having this conversation again. Just let me out of the car. Sort out what you really want, then we’ll talk.’

‘I’m not stopping you,’ he says.

‘But… God!’ And I throw open the door, scramble out – it’s almost impossible to leave these low-slung sporty things gracefully – and slam the door hard behind me. I can imagine his wince at the sound and enjoy a small sense of childish satisfaction.

Fishing in my bag for my keys I see that I still have Mrs P’s. Now I would definitely have to go back.

20

Hunting, sniffing, trapping

He can't believe he'd let her get away. Only seconds faster and he would have had her. The anger makes his head throb. Everything looks grey and the buzz of insects scratch and crawl through his mind. He'd hidden in the bushes almost as soon as he'd realised he couldn't smash the door down. With the arrival of the police car, he'd made a swift exit, trotting up the road and concealing himself amongst the rolling grasses of the Downs along with all the other walkers.

He must have trekked for over an hour before he felt himself under control again. He'd cut her jacket into pocket-sized squares so he could take one with him. He takes it out now and holds it to his nose, breathing deeply, closing his eyes and imagining her sweet face.

It's only a matter of time. He's getting to know all her haunts. The library, Bedminster and up and around Clifton. It had been pure luck seeing her here. No, not luck, she's as drawn to him as he is to her. Destiny. Their love was meant to be.

Sometime soon, very soon, he would have her to himself, his angel princess, his rose. But for now, he would just enjoy the hunt.

21

Once I'm safely in the flat, I send Nick a short text thanking him for coming to get me. I feel guilty for having been so nasty to him. And for hitting him. That's shocked me; there's no excuse for that. But I know what Becks would say – that it was about time I knocked some sense into him. He just made me so angry that I lost control. Not good.

Checking the time, I see it's just after half seven. *Oh God, no time to make something special.* Opening the kitchen cupboards one after another, I realise there's really nothing to eat. Some penis-shaped pasta that someone had given Becks for Christmas, cereal, and some tins of things that had seemed a good idea at the time but that neither of us really wanted to eat. I find an incredibly old onion growing long green tendrils hiding behind a box of chocolate Krave and chop it in half. Perhaps about a third is usable? That gets chopped up and dropped into a pan with the last dribble from a bottle of garlic olive oil. I add a tin of tomatoes that includes garlic and herbs – *lucky find there* – and some black pepper in an old grinder that's gummed to a shelf. That would pep things up a bit. Also a small dollop from a tube of harissa 'hot hot' paste that was lurking in the back of the fridge next to some yellow and white yogurt pots featuring Goldilocks and the Three Bears. It has a dark crusty ring around the cap that I wipe off first, but the contents seem an okay colour. I don't dare check the sell-by date of any of these items. Sell-by dates are just suggestions anyway, aren't they? I'd read about people who had eaten stuff they'd found during expeditions at the North Pole that were about fifty years old and it hadn't hurt them. I don't have any cheese, and there's no way I'm going out to buy some, not after what happened at Mrs P's. Boiling some water I drop in all the penis pasta. Embarrassing, but needs must.

Everything was just about ready; the penises al dente, and the tomato sauce looking and smelling more than edible, and my bedding moved from the sofa onto a chair by the window, so the flat was tidy enough when the doorbell rings.

'Hi?' I call into the entry phone.

'It's me, Mark.'

Feeling a sharp pang of electricity that pierces my stomach and runs straight up my body to my fingertips, I press the door release button.

I hear him coming up the stairs, fast. It sounds like he's taking two steps at a time. As he comes into view, first I see he's smiling a happy broad smile and next I see a bunch of flowers in one hand and a bottle of wine in the other. His enthusiasm reminds me of a large springy dog returning a stick to its owner. He hands me his offerings and we share an awkward moment trying to hug without squashing the bouquet or getting bashed by the bottle.

'Mmm,' he says into my hair. 'You smell great. And the cooking aromas too,' he adds as he pulls back to gaze at me.

I think about the penises and blush. Do we know each other well enough for this kind of culinary kinkiness?

‘I had a bit of an unforeseen rush,’ I say. I don’t want to explain about my narrow escape – or Nick. ‘So supper was a bit dragged together with whatever I could find in the cupboard. Sorry.’

‘I’m sure it’s great. I’m not much of a cook, so anything has to be an improvement on tinned meatballs and frozen ready meals.’

Ushering him in I get him busy opening the wine while I find glasses – mismatched and chipped – and cutlery. We sit up at the breakfast bar and clink glasses of freshly opened red wine.

‘Cheers,’ I say taking a sip that quickly turns into a gulp. Heat from the strong red wine being definitely what the doctor ordered after the evening I’d had.

‘Better?’ he says with a questioning look on his face.

‘You have no idea!’

He smiles. ‘Hard day caring for the needy?’

‘Something like that,’ I say and take another gulp of wine before dropping off my stool to dish out supper. If I kept drinking like this on an empty stomach there was going to be trouble.

I hold his plate piled up with soft pale members and sick red tomato sauce and look from it to him. Am I really going to feed him this?

‘What?’ He makes his half-smile and I laugh.

‘This,’ I say and present his plate with a flourish.

He stares at it for a good five seconds. ‘Are those…’

‘Yes,’ I say. ‘Sorry, I’m rubbish at grocery shopping and so is Becks. We just eat on the run, so this is all I could find.’

‘I’m sure it all tastes the same whatever the shape, but I have to confess this is a first.’

And now we’re both laughing. The penises have lost much of their shape in the cooking so they really could be anything. Someone once told me there are two kinds of boyfriends. If you’re making something in a blender and forget to put the lid on; one kind gets angry and shouts, the other laughs and helps you clean up the mess. I know which type I prefer and I get the impression Mark is that kind.

After we've finished our supper we take our drinks and nestle into the sofa and talk. I tell him about my mum, how it hurt when she left me. How my dad had retreated into himself and his long deep depression.

'It must have been lonely for you both,' Mark says. 'Hard for your father raising a child on his own. Are you still in touch with your mother?'

'Yes, but she's always lived overseas. Romania at the moment, funnily enough.'

'So you don't see her? Does she ever come to England so you can stay with her?'

'She's been back occasionally. Dad won't travel to see her so never took me to visit. I tried to fly out to America to visit her once. I even got as far as the check-in gate, but I panicked. I'm terrified of flying and she never seems to be close enough to visit by boat or train. So we haven't managed it. We Skype, write and Facebook. That's about it. What about your adoptive parents, do you see much of them?'

'Not for a while. They live in Salisbury, but I catch up when I can. Lately, with the dreams and everything, I want to know more about my childhood. What I was like when they first got me, and if they know anything about the orphanage. I feel as if I've been remembering more, so I'm beginning to question more. And I want to see for myself what the place looked like because all I have at the moment are vague impressions.'

'Of what?'

'Since we started our sessions, I see and hear things unexpectedly. I mean really see them, as if they're in the room with me. And my dreams are so vivid.'

'What kind of things?' I ask while topping up both our glasses.

'Children, silent grey dirty children. They have shaved scalps and huge eyes.' He shakes his head. 'I've seen lots of these sorts of images online but I'm sure they're the children that I lived with because I feel like I recognise some of them as if I might remember their names any day now. I hear banging doors and shouting, I feel frightened by them, and it's made me jumpy. Someone dropped a book on their desk today at work and I almost leapt out of my skin. Perhaps that's just the constant tiredness. I wake up every few hours freezing cold and starving. Although once I get out of bed – for a blanket or something to eat – it's gone, I'm fine again, no cold, no hunger. It's like I'm being haunted by my past.

'Last night I woke up and there was a woman leaning over me, staring right at me. Frightened the hell out of me. When I turned on my bedside light she was gone. Bit of a dream I think, I couldn't have been properly awake yet.'

'Who do you think she was?' I ask.

'Oh, I know. I recognised her immediately, that's what made me so scared.'

'Who was she?'

'Felicia,' he says.

'You mentioned her before; you called her everyone's mother. Do you know who she was?'

'She was one of the matrons who cared for us.'

'So shouldn't that be a nice memory?' I ask.

'No, I was terrified. But I had such a strong feeling of loss too, so I'm not sure.'

'We could try and find out with the EFT. Take you back and find out more about Felicia.'

'I'd like to try. I want to understand what's going on with me. I feel like I'm trying to put together a jigsaw puzzle from several different sets that have been thrown together without a picture to refer to. I'm positive that deep down I know the answers. It's like having a word on the tip of your tongue, only you can't remember it.' His face shows his sense of frustration as fine lines crease his brow.

'Okay. Let's start with the set-up line. How about, "Even though I can't quite remember everything, that's completely alright".'

He nods and I move over on the sofa to face him. We start tapping, him mirroring my movements, gradually working our way deeper into his memories of the orphanage. As new thoughts bubble up, he relays them to me and I add them to my spoken lines, elaborating and developing them to help him bring out even more. EFT is great like that; stuff just seems to surface when the person feels ready to deal with it.

'I remember her,' Mark says, his eyes widen in surprise. 'I can imagine her really clearly like it was yesterday.'

'Tell me about her.' I'm excited and happy for him, this is a real breakthrough.

'She's tall and very thin. High cheekbones. Her hair is long and grey, always in a ponytail. But she's not old, so prematurely grey maybe?'

He gives me a questioning look and I half-shrug. 'What colour were her eyes?'

'Grey-blue.'

'What do you feel about her?' As I ask these questions I lean forward, push his hands down onto his lap and gently tap on his pressure points for him.

'Love, I think. It's confusing. I love her, but I'm terrified of her too.' His face clouds, his eyebrows drawing down in an expression of deep unhappiness.

I tap on the point above his eyebrow and imagine I could feel the knots of muscles bunched there by his unhappy drawn face. 'Why terrified?' I ask, tapping now beneath his eye.

'She hurts me, and the other children. But she loves us too, especially me and Dragos.' He seems surprised at this sudden memory. 'She gave us food, that's Dragos and me. She said we were her special ones and gave us extra food. I was always hungry, everyone was, I was so hungry it was a pain that never went away. That's why I wake up starving, isn't it?' His green eyes gaze into mine, large and innocent as a child's.

I nod, not speaking in case I interrupt his flow of memories, I just keep tapping on his pressure points, willing him to stay calm and remember more.

'But I'm scared of her. Dragos is too, but he's bigger than me and he doesn't get things wrong like I do, and… she hurts us. We have to be completely quiet and not move a muscle or she hurts us. She bites. Oh!' He stops, his mouth open in shock. 'She was…' He shakes his head and I see his eyes shine with unshed tears. 'I remember… terrible things. She… she… she should never have been allowed to… We…'

'Mark,' I say keeping my voice soft and low. I start to tap on the top of his head saying, 'Even though Felicia did these things to me, I am safe now.'

I feel my fingers run through his hair as he abruptly stands.

'I can't… Sorry… I just…' His eyes are wide with panic.

'Mark, please sit down. Let's run through the sequence.'

He shakes his head and grabs his jacket where he'd hung it near the door. 'I'm really sorry, I can't do this now.'

And then he was gone, pulling the door shut behind him.

The flat feels lonely now that Becks is away. I keep worrying about what has just happened with Mark, and I can't stop thinking about Nick. I wish I could talk everything through with someone. Becks preferably, only she is biased against Nick.

My head's buzzing with all that Mark has told me. I get my notebook out. Writing it down helps me make sense of it. From his reaction, I would say that Felicia was most likely sexually abusing him, but to be sure I'd need to get him to talk about it further. Poor man, no wonder he'd blocked it all from his memory. Was I really the person to help him with this? It's turning out to be a bit more serious than a bout of insomnia. Maybe I should suggest he spoke to Carey. She has so much more experience than me. He said that Felicia bit him. And that's what has really struck me. The biting and the wolf tattoo. I need to talk it all through with someone but I'm not sure I'm ready to voice my suspicions about Mark just yet.

And I still feel bad about hitting Nick, especially after he'd come to my rescue.

Did I really believe that the hooded attacker could be Mark? I shake my head. Stupid; I would have recognised him, wouldn't I? Oh, I wish I could talk to Becks.

I miss Nick too, and the way we were. We could rebuild it couldn't we, back to how we were? I wish I could just make up my mind about him, and stick to it, and stop all these seesaw emotions.

And what if Mark is the Bristol Beast, who am I fooling? I can't deal with stuff like this. I'm not even a fully certified practitioner. At best I'm a carer who's found another way to be more caring. I google Bristol News and see a breaking news update that the police have brought a man in for questioning regarding the attacks. A feeling of relief floods through me. I'd really thought it might be Mark, hadn't I. God, selfish too; I'm more relieved finding out that it can't be Mark than considering the Beast's poor victims and any new ones.

But still, I shiver inside. It could be him, couldn't it?

I push the thought away.

Maybe I should be concentrating on Nick. If he really loves me, he needs to show it, at the very least move out from living with Kate and see if we can start something again. I can't let him move in though, no way, not yet. If I call him and apologise for earlier, that might be a step in the right direction, maybe?

Picking up my mobile, I phone Nick and I listen while it rings, and rings, eventually going to voicemail. I hate leaving messages; you can't take it back when you get it wrong. I end the call and send him a text instead saying 'Sorry about earlier. Can we talk?'

It's nearly ten by now so I don't think he'll get back to me until tomorrow. I stare at the washing-up. It isn't going to do itself, but I just don't feel like it. I'm still shaken up by Mark's EFT session and too many thoughts are buzzing round my brain to deal with anything useful. Instead, I go and run a bath, putting candles around the edge – the full works.

Tying my hair into a messy bun, I slide with a grateful sigh into the steaming water. Bliss. My eyes close and as I drift off to lovely places in my head, the door buzzer goes.

What?

In my haste, I slosh water and the now sodden candles tumble into the bath, leaving thin soot trails across the surface. Great!

Grabbing a towel I pad wet footprints across the floor to the entry phone. It could be Nick or Mark. Both possibilities speed up my heart.

'Hi,' I say into the phone.

'Hi, it's Kate. I… I'm so sorry, I know it's late, but we need to talk.'

Now my heart is completely in my mouth. I think I might actually drop dead here and now. *Kate, what the hell?*

'Please.'

I can hear the plaintive tone in her voice. As much as I hate to admit it, it must have taken a lot of courage to be here. I push the buzzer and open my flat door, waiting for her to appear up the stairs.

She's apologising as soon as she's in view. 'Oh God I'm sorry, you were in the bath. I shouldn't have come.'

I open the door wider. 'Probably not, but you're here now.' There's an angry note in my voice and I take satisfaction in seeing her wince. Okay, so I'm a bitch but it's not like she doesn't deserve it. I've wanted so badly to tell her a few home truths, and here she is. I just need to relax my jaw a little and let them spill out.

She's standing in the middle of my living room, white hands clasped in front of her looking how I imagine a rabbit does in the dazzle of oncoming headlights. I should invite her to sit down, but I don't.

We just stand and stare at each other. She's very pretty. Not that I didn't know that already, it's just that I've never had a chance to properly look at her before. She seems very young, although she's probably only a couple of years younger than me, about twenty-three I guess, and pale. Pale hair, pale cheeks.

'I'm sorry,' she says and I wonder what she's saying sorry for; disturbing my bath, being in my flat or stealing my boyfriend? 'I shouldn't be here. Nick will go crazy, only…'

She's so uncomfortable. I'm beginning to feel a bit bad deep down to my core.

'I know he's been to see you and I…'

Oh right. The small sympathy I've been brewing shrivels up with a hiss. So she wants to warn me off her boyfriend. Not so hot when the boot's on the other foot, is it? Anger creeps up my gut like a stalking cat.

'I'm… I need to talk to you because…'

She keeps stopping mid-sentence, it's driving me crazy.

'You're scared of losing—'

'I'm pregnant,' she says cutting me off, and I stare at her open-mouthed.

'Sorry… I'm pregnant. Nick is… Nick is finding the idea difficult.'

'Difficult!' I repeat, my voice incredulous. *Oh my God, it's happening again.* 'Did you know what he did to me?'

She bites her lip and nods. 'He told me you'd been pregnant, just after you lost the baby. I'm so sorry.'

'Stop saying you're fucking sorry,' I shout and she flinches. 'I'm sorry,' I say, and we both laugh, a shaky lunatic sound that has little to do with joy. 'How far gone?' I move to sit on the sofa. I motion her to join me, which she does with small hesitant steps, lowering herself to the cushion with the care of a bomb disposal expert. Perhaps she thinks it – or I – would explode at any moment, which I just might.

'Four months,' she says.

'How long has he known?'

'A couple. I think he thought I might have an abortion, or lose it like you did—'

I interrupt her with a derisive snort, *thought he'd get lucky like last time, the little shit.*

'But now I'm in the second trimester…' she continues.

I recognise the jargon; she's been reading up, just like I did, while it still mattered.

'And you think he's about to do to you what he did to me.' My words are like a slap and she puts her head in her hands and starts to weep.

I can't hold her or even touch her. It's the truth and it hurts us both.

Bastard.

I can't believe that he's been reeling me in. I wished I'd punched him rather than that puny slap.

'Shit,' I say and Kate peeks at me through tear-sodden eyes. 'He can't be allowed to get away with it.' I feel sick at the hope that lights up her face. *Fucking bastards, both of them.* My anger has focus and I'm losing control. Kate has it all; the man I'd loved, the baby I'd craved, the family I so desperately yearned for, ever since I could remember. Only none of it's real because Nick's a slippery shit who isn't prepared to take responsibility for those who love and need him. *Just like my mother.*

And he was about to use me as his scapegoat.

'Kate. I'm just so angry right now I don't think I can have this conversation.' I wrap my arms around my body and rock back and forth, trying to calm the fury threatening to detonate.

'But I don't know—' she starts.

'Just go,' I say.

'But…'

'If you don't leave right now, I'm not sure I can be answerable for my actions.'

'Oh!' She stands up fast and backs a few steps towards the door.

'I'll think about it. Send me a text and when I'm calmer, I'll ring you. We'll talk, okay?'

She nods and bites her lip. Now she looks about twelve and I nearly scream.

'Please, Kate, go.'

As soon as I hear the front door downstairs shut with its familiar bang, I let out a howl of pain and attack the couch with the anger of a rabid beast. I fling the pillows and then run at my duvet, grunting with exertion as I throw it across the room. I rush into the bedroom and rip the bedding off before manhandling the double mattress across the room. I rip the curtains off the pole, throw open the wardrobe and with a primal scream, fling all

Becks' and my clothes around the room. Everything is everywhere like the gutted mess of an eviscerated animal.

Except for the bedside lamp.

A lamp of particular ugliness picked out by Nick during a trip to Ikea so many months ago. I hear a guttural growl that came from deep in my throat as I launch myself at that horrible symbol of our unity. But my feet tangle in the strewn linen and I fall, heavy and swearing, beside the empty bed base.

'Fuck, fuck, fuck,' I shout, struggling to regain my feet. As fast as it had come, all the bilious fury spills out of me and I lie spent amongst so much twisted material, naked except for what has wrapped itself around my ankles.

Calm; a moment like the eye of the storm, all I notice is my laboured breathing. Then a wave of sobbing rolls over my consciousness, and I'm lost to all but that.

I must have cried myself to sleep because I wake some hours later, shivering as the cool night air goose-bumps my flesh, Kate's tear-blotched face filling my mind. No more sleep then.

I get up and survey the mess around me. So much destruction. I'm almost proud, and more than a little shocked. I didn't know I was capable of this kind of thing. I've never done anything like it before. Normally I keep everything bottled up. I cry, true, but screaming and throwing stuff around, not me. I do feel better, lighter somehow. Something has cracked and allowed the floodgates to open. Yes, I feel good. It's a big ugly mess but I needed to do that. Damn Nick, he has a lot to answer for.

Grabbing up a few recognisable clothes from the floor I cover my nakedness. Then I drag the mattress back onto the bed base. God, it's heavy. Had I really flung that across the room? The curtains I'd think about later. Hopefully, I hadn't broken anything. I pile everything onto the bed and go stare at the sitting room. A mess, but not so bad. I pile my bedding back on the sofa and think about a cup of tea.

As I stand waiting for the kettle to boil I stare at my shelf of stolen objects. Little houses and doll's house furniture that generally involved babies. Shit, it isn't hard to analyse – my crazy mind has been collecting home and family. Now my pain has been exorcised I can see these things for what they are, totems for my lost family – Nick, baby and me or Mum, Dad and me. Our minds are strange, only it did make sense in an odd way I suppose. I don't understand why they had to be stolen though. None of them had been that expensive even on my meagre income. Starting tomorrow – no, today actually, as I can see from the clock it's nearly five – I'll start returning them to the shops: a kind of reverse shoplifting – that sounds almost fun!

Giggling, I hug myself. Okay, I need to sit down with my tea and work out just what the hell is going on and what I'm going to do about Nick. And Mark. I really need to get him to talk to me. He left in such a state; I can't bear to think of him dealing with that alone.

Then I'll try and have a bit of sleep if I can.

22

Dream

Kate holds a tiny newborn in her arms. It's my baby but I'm letting Kate take her. I have all the stolen things in a wicker basket and I give them to Kate for the baby to play with. Nick is hiding somewhere and we're searching for him because the basket is getting too heavy for Kate.

My father is playing his guitar. I can see the music he's playing; it comes out of the strings like holographic threads of light.

'That's beautiful,' I tell him.

'So are you,' he says and hands me the guitar.

I play a tune so lovely that the music wraps around us both and we are laughing. But then Nick runs in and starts ripping up the glittering threads. He keeps saying over and over, 'Not this way, not this way.'

23

My new-found high lasts for most of the morning while I do the rounds. I visit my service users in body only, as my mind is busy elsewhere. If they notice I'm distracted no one says, except for Pauline sitting in her yellow glowing home.

'Are you alright, Astrid love?' she says searching my face with concern.

I hug her. 'I'm fine. Sorry, my life's a bit of a muddle right now.' I add at her worried expression, 'Don't worry, I'll be back on track in no time.' I make what I hope is a reassuring smile.

Having none of it, she waggles a fat knobbly finger at me. 'You can't care for others if you don't look after yourself too.'

She's right, I'm a mess and I mean to sort myself out.

I go to the library mid-morning and treat myself to a frothy coffee. Settling into one of the comfy black leather couches I get out my notebook to see if I can't sort my thoughts out by making them into bullet points.

Nick - Bastard
Kate - Pregnant

Mark - ?

My explosion last night had sorted out one problem for me, I definitely don't want Nick back. I write:

Nick - Bastard - definitely X !!!

That feels good. Maybe a little self-indulgent revenge would be okay, wouldn't it? Actually, I wouldn't have to do much, just keep him thinking I might take him back and he would do the rest himself, like a windup toy on self-destruct.

But what about Kate? Did I owe her anything?

No, I don't, so fuck her!

That isn't right though, is it? Whatever happens between her and Nick she's going to keep that baby, but ideally with Nick at her side? For my own sanity, I need to help him understand his responsibility to Kate and their child. I'm the product of an abandoned childhood; I don't want to add to someone else's abandonment. If I could help Nick rather than kick him in the teeth – appealing as much as that was – I would ultimately be helping myself move on. I write this down too. My notes are getting me somewhere at least.

Sounds alright on paper, but am I really strong enough to do it?

Nick has hurt me so badly.

And now Kate is having his baby.

I feel the sting of tears. This child would have been the half-sibling to my own baby. Always the pain for my lost child, I need to let her go too and lay her to rest. In order to move on, aiding Nick and Kate would ultimately help me. If I have any feelings for Mark I can't focus on any new relationship while Nick still lingers in my life.

And I am interested in Mark aren't I?

Mark - ?

Just seeing his name brings up a slideshow of his best moments, especially kissing in the moonlight. Yes, I am interested in Mark, but I need to help him too. Yesterday he'd practically bolted out of my flat. We need to work on just what he has remembered. And I need help too, to sort it all. With Becks away, I don't have my trusty sounding board. No one understands me like she does, except Carey maybe? Nodding to myself, I knock back the dregs of my coffee and leap to my feet. Spinning on my heels, I encounter a grey blur of a figure who slips behind the central aisle made up of black wooden bookcases before I can get a proper look at him. A shudder runs through me as I remember the hooded man who had chased me across Mrs P's front yard. I move fast to the bookrack and peer around it. Nothing, just a surprised elderly gent clasping a stack of large hardback books to his chest. I'm seeing things now. Must be the lack of sleep.

Shoving my notebook into my bag and slinging it over my shoulder, I head through the cooling shadows of the book aisles and out into the midday sunshine. Stopping by the black metal statue of Raja Ram Mohan Roy I notice his hat for the first time. It looks a bit like a fruit basket, I'm surprised no one has filled it with apples or something, doing a bit of 'touching up' like the students do to some of the other statues in Bristol. After all, the Queen Vic statue, a grey stone bell-shaped bulk which stood outside that big swanky hotel, was always in for it. Squinting in the sun as I stare up at him, I realise that I forgot to put on a hat this morning.

I phone Carey and explain in brief my dilemma about Nick. A wave of gratitude floods through me when she agrees to see me after my lunchtime appointments, at half one. Knowing Carey is available and just having someone to tell it all to, helps so much. I glance up to the golden unicorn slim and proud on the roof of the City Hall and smile. It fits my mood exactly as I walk across the grass to the Park Street bus stop.

My next round of visits go by with cheerful ease and when I've finished all the lunches I almost run to Carey's. I'm talking as soon as she opens the door, my voice gasping as I struggle to catch my breath and speak at the same time.

'Oh, thank you for seeing me at such short notice. I think I was going crazy!'

'Astrid,' she says, laughing, and pulling me into a hug that tugs me off the doorstep and into the natural cool of her hallway. It's a calming pale peach with stripped pine floors. Her walls contain a few large close-ups of her kids, artfully captured in soft focus sepia, making them seem like children from a lost age.

'Come on,' she says, ushering me into her sitting room. I can smell incense. It's a head-spinning mix of something deep and woody, a hint of wet earth with sweet undertones. 'I was just finishing a meditation,' she says, going over to open her white thin cotton curtains and slide up the window a bit. Distant traffic noises blur with the loud squawking of seagulls. 'Do you hear them? I always think the weather's on the turn when they make a lot of noise like that.'

She points at the couch. 'Make yourself comfortable while I get us both a glass of water.' Smiling she turns, heading off to the hallway and kitchen that I know is at the back of the house. It's a tiny space with everything close to hand and I can imagine her calm and neat as her surroundings, collecting glasses and filling them with cool clear water. Swallowing, I find my throat is dry from all the rushing today, and from the shouting last night. I'm genuinely grateful when she returns, in a swirl of long pale cream cotton, her top slit up the sides above cropped white leggings. She hands me the water, which is just as cold as I hoped it would be.

'Better?'

I nod, still sipping.

'Good. Now tell me, what's up?' she says, settling herself down beside me.

I explain about Nick, how he's been trying to persuade me to get back together with him, and about Kate, her visit last night, and how I'm hoping to sort both of them out somehow.

'Okay,' says Carey pushing her hair back behind her ear. 'Quite a tall order. First let me say, brilliant, brilliant you, for this understanding. You have come so far, you should be proud of yourself.'

At these words I do feel something strong and happy well up inside me, filling my chest with a bubble of emotion, but besides that is an unexpected gush of tears. I cover my face with my hands and my shoulders jerk as I fail to hold back the flood of crying. Carey hugs me tight for a few moments and then passes me a box of tissues.

Sniffling and gulping for air, I try to explain. 'I know I need to let him go. I know he's not good for me, only…' My breath hitches and I lose the words.

'Astrid, it's a sad fact that a toxic relationship is a lot harder to get over than a healthy one. Inside you know you're doing the right thing. By helping Nick move on you're giving yourself permission to move on too. Does that make sense?'

Nodding, I twist and scrunch the damp tissue in my hands, staring down into my lap, my knees pressed together as I huddle, miserable and lost.

'What you have to ask yourself is, why does Nick run away from responsibility?' she says.

I shrug. I know quite a bit about his family, they seem alright to me. Not as fucked up as mine, anyway. Do you ever really know someone, though? I'd thought I knew Nick. I'd thought I could count on him, but I'd been wrong.

'Kate and Nick aren't your responsibility, you know that don't you?' says Carey.

I nod.

'It's their life path and their lessons to be learnt. Knowing that you have to let Nick go is enough, you don't have to fix them.'

She's right. Maybe it's enough just to tell Nick I'm not interested, then he would be forced to deal with his situation with Kate.

My mobile rings, cutting into my thoughts.

'Sorry,' I say getting it out of my pocket. 'I forgot to turn it off.' It's an unknown number so I silence it and put it away in my bag.

'Shall we tap on your feelings for Nick? Clear the cobwebs a bit?' she asks.

'That would be great.'

'Okay.'

Carey and I settle ourselves to face each other.

'Even though I have this hurt in my heart about Nick I completely love and accept myself,' began Carey.

I follow along, repeating her words and mirroring her tapping actions. Slowly, calm reasserts itself along my body. Our voices are like low murmurs of meditation and I feel able and in control again. Not like before, which was all hot flush of determined activity. No, now I'm centred and self-contained. I feel upright – if that makes sense – whereas before I had been all over the place.

When we have finished, I pay Carey and she walks me to the door.

'From the young woman I met just six months ago, you are now well on the way to the person you want to be,' she says. Smiling, she hugs me. 'You make me so proud.'

It's a strong afternoon sun that slits my eyes as I trot down her front steps. I turn to wave and see she's looking with a frown at something away over my shoulder. Instinct turns my head in the same direction but I see nothing; just a quiet street, a few parked cars, net curtained windows opposite, and a woman walking her dog.

'What?' I ask turning back to Carey.

'I thought I saw… Oh, forget it. Off you go. We'll catch up soon, then you can tell me more about how you've been getting on with your test subject, the one with agoraphobia.'

'Lil,' I say. She's right, I have been losing focus. I have a shedload of writing up to do for my course and a plan for my next visit to Lil's. I would need to see Mark again – my heart skips a little at this thought. Perhaps we could untangle what had come up for him last night. I remember that I had wanted to talk to Carey about him, get her opinion on the best way forward. But the music of my ringtone cut in. Waving a last goodbye to Carey, I set off down the street, rootling in my bag as I go. It's the same unknown number. 'Hi.'

'Miss Alden?'

'Yes.' I feel cautious. I hope this isn't my mobile service provider. They are always trying to drag me into long conversations about upgrades to my package. I wish they'd get it; I could barely afford what I had already.

'Detective Inspector Reid, miss. I understand there was an incident yesterday evening. You were chased by,' I hear riffling papers, 'a man in a grey hooded top in Downside Road, Clifton. Is this correct?'

'Yes,' I say, slowing my pace to hear him better.

'I understand you had some strong impressions about this man?'

'Sort of.'

'I would be most grateful if you could meet with me to discuss this incident. Either at the city centre Bridewell Police Station or I'd be happy to come to your home if that's more convenient?' His voice has a smoker's rasp, plus a hint of London accent?

'When?' I ask.

‘As soon as possible, miss. While it’s all fresh in your head.’

‘I’m at the bottom end of Redland at the moment. I could be at the centre in twenty minutes or so, depending on the buses.’

‘That would be perfect, miss.’

‘Do I just walk in and ask for Detective Reid?’

‘Yes, miss. The front desk will take care of you.’

Click and he’s gone. I up my pace for the bus stop. Detective Inspector Reid; I imagine a middle-aged man, shortish, a bit overweight, smelling of stale cigarettes. He wouldn’t wear a uniform. My mind flicks through a variety of crumpled jackets in varying shades of brown until I settle on a tweed one with corduroy elbow patches, a bit like our English teacher at secondary school.

There are a couple of people at the stop before me. I stand in line and continue my mental descriptions of DI Reid. He’d be divorced but still loved his wife; the pressure of the job had pushed them apart, that’s why he moved to Bristol.

A man joins the queue, standing a few feet away from me. I glance briefly but he’s mostly turned away from me with his hood up.

His top was grey.

Stop it, lots of people wear grey, especially men for some reason. I look to my left and study the two women ahead of me in the queue. They’re chatting to each other, elderly, both leaning on their granny trolleys. One has a typical navy tartan design, the other’s is more funky – bright yellow shiny plastic with a few battered fake flowers fixed to the lid. That would be me one day. I smile. By then I won’t care what people think so I could let some of the crazy show round the edges.

There’s a light brush against my arm. The man has moved up close and his body must have touched mine. I edge over towards the elderly ladies. Should I walk to the next bus stop? What if he follows me?

There's the loud hiss of brakes as a huge double-decker bus comes to a stop beside me, cutting into my thoughts. I huddle behind the two ladies like their unfortunate forgotten cousin and follow them onto the bus. They settle into the front seats reserved for the elderly and disabled and I slide into a seat just behind them. I watch for the man but he doesn't get on. Peering out of the window I search the street. It's empty. He's gone. Maybe this isn't his bus and he's decided it would be quicker to walk; I'd done that a million times hadn't I? No denying it, I'm still shaken up by my experience yesterday. Talking to the detective would probably help. He might have some useful advice. Perhaps I should take some self-defence classes like Becks said. We'd find one together when she was back. It might even be fun?

The ladies disembark outside the back entrance to Primark and I jump off at the next stop doubling back on myself for the city centre police station. It's relatively new – the old one has been converted into a nightclub and gallery – and has a high tech space-age feel to it. Walking up to the front desk, I'm greeted by a crisp WPC who appears only just out of secondary school. She buzzes through on a complicated phone system and has a brief conversation before telling me that I should take a seat as DI Reid will be down in just a moment. There's a sort of black fake leather bench along one pale grey marble wall and I go and perch, the cool hardness reinforcing my sense of not belonging.

I've hardly been there more than a minute when a tall, thirties something black man, wearing a dark suit over a white T-shirt strides towards me, his hand extended.

'Miss Alden?'

I stand and shake his hand. 'Detective Reid?' Apart from the smell of cigarettes, which is faint and spicy and not unpleasant, he's nothing like I'd imagined.

'Yep. Let's go to an interview room. There's one free just up the hallway from here.' He turns to the reception desk. 'Could you have WPC Pettit join us in room 12A. Ask her if she'd rustle up a couple of coffees, or tea?' he adds turning to me.

'Just water, please.'

'Water for Miss Alden, coffee for me. Thanks.' He turns and heads up a hallway to the left and I follow, a nervous itch settling on my neck.

Once we're seated in a sparse room that holds only necessities, Reid smiles. He reminds me of David Oyelowo. I wonder if his co-workers comment on it.

'Thank you for coming so promptly, Miss Alden.'

'Astrid.'

He nods. 'Astrid. Thank you. I was keen to talk to you as soon as possible because of the correlations between yourself and the attack on Miss Patterson.'

'Becks.'

Again the curt nod.

There's a knock at the door. 'Enter,' says the detective.

The door stutters open with a WPC, her arms full, struggling to get in. I recognise her as the policewoman who came to my rescue at Mrs P's, WPC Sensible. She must have used her elbow to push the handle. Reid goes to her aid and to my surprise she blushes. Interesting.

'You remember WPC Pettit from yesterday evening, Astrid,' he says putting a white plastic cup of water down in front of me.

'Yes,' I say and smile at her. 'Hi.'

She gives me a slight smile in return. 'I hope you feel less shaken up today?' she asks.

'Sit down, Pettit,' says Reid and the WPC pulls up a chair next to him. He takes a yellow folder that she's laid on the desk and opens it, pulling out a couple of sheets. 'Okay, let me just scan Pettit's notes to refresh my memory.'

Pettit and I sit in silence as Detective Reid reads.

'Right,' he says and Pettit opens her notepad, her pen poised. 'You share a flat with Rebecca Patterson, is that correct?'

'Yes,' I say. Butterflies begin to rise in my stomach.

'And you say a man in a grey hooded top followed you up Upper Belgrave Road and then into Pembroke and Downside Roads where he then chased you to the front door of…' He stops and checks the notes. 'Bridgewater House, number five B, of Downside Road.'

'Yes.'

'You believe that before he started to follow you that this man leant towards you and seemed to sniff you. Is that correct?'

'Yes.'

'You see, Astrid, I have a number of concerns here, that I must clear up before I can proceed.'

I nod, and take a sip of water as my mouth is suddenly dry.

'It is either an extraordinary coincidence that the same man, or one with oddly similar behaviour patterns, targets both women who happen to live together in the same flat.' He leans forward and I feel his presence as an intense cloud of maleness. Too strong, too much.

'Oh, Becks and me, we're not together, together.' I make bracketing mimes with my fingers. He stares at me and I feel a blush coming. *This man assumes nothing*, I think.

'Or that this man is known to you both, or he knows of you both. In either case, you may have invaluable information to help us apprehend him.' Reid stops and takes a sip of his coffee, which allows Pettit to catch up with her frantic scribbling.

‘Or,’ he stops and looks at me with cold blank eyes, before continuing, ‘You have made this up, for whatever reason, not to be left out of your friend, Becks’ limelight.’

His presence looms over me and my cheeks burn. How could he think I’m making this up? That’s just sick.

‘So you can see why it’s important that we talk, Astrid.’

I wish I hadn’t told him my first name now. He’s kept to Detective Inspector Reid, keeping the advantage I guess. To think I rushed here, I should have made him do the running – not that I wanted him in my flat. ‘Why would I make this up? It was horrible. I was terrified.’

‘We have made a few enquiries. I understand you have been through a breakup?’ he asks glancing down at the notes in the folder.

‘I don’t see what that’s got to do with anything.’ My voice seems to be rebounding off the walls of this empty box of a room.

‘And that you suffered a miscarriage.’

I jump to my feet and I start a little at the sound of my chair upending on the floor behind me. I lean over the desk towards him and ignore the sound of Pettit’s chair scraping as I keep my glare set on Reid.

With horrible calm, he returns my stare. ‘Sit down, Miss Alden, you’re not under investigation here. I just want you to understand some of the possibilities I’m considering. Do you get me?’

I straighten up.

‘You see, if this man does know you both then you could be in some considerable danger. So I need to eliminate all possibilities. Believe me, I would prefer it if you were making it up. At least I’d know you were safe.’ He says this last with almost a smile.

And now I think I can see the man beneath the hard veneer. His eyes are tired. He has seen bad things and he would rather not see anymore. I nod and take a deep breath.

Setting my chair upright I sit down and take a gulp of water. 'I thought you had someone. The news said you'd taken a man in for questioning?'

'We follow every lead we get, Astrid. Any line of enquiry has many possibilities that need close scrutiny. Anything you can add to that can only help give us a clearer picture,' he says.

I nod, a weight settling between my shoulder blades. 'What do you want to know?'

We talk for ages about everything. Talk about hanging out your dirty linen; it's hard, bringing out my last year of pain to these two strangers. I explain all that's been going on since I bought the flat with Nick to the present day. I don't feel judged by Reid, he's heard worse I'm sure. I want him to understand who I am. I'm not the kind of person who would make up something like this, cry wolf so to speak. My life is – was – a mess, but I'm not fucked up, and I'm getting it all sorted now. After what feels like hours we finally seem to have got to the end.

'Lastly, Astrid, can you think of anyone who might hold a grudge against you or Miss Patterson?'

'Apart from Nick or Kate, and I don't think either of them is capable of anything like what happened to me or Becks, no.'

'And both you and Miss Patterson work in the caring sector. Have either of you come across anyone in the line of your work who might be…' He hesitates. 'Of an unusual nature or who might be taking a particular interest in either of you?'

I think of Mark and experience a churning charge of nausea. Patient confidentiality, is it appropriate here? Would Mark attack Becks? Wouldn't I have recognised him even with the hoodie?

'Yes?' asks Reid.

'I told you I was sort of seeing someone called Mark Osbourne.'

'Yes,' says Reid.

'He's also one of my test subjects for my EFT practice.'

'And what prompts you to mention him?' he asks.

I glance from Reid to Pettit and back again. 'There are some… similarities.'

Reid tips his head in question. 'Like?'

'He has a wolf tattoo. He…' *This isn't right.*

'Please, Astrid.' His voice is firm.

'He has disturbing dreams about wolves and…' I can't say more, it's just too wrong. 'And stuff,' I finish lamely. 'Look, Detective, I know him. He's kind and gentle. Oh God, I shouldn't have said. It's not fair on him, he trusts me.' I feel hot and sick. What have I done?

'It may be nothing as you say, but we have to follow every lead. It's not just about you, or Miss Patterson. There's another woman who has been hurt and there may be more to come. I appreciate your dilemma. Hopefully interviewing Mr Osbourne will just be a chance for us to eliminate another man from our enquiries. That seems alright doesn't it?'

I have to agree, but I feel terrible. I have taken Mark's fragile trust and trampled all over it.

I give Detective Reid Mark's mobile number.

In return, he gives me his card. 'Please put my number, and the station's, on your phone. Ring us if you have the slightest concern. Keep safe and be aware. I understand your work takes you out and about all over Bristol, but please be extra vigilant until we have made some progress with this case.'

We all stand up and I shake hands with them both.

'Thank you, Astrid, for your time. WPC Pettit will show you out.'

24

Hunting, sniffing, trapping

The library is where he will find her. He waits at College Green, sitting on the grass and listening to the thumping music from the iPod until he sees her, so bright she lights up everything around her, and then he follows.

She goes to the library cafe and sits drinking coffee and writing notes in her book.

Hiding behind the end of a tall bookrack, he picks a book at random and pretends to read. This way he can watch her, peeking up through his lashes, the hood of his eyelid dimming the top half of his vision so that she becomes a fuzzy blur of indistinct loveliness. All too quickly it's not enough just to look. *She's so absorbed, she won't notice,* he thinks and inches forward until he's standing behind her chair. Leaning a little forward he can smell her hair and drink in her amazing aroma. It calms and excites him all in one.

She makes a sudden movement, shifting to rise from her seat, and he barely straightens fast enough to avoid her hitting the back of her head on his mouth. Moving with swift strides he retreats to the long bookshelves and ducks behind them, nearly knocking down an old man. He keeps moving, on to the next tall set of shelving, and then the next before he risks stopping to check for her.

Peeking around, he sees her walking with fast purposeful steps down the aisle and out through the entrance hall.

Hurrying after her, he stops and waits in the gloom of the hall as he can see her, standing just outside the library front door staring up at the black metal statue in the square. When she moves off, he follows, keeping at a careful distance.

She goes from place to place like a bright butterfly. Her hair is free to catch the wind today. He likes the long layered tresses – dark like mahogany with some copper lights that catch the sun in bright flashes – and longs to run his hands through it. Her hair will be soft like silk, he feels sure of that, and he can see her body is lithe and nimble. When he gets her to a quiet place, where no one can disturb them, he will learn every part of her, search out the scent of her secret places. When she goes to the bus stop he follows and gets on the bus behind her, nipping up the staircase and hanging about on the stairs until he sees her pass, heading for the exit, then he follows. She seems distracted and it's easy to keep up with her threading her way through the busy streets.

As he hangs about each of the places she visits, waiting for her to re-emerge, he imagines how it will be, when it's just the two of them. He won't need to pretend with her; she knows him, just like Felicia did. He can see her clever knowing shining out of every pore of her. He won't need to teach her with cruel bites like the others, because she is already perfect. She will *want* him to love her, in his special way. Just thinking of what they will have warms him deeply and he begins to sweat. Trickles run down the nape of his neck and irritate in an unpleasant set of ever increasing lines down his back so that he squirms and tries to scratch through the thickness of his clothes. He wants to take off his heavy hooded top but doesn't want the risk of anyone seeing his face. He wipes the back of his neck and rubs off the sweat now glistening on his palm onto his jeans. Glancing up he sees her, with her back to him, talking to a woman at the door; a small blonde woman, who peers at him with a piercing sharpness that makes him turn, duck his head and walk fast up the next street.

Stopping, he edges back until he gets a view of her walking down the road, busy with someone on her cell phone. He follows, gradually catching her up. When she joins a bus queue he walks up and stands behind her. His heart is beating so fast he's worried that she'll hear it. Turning his body away so she won't see his face, he holds his breath, listening for her heartbeat. She's too far from him. He edges closer until their bodies touch. An electric thrill runs up his arm before she shifts away from him, moving closer to two gossiping women. He can't risk getting so close again, not just yet.

When the bus comes she gets on with the two women and sits near the front. He can't get on, he feels she's watching out for him. As fast as he can, he heads back the way he came.

He will just have to catch up with her later. He knows most of her habits now, all the regular areas she visits, so she can't avoid him forever.

25

I went straight home. The interview with Reid has wiped me out. Phoning work, I tell them that I'm ill and can't do any of my teatime slots.

It's not a lie, I'm really not myself.

Making a cup of tea, I get lost for a moment staring at the shelf of little thefts. Perhaps if I start being proactive about my life I'll feel less empty. Okay, I'll drink my tea, sort the bedroom, take back a few of these weird stolen things – Nick's right, they are ugly – go to Mrs P's and see if Sir Lancelot is about. If I can find a picture of him at her flat I could put up some posters in case someone has found him. And I'll ring the hospital and see if I can find out how Mrs P's doing and when they're going to let her out. I couldn't bear it if she came home to find her cat gone. I'll ring Lil too and see if she's ready for another EFT session. Also Mark; we should arrange another meeting. Picking up my mobile, I find I can't bring myself to either ring or text him. I start a text – 'Hi if the police' – and then delete it. 'Hi, when the police talk to you, I'm sorry I,' I delete that too. Some things need to be said face to face. Sighing I text him – 'Please ring me.' I could sound him out on the phone.

While I'm clearing up the tip that was the bedroom my mobile rings. Because I'm standing on a chair, trying to rehang the curtains, I twist my ankle a little in my haste to answer it.

It isn't Mark.

'Hi Kate,' I say, my voice as flat as I feel.

'Hi.' She sounds nervous. 'I wondered if you'd had a chance to think about things?'

Like I'd thought about anything else! I sit on the bed and push my hair out of my eyes. 'Yes, and no. I think you and I should meet up again to discuss stuff.'

'You do?' Her voice sounds hopeful.

I swallow back the cramp in my throat. 'I'm not sure how best to sort this out. Give me a couple of days to think a bit more. Can we meet the day after tomorrow, Thursday?'

'Where?'

I search my mind. It has to be where no one knew us and easy for me between service users. 'City Centre Library off College Green.' The only person likely to catch us there was Mark and he wouldn't say anything to Nick. 'At twelve.'

'Okay, brilliant. Thanks, Azza, this is really amazing of you.'

'Yeah,' I say. I hope it is because part of me still hungers for revenge.

Hanging up, I scan around the bedroom. Apart from the curtains it's all looking good. Then my glance catches the bedside lamp. God, I hate that lamp.

Walking back into the living room I take in all my possessions. A lot of cheap tat that Nick and I had collected. Actually, I hate most of it. And the flat's too small. Thinking back I remember it was Nick who had chosen it. I'd wanted a property we'd seen in Bishopsworth. It was an ex-council two-bed house with a long narrow garden. Nick felt it was too far out of town, which it was, but only by a fifteen-minute bus journey. He'd wanted this Victorian converted first-floor flat with its bags of original features. Features such as sash windows; pretty, but noisy – they rattle in the wind and at night every sound from the street came in – and they didn't keep out the cold. All the flats, above and below, had stripped floorboards, so no soundproofing. The couple above seem to stamp around in hobnail boots and drag bits of furniture about incessantly. My living room is big with beautiful plaster coving plus an extravagant ceiling rose, but the bathroom is a tiny windowless box and the bedroom poky. This place was Nick's choice and I suddenly realise that I hate it. It was a prison and I had shut myself in here to wallow in my pain – keeping it because I knew Nick wanted it.

Wow, I'm as much imprisoned in this place by my perceived loss of Nick and our 'could-have-been' as Lil is by her agoraphobia.

I need to get out.

Grabbing an assortment of little objects off the shelf, ones I had stolen from Park Street and Clifton areas, I head out into the late afternoon sunshine.

First I went to a shop in Park Street that sold an odd assortment of unnecessary objects. The kind of stuff you buy in a panic for someone you don't know that well for Christmas – it's funny and it's cheap. I'd nicked a miniature garden from there. It had a small solar strip so that a minuscule baby Bambi and Thumper wave a continuous welcome from the edge of a tiny frozen pond. I walk to a dim area at the back of the shop and get the garden out of my rucksack. Feigning interest in some objects on a shelf I place my thieved thing in amongst them. I can't see any more of this type around; they must have sold out, so I guess the shop assistant will be pretty surprised when she sees it. I carry on like this, sauntering into shops, poking about, pretending to look at the merchandise while secreting stolen goods back onto shelves. It makes me feel good, and light-hearted too. I wish I'd done this ages ago.

It's about six by the time I get to the top of Blackboy Hill. I have a deli wrap and a carton of juice in my bag that I'd bought on the way so I cross at the lights and walk on the soft bright grass of the Downs. There are a few people about, some just chilling like me, others busting a gut jogging and doing stretching exercises. Good for them. I have found all the walking over the last ten months working for Your Home Care very therapeutic and I'm definitely a lot fitter.

Sitting down I take out the wrap, tear off the packaging and bite into it. Soft and yummy. Chewing, I peer around me. This must be a nice area to live in, being so close to the park. Too many cars though, circling around the edges of the large green patches. I watch a heavily pregnant woman struggling with an overly enthusiastic dog. The dog sees my wrap and makes a beeline for it. Stuffing the last of it in my mouth, I jump to my feet.

'Milo, no,' she pants. Her voice sounds hoarse; perhaps Milo needed a lot of discouragement on their walk.

I can't speak for humus and flatbread gummed to the roof of my mouth, but I smile and pat Milo – what is it – a labradoodle?

'I'm so sorry. Don't worry, he doesn't bite.'

I swallow my wad of wrap and the yellow dog licks my hands. 'No worries,' I say just as much to her joyful pet as to her.

Pulling at his collar, she drags Milo away across the Downs. Watching them go I think about how overheated she looks. I hope Milo won't be a problem when the baby arrives. Smiling, I pick up my bag and set off across the grass towards Mrs P's flat. When I get to the point where I had seen the grey-hooded figure, I stop and stare across the road. No one like that there today. After crossing the road, I again check the pavement up and down the street. Some people, but no one that particularly stood out. I carry on a few metres before turning into Pembroke Road and then first left for Mrs P's street, Downside Road. There, I start calling and making kiss-kiss noises.

'Sir Lancelot, Sir Lancelot.' I feel like an idiot but the street is empty, so no witnesses. Poking around in the undergrowth I call again and again. No cat. I do the same all around the car park area of Mrs P's building. No cat. Sighing I let myself into her downstairs front door.

Upstairs smells stuffy and hot. I open a few windows and put some hard stale bread out for the gull. He tries a bit, drops it and marches up and down the dark grey ledge calling in his harsh seagull tone.

'Not up to your usual standard?' I ask him. He turns his head and pierces me with his bead-like eye. 'So sorry, I'm sure.' It squawks and flies off. *Can't be that hungry then.* Perhaps there is a whole legion of old ladies feeding it gourmet suppers around Bristol?

I empty out the cat litter trays and refill them with fresh from a bag she keeps under the sink. Where would I find a photo of her cat? Checking the surfaces and opening drawers around the flat feels terrible. I'm invading Mrs P's space, but I keep reminding myself, it's for a good cause. Finally, I strike gold. A drawer full of albums and loose photographs. At least a dozen are of the cat. I choose one and put it in my backpack before fixing the windows open at their minimum in case of rain and then head back down the spiral staircase.

Opening the front door, the first thing I see is a man slouching under a tree by the car park entrance. A shiver runs through me. He wears a dark hooded top, his face in shadow and his hands in his pockets. He straightens up and takes a step towards me.

'Excuse me?'

I jump with a scream caught in my throat and turn to see a woman's face poking out of a car window just some ten feet from me. Glancing back at the man I see he's stepped away into the shadows, his shape now barely discernible through the dappling sunlight.

'Sorry to startle you. I'm a friend of Dorothy Percival's. I just saw you come out of her door. I wondered if you could let me in, as I know she finds it difficult to get up out of that chair of hers to press the buzzer,' she explains as she climbs out of her car, smiling and extending a hand. 'I'm Poppy, an old friend of hers. We went to school together.'

I shake her hand. 'Astrid,' I smile. 'I'm one of her carers. I'm sorry, you can't have heard, she's in hospital. She asked me to look after… to, you know, look after everything while she's away.'

'Oh dear. Poor thing, is it serious?' says Poppy her face full of concern.

'A fall that resulted in a broken hip.'

'But her cat.'

Eek. I don't want to say he's lost in case it gets back to Mrs P. 'He's good. Fat and lazy as ever.' I smile and almost cross my fingers behind my back.

'Oh well, I suppose I should visit her in hospital.'

'I'm sure she'd love that.' I peek over to the gate but I can't see the man.

'Do you know where?' asks Poppy.

'I don't know for definite but I expect she's still in the BRI.'

'Which one is that? I'm not from Bristol you see. I drop in for a bit of shopping occasionally and visit a few old friends. I lived here for twenty years but that was a long time ago now.' Her face crinkles with a light smile.

‘It’s back towards the city centre.’ I scan the entrance. Is he waiting around the corner? ‘If you like I could direct you? I’m heading off that way in any case.’

‘Oh, if you’re sure I won’t be taking you out of your way?’ Poppy says. Relief floods through me, she’s my unexpected knight in shining armour just as much as I’m hers.

‘No that would be fine, honestly, you’d be saving me a bus fare.’

‘Well in that case…’ Poppy turns and indicates that I should get in the passenger seat of her small blue car.

As we drove out of the entrance I peer up and down the road but the hooded figure is gone. Was he a figment of my imagination? He was probably nothing to do with me, just someone trying to find an address in this road and I had put two and two together and made five million. I never was good at maths.

I direct Poppy down Whiteladies Road and then to curve round to the left to reach Perry Road which is the one just before the hospital. I hop out at the lights and tell her to take her first left and immediate right where she would hopefully find a space in the hospital car park. I ask her to give Mrs Percival my love and tell her everything is fine at her flat. We wave goodbye just as the lights change and Poppy drives off.

Now I’m pretty much in the city centre, which isn’t where I want to be, but I don’t think I could have walked out of Mrs P’s car park. Not with that man there. I’ll just have to find a printer around here and make some fliers, if there’s any still open at this time. Tomorrow I had service users to see up in Redland and Clifton so I’d put the posters up then.

Should I tell the police about the man at Mrs P’s? What was there to say; I saw a man lurking in the entrance. What could they do about it; it wasn’t as if I saw his face or anything. I couldn’t give them a description.

No, I would just have to keep my wits about me, as Reid said, and wait to hear back from him whether he had dug anything up that connected Becks and me to the Bristol Beast. Next time, if I saw the hoodie man again, I'd take a picture.

26

Hunting, sniffing, trapping

Sitting on a bench on a cement island between the streams of heavy traffic in the city centre he takes in the architecture and the humanity around him. A lot of grey alleviated by shallow areas of water where mini fountains dotted within the rectangular pools kept the water moving. There's a static van selling food and drink. Cyclists weave through the crowds who seem to be milling aimlessly about. He keeps watch on both sides; the bus lanes, should she come that way, and the pavement up Park Street if she'd decided to walk. Everyone seemed to be eating. Why were they always putting stuff in their mouths like that? They didn't understand hunger, not like he did. That gnawing pain that constantly filled the mind. Dizzy spells and tiredness from lack of protein. Food had been an all-engrossing obsession of his childhood. Now he could have anything he wanted, but a small part of him worried so he kept something with him in his pocket at all times, just in case. Like now. Watching all these people eating he felt hungry, but he dare not leave this bench in case he missed her. Pulling out the snack bar from his pocket he tore open the wrapping with his teeth. The chocolate outer layer around the wafer was melted. Grimacing he licked the plastic clean and most of what had got on his fingers. His senses prickled. Glancing to his right he saw a child watching him. It stood motionless amid the human traffic, a small boy of about seven or eight, with dark dusty hair and dirty knees sticking out from bright coloured shorts. Feeling a stir of desire he shifted in his seat. It was the fear starting to grow in the child's eyes that made him want to steal it away, somewhere quiet so that he could re-live some of his memories and relieve the tension that had built up so strong inside him. This child, so small and skinny, reminded him of someone, someone he'd known long ago, and hoped to find again to complete his lost family. So many cities he'd searched for them, he would never give up.

There's a shout and a bigger boy runs up to the smaller one and grabs it by the arm, pulling it back to play in the shallow waters.

The child went, turning its head to peek at him for a moment before he is forgotten.

He turns back to watch for her, his shining one. He had caught up with her earlier, as he thought he would. He'd heard her calling for something and he'd seen her looking in the bushes. What could she have been searching for? She'd been at that house, the one where he'd nearly got her last time before the police came. He'd watched her go in and waited in the shadows. Not well enough because he was pretty sure she'd seen him when she came out. He knew fear, even with the expanse of car park between them he'd smelt it on her.

But she'd got in a car and escaped him.

Clever girl. He likes that she is making it hard for him, all the sweeter when he finally got her alone.

27

I was lucky and got some good A4 posters made quite cheaply, only in black and white, but they'd do. I also bought some pin tacks, sticky tape and a pack of A4 clear plastic sleeves. When I got home I put the posters in the sleeves and sealed them with the tape. Tomorrow I'll put them up and hope someone contacted me with some good news. Then I get my laptop out and check a few rescue centres and phone all the local ones. No one has handed in a cat matching Sir Lancelot's description, but they all take my details just in case.

Next, I call the BRI and ask if Mrs Percival is still there. After a few moments of empty air, the receptionist puts me through to a ward. It takes an age for anyone to answer. Finally, I get a slightly out of breath nurse who listens as I explain who I'm looking for and if she knew how long Mrs P would be with them. She assures me that Mrs Percival will be with them for quite some time yet, especially considering her unsuitable living arrangements. Perhaps I could call back in a week and there would be more information then?

Relieved with the knowledge that I have some time to find the missing cat, I ring-off and poke about in my fridge for a snack. As I haven't been near a supermarket for days, I shouldn't be surprised that I can't find anything to eat. I check my phone. It's nearly seven o'clock. Why haven't I heard from Mark yet? A pang of guilt runs through me. After the abrupt end to our session last night, I feel worried – just what has he remembered? When Detective Reid gets hold of him he probably won't speak to me ever again, and who could blame him?

I ring Lil. She's enthusiastic when I suggest I come round for a follow-up EFT and Matrix session.

'Oooo, yes please, Astrid love. I've got ever so much to tell you.'

Her excitement is a balm to my sense of gloom about Mark. I say I'm just going to the supermarket first and ask if she needs anything. Lil has a list of last-minute wants and I write them down on the back of the old bank letter envelope I'd left on the kitchen counter.

Half an hour later I'm round at Lil's. I let myself in, say a quick hi to Lil lounging on her sofa as usual, and lifting the shopping bags high out of reach of her mutts' inquisitive noses, I take them off to her cramped kitchen. Filling two glasses of water, I bring them into the lounge. We hug a proper hello before I settle down beside her.

'Tell me how you've been?' I ask.

'Oh, I've been so looking forward to seeing you. I've had such a lovely few days. I've been working on the garden.'

'That's fantastic, Lil. No anxiety?' One of her little dogs is trying unsuccessfully to jump on my lap. I lift him up and hold him away from licking my face. 'You wriggly thing,' I tell him before squashing him down into my lap and stroking the soft fur of his ears.

'Don't put up with any of his rubbish. Stop that, Angus,' she says to him. 'No it's been fine, almost as if it never was. I haven't been bothered hardly at all. No going out the front, mind. But to have the use of my garden again, that's so lovely that is.' She grins and takes a sip of her water. 'It's got awful overgrown. Stingers, brambles an' all sorts, bit too much for me. I've found a bloke what does. A friend recommended him. He came by this morning and hacked it all back. I'm that happy, Astrid, I could burst.' She grabs me into a warm hug, squashing her little dog between the two of us. When she lets go, Angus hops off my lap in disgust and trots out of the back door into the garden.

'So would you like to try some more Matrix Re-imprinting? Maybe we could get you out the front door next?' I ask.

'Oooo, God.' She shivers. 'Do you reckon?'

'World's your oyster, Lil.'

She grins. 'We'll give it a go. I'm willing if you are,' she says with a cackle.

At least she's more positive. I hope she can keep that up.

Getting out my notebook I check how we finished our last session. 'Do you mind if we turn the TV down?' I ask and she uses a black remote to mute the telly with its ticker tape of gloom. I notice that a lot of my service users have their tellies on all the time. I wonder if that is bad for them, the constant distraction, or is the noise like having company in the house?

Going through her mood checklist with her I find her scores have improved quite a bit.

'Okay, Lil, we'll do some Matrix Re-imprinting like we did last time.'

She nods. Her other little dog trots up and whines at her. Lil lifts him onto her lap and strokes his head. It's missing most of its teeth so its tongue hangs out of one side of its mouth as it pants with fast little breaths.

'This time, though, I want you to have someone you trust with you.'

'I trust you,' she says, her expression perplexed.

'Thank you,' I say smiling. 'That's not what I mean though. Imagine someone that you trust and feel comfortable with. It can be anyone, especially if it was someone you felt close to as a child.'

Lil ponders for a moment. 'Miss Hills,' she says. 'She was my favourite teacher at primary school. She taught us everything but she was especially good at art. I'd like her with me.'

'That's good. Can you tell me what she looked like?'

'She was pretty with nice curly red hair. She never got cross, even when I made a mess. I loved her bangles and rings. They were silver and she wore lots of them all jumbled together. The bangles made a jingling noise when she moved.'

'That's perfect, Lil, keep Miss Hills in your mind. Now I want you to tell me about a time that really upset you, but this time you'll have Miss Hills with you. Because these are our rules if anything gets too bad or upsetting, we can freeze it; stop the memory with everyone frozen still.'

'Like musical statues?' asks Lil. Her voice has already taken on a child's lisping lilt. 'Yes, just like that. And we won't start the action again until you're ready.'

'Alright.' She puts her dog down and shuffles round in her seat to face me.

'Now tell me. Why do you think you can't go out to the shops? What happened to frighten little Lil?'

'I'm not sure how it started. I feel like I was always anxious, it just got worse over time.'

'Close your eyes. I'm just going to tap on your meridian points. Now, imagine you as a little girl, like we did last week. Can you see her?'

'Yes.' Lil nods, a slow movement of her head like a sleepwalker.

'How old is she?' I ask as I hold Lil's hand tapping on the side of it before moving to the point at the top of her head.

'Five, nearly six. She's got Tiggy with her so she must be not quite six.'

'Who's Tiggy?'

'That was my favourite toy. A plush brown mouse in a blue dress, like the one from the Cinderella cartoon. I loved her so much.' Lil is smiling, then her face crumples. 'Tiggy's been gone a long time now.'

'What happened to Tiggy?' I tap a gentle rhythm through all her points as we speak.

'Little Lil is crying.'

'You tap on her, just imagine you're tapping on her as you feel me tapping on you. Ask her why she's crying.'

'She had a very bad day out with Mum. It was meant to be the best day ever.' Lil is sniffing and I quickly grab some tissues out of my rucksack to give her. 'Why was it the best day ever?'

'It was her birthday.'

'Little Lil's?'

'Yes.'

'So it was an outing for her birthday?'

'Yes. Her sixth birthday.'

'Would you like to bring Miss Hills in to help, would little Lil feel better if Miss Hills was there to help?'

'Alright.' The sniffing has calmed a little but her bottom lip still twitches, and a concertina of dimples are forming along her chin.

'Remember what she looked like, can you hear her bangles jingling? Ask her to hold little Lil's hand.'

Lil smiles and I know she has the image clear in her mind. 'Ask Lil what happened on her special day out.'

'Mum was taking me shopping for a new outfit and a birthday tea. I took Tiggy too. We went on the bus to the centre and went to the big M&S. I lost Tiggy. We looked everywhere but we couldn't find her. I was so worried about Tiggy all alone in that big shop. Mum got cross. She said someone would find my Tiggy and hand her in, we could come back for her another day. Mum needed to get going with our shopping and tea. But I couldn't leave M&S without Tiggy so I ran away from Mum. I looked everywhere. I couldn't find her. I couldn't find Mum. I needed a wee. I was so scared. There was noise and people everywhere.'

Lil's crying and wringing her hands, the tissue is a shred of twisted wisps in her lap. I feel a stab of anxiety; she's so upset, that's not how we're supposed to make our service users. If any of this gets back to head office I could lose my job, I haven't asked anyone if I can do EFT with their clients. And I doubt they'd give me permission if I did.

'Stop the scene now, Lil. Make everyone just freeze in place like musical statues.'

But she's not listening because I've lost her in her past of pain.

'Lil, please.' I rub her arm and give her the glass of water.

Lil gulps back a mouthful. Her breath is hitching and I think she might choke.

'Have you stopped the scene?' I ask her.

Sniffing hard, Lil nods. I give her a fresh tissue and run through a sequence of tapping and ask her to imagine herself tapping on little Lil. 'Tell her it's alright. We've stopped everything so we can relax. What does Miss Hills say?'

'She…she…she says poor…poor little girl, so scared and alone.'

'Now ask Little Lil to imagine she's still in M&S but she has Miss Hills with her.'

'Alright.'

'How is she feeling now?'

'Not so scared.' Lil takes a deep breath.

Thank God. That felt like a close call. 'Are you okay to start again?'

She sips her water and nods.

'I hid amongst some clothes,' she says. 'Under one of them circular hanging racks. I needed a wee so bad and I couldn't stop crying. I'm ashamed to say I couldn't hold it no more and I wet myself, right there in the middle of M&S, under a clothing display thingy. M&S isn't so special now but back then it was ever such a smart place. I was so embarrassed. I was wearing white ribbed tights and a red and white gingham smocked dress, I remember that.'

I can see the surprise on Lil's face that she's remembering everything so clearly. I know that part of her is right there, in M&S, re-experiencing it all as if it were yesterday.

'Because my tights were wet they made my legs rub and be sore all the way home,' she says.

'So your mum found you?' I ask.

'An assistant found me, a nice young woman. She took my hand and said that I should come out as my mum was worried about me.'

'So she took you to your mum?'

Lil nods, biting her lower lip.

'Remember that Miss Hills is with little Lil and we can stop at any time,' I say as I tap round all her points again. 'What happened when you came out?'

'She took me to Mum. Mum was that angry. She didn't say nothing, not till we got outside. Then she slapped the back of my legs, that's how she found out I'd wet myself. She wouldn't sit next to me on the bus home, because I was a nasty dirty girl. I thought they must all know, everyone on the bus, that I was a nasty dirty girl like Mum said I was.'

'And Tiggy?'

Lil shakes her head, tears popping out from beneath her eyelashes and rolling down her plump cheeks to drip onto the yellow T-shirt top that's stretched around the beach-ball curve of her stomach and breasts as she hunches over in a shape of ashamed misery.

I can't help myself. I wrap my arms around her and she cries, loud and heaving onto my shoulder. We stay like that for a few minutes. Her crying upsets her little dogs who come hurtling in and try to climb into her lap, scratching her bare thighs with their hard claws. Lil pulls away from me and scoops them into her lap. They jump all over her leaping up to lick her face. Laughing, she hugs them to her chest as they wriggle and waggle their happiness, squeaking yaps and sneezing for all they are worth. Cuddling her babies with her head bowed, I nearly don't catch what she says.

'What must you think of me?'

'No, please, Lil. I'm so happy you've told me. You were little, and you were scared. Lots of children get caught short like that. I can remember laughing till I wet myself with my best friend at secondary school, and we were fourteen. You were only six, only just six.'

Lil still won't look at me. I hold out her glass. 'Please, have some water. You've got the chance now to turn this horrible memory into a nice one.'

Lil peeks at me over the top of one of her dogs' heads. I gesture with the glass. She takes it and sips.

'Did you go straight home from M&S?' I ask.

She nods.

'So you didn't get your birthday tea.'

Lil buries her face in her dog's fur.

'Can you imagine what your birthday tea would have been like if you had been allowed?'

'Yes,' she says still hiding her face.

'Put the dogs down and finish that glass of water,' I say picking up my own glass and having a quick sip. She does as I ask and the dogs trot off towards the kitchen. 'What tea shop would you have gone to?'

'Mum said we could go to the Wimpy. I was going to have a knickerbocker glory. I'd never had one before but I'd seen them in pictures.'

'Shall we make a memory where you go to Wimpy's and have a knickerbocker glory?'

'But my tights were all wet,' says Lil.

'This is your new memory, it can be any way you want. What do you think should have happened?'

'It…it's a lovely day.'

I nod at Lil encouraging her.

'The…the sun is shining and Mum lets me take them off and throws them away. She buys me much nicer, new pants and socks.' She stops and looks at me. 'Mum would never have thrown them away.'

I laugh. 'This is your special day and she wants you to be happy, so she throws them in a tree.'

Lil giggles and then the sadness pulls the corners of her mouth down again. 'Tiggy,' she says in a whisper.

'Okay. Imagine something nice for Tiggy.'

'Tiggy was found by a little girl called…Caroline. Caroline loved her so much she kept her safe in her bedroom and tucked her up beside her in bed every night.' Lil smiles. 'I'd like to imagine someone loved her as much as I did.'

'Brilliant. Now shut your eyes again. I'm going to tap on you.'

'And I'll tap on little Lil,' adds Lil.

'Maybe Miss Hills would like to come to tea too?'

As I tap, Lil describes a beautiful tea at Wimpy, which used to be in the town centre when she was a little girl. I have no idea what Wimpy was but I get the impression it was something like McDonald's, only nicer and more intimate. The knickerbocker glory was the most amazing anyone had ever seen. Miss Hills had one too. Lil's Mum had a cup of tea and a donut. Everyone was happy and smiling.

'Now whenever you think about that day out in M&S, I want your mind to go straight to eating an ice-cream sundae at Wimpy.'

Lil laughs and shakes her head. 'I'm amazed by you, Astrid. You're a lovely person.'

It's my turn to be embarrassed. 'Don't think it's all about me. You did all the work, Lil. You faced your fear and made it into something golden. I think what we worked on today was a key event in your life. What's called a primary event. It's possibly one of the first scary outside events that started you on the road to anxiety attacks and agoraphobia. If you keep remembering it as a lovely day at the Wimpy, it should have a knock-on effect in lessening a lot of your anxiety overall.'

Lil's mutts are barking at something in her garden. We both stand up to look. I can't see anything that might have excited them. They're such hyperactive little beasties it could have been anything.

'Shall I make us both a cup of tea?' I ask.

'Oh, that would be lovely. There's some Battenberg in the tin by the kettle. All that talk about knickerbocker glories has made me peckish.'

I go to her kitchen and make us both a cup of tea, remembering to load Lil's up with a tooth-rotting three spoons of sugar, before I bring them, with a slice of cake for her, back into the lounge.

'You not having cake?' asks Lil as she takes the saucer with the pink and cream geometric cake I hold out for her. Her gaze is set on the slice and not me.

'Too hot for cake, thanks.'

Lil breaks off a square and puts it in her mouth. 'Do you think I'll be able to go down Asda now?' she asks, her voice muffled round the Battenberg.

'Don't push yourself, start with little steps. Take your dogs out to the front garden and see if you can walk them up the road a bit? Just go with how you feel. What happened when you were a little girl had a big impact on you. Don't expect to get better overnight, but you're an adult now, the little girl inside has been trying to protect you. Thank her and tell her you're okay now, you don't need her protection anymore.' I put my empty cup down on her cluttered coffee table. 'Do you want to try now, with me with you?'

'Oh no, I'm not sure…' Lil's voice holds a tremor of fear.

It's a lot to expect and I shouldn't have asked. I just got carried away in the moment.

'I'll tell you what,' says Lil. 'When you're ready for the off I'll come to the door with you, peek outside and see.'

'That would be brilliant.' I feel so excited and proud of her, and me if I'm honest. I feel we have really achieved something at this session.

I chat with her while she finishes off her tea and cake, and then I gather up the mugs and Lil's saucer and put them in the sink. I get my bag of groceries that I'd left on the counter out of reach of her pets and wait while Lil puts on her slippers and stained blue flannel dressing gown. She pulls it around her ample tummy and ties up the belt.

'Ready?' I ask.

She nods and we go out to the hall to her front door. At the sight of it, Lil grasps hold of my hand, squeezing hard as I open the door. I step out onto her cement path and she puts one slippered foot out on her step. One of her little dogs comes and sticks his head out.

'No, Charlie, come back.' There's fear in her voice.

Releasing her hand, I pick up the squirming pet and put him in her arms. 'I'll ring you in a couple of days and you can tell me how it's going.'

I wave goodbye as she shuts her door. She hasn't made it outside, but she has tried. It's a good start. I feel sure that now she would be able to move forward in her life. All those years stuck indoors, it's mind-blowing. Better late than never I guess.

I feel light and happy as I walk the twenty or so minutes home. Today I have really achieved something.

28

Hunting, sniffing, trapping

He'd waited so long the cold had seeped into his bones as the sun went down.

So she wasn't coming this way today.

He'd be back here again tomorrow.

Getting up his legs feel stiff with cramps. The sense of disappointment is bringing him down despite the music from his iPod that encloses him in a dense fog of heady beats. He knows all the words by heart now and sings along in a low gravel tone. No point being loud and bringing attention to himself. Hunger gnaws like a busy rat in his gut and he wonders what to eat. There are plenty of fast food places across from where he's been sitting and watching their passing trade has been painful on his empty stomach. He crosses the road and goes into the first one he sees, a chicken and chips joint.

Taking his order he starts up Park Street and eats straight out of the box as he goes. The food is slick with grease but he doesn't care. At this point, anything would have tasted great.

He thinks about his angel. Where she is and what is she doing? He tries to imagine her at home, perhaps cooking a meal or watching TV. Maybe she's going out with friends? Not with a man, though. A knot of anger grows in his stomach. If she's seeing someone… He bites into the piece of chicken he holds in his clenched fist and hears the bone crack. Spitting this bit of hard shard and flesh onto the pavement he ignores the expressions of surprise and disgust from a group of women walking towards him and crumples up the remains of the carton. He isn't hungry anymore; his stomach is too full of bile for food.

29

My mobile starts ringing just as I open my front door. Hurrying inside, I slam it shut behind me. It thuds like someone has crashed into it from the outside, which, after my horrible experience, actually makes me scream. It's just the wind though, huffing and puffing fit to blow the whole house down. Autumn will be here soon and the wind has picked up lately.

My phone's getting louder, echoing around our communal hallway, demanding my attention. I scrabble around my rucksack and fish it out. When I see from the caller ID that it's Nick, I chuck the phone back in my bag in disgust. By the time I get upstairs and into my flat, I see he has sent me three messages.

- 'Just returning your call. When are you free to talk?'
- 'Are you feeling better?'
- 'Can't stop thinking about you.'

'Fuck you,' I say to his messages and throw my phone on the couch.

It starts ringing immediately and I wonder if the fall messed with something. It'll only be Nick. Ignoring the insistent music of my ringtone, I put the groceries away. After I've washed up the pile in the sink, I'm going to have cheese on toast topped up with coleslaw. My stomach rumbles. Maybe I should have had the cake Lil offered, as it's almost nine now and I'm over-hungry.

The washing-up sits dripping on the chrome drainer and I have just sat down with my toasted cheese when my door buzzer goes.

Taking a big bite I go to the window and peek out. Nick's car is parked outside and he steps into view before I have time to duck. He waves at me and points at the front door.

I definitely don't want to be doing this now. Fucking hell. Looking at my meal I realise I have just lost my appetite as knots of anxiety are twisting my stomach. Just because you know someone is a lying shit doesn't turn off all those crazy feelings for them. Maybe my emotions are just as strong, only a bit different now. Closer to hate than love.

I don't want to deal with this, not now.

The buzzer goes again spiking a lance of panic through my gut. Picking up my phone I start to tap in a text telling him I'm sick, that I've got a stomach bug, best if he stays away. Then I hear the key in the lock.

'Hi.' Nick stands in the doorway managing to appear sheepish and triumphant at the same time.

How could I forget he had a key? Why hadn't I changed the lock months ago? First thing tomorrow I'm calling the locksmith.

'I was worried. You weren't buzzing me up,' he says.

'I… I'm sick. I was just sending you a text.' I hold my mobile out like it's a cross warding off a vampire.

'Sorry to hear that.' He pushes the door shut behind him and takes a step towards me.

Stepping back I keep the phone up between us. 'Don't. It's a real nasty one. Puking, diarrhoea, the works.'

'You look okay.'

'Don't you think I know when I'm sick,' I snap.

'Sorry.'

We stand staring at each other, an awkward chasm opening up.

'I need to talk to you,' he says.

'Can't this wait?'

'No, not really.' He steps closer, his hands patting the air like he's trying to reassure a wild animal.

'I need to know, Azza. Do you want to get back together? You keep giving me mixed messages. A couple of days ago you were all over me, and then you hit me. What's going on? You can't blame me feeling confused.'

'Hardly all over you,' I mutter.

He raises an eyebrow and my face flushes.

'I had the impression that you wanted me as much as I want you.'

You want me to get you out of this mess with Kate more like. I'm so torn; should I just reject him now, or wait until I had spoken to Kate?

Actually what difference would it make?

'No,' I say.

'Sorry?'

'No. I don't want you.' I look him up and down with an expression of disgust. 'I don't want any part of you, and I don't want you in my flat.'

His face goes a deep cherry red, which, with his hair, makes a scary impression of a cartoon character from Bugs Bunny, only I'm not in a laughing mood.

'I thought—'

'Well, you thought wrong. Go, go on. Get out.' I point at the door. 'And you can give me those keys first,' I add.

'No. I have as much right to them as you. This flat is half mine and I can live here if I choose. I didn't want it to come to this, Azza, but I need you to get Becks out of our bedroom. I can move in here if that's what I want and you can't stop me.'

'What? You'd want to live here, with someone who can't stand the sight of you? What about Kate, are you moving her in here too?'

He seems shifty then. 'I can if I want,' he says with a defiant lift of his chin.

Oh, but you don't want to, do you. 'And where's Becks supposed to go?'

'That's her problem.'

'So you're just going to force your way into my life are you?' I can't believe he's being like this.

'If I have to,' he says trying to stare me down.

'Becks is away. She went this morning and won't be back for a couple of weeks,' I say, knowing she'll be back a lot sooner, but I need to buy some time.

'You'll have to pack her stuff for her won't you?'

'I just can't believe you're doing this.'

'Believe it.' He looks smug. I want to slap that expression off his face. 'I'll bring my things over at the weekend.'

So he's planning to leave Kate that quickly. Did she know? 'I need more time.' My voice is cracking. Tears are welling up and blurring my vision. 'Please.' How I hate having to beg him. 'Please, wait until Becks is back so we can work something out together.' I wipe at my eyes, sniffing.

He steps forward and puts his arms around me. God, I hate him, but I let him hold me while I cry. His cheek is pressed against the top of my head.

'Okay,' he says. 'Only until she's back. When's that?'

'Not sure. I'll text her.' My voice is muffled against his chest.

He moves away and lifts my chin. 'Don't shut me out. You know how I feel about you.'

It's my turn to look shifty. I say I need to wash my face and hide in the bathroom until I feel more in control of my emotions again. When I come out he's in the kitchen area, peering into one of the overhead cupboards. Seeing me he quickly shuts it, his expression guilty. *Working out where to keep your stuff and that bloody cappuccino machine*. That was one of the first things he'd taken with him when he'd moved in with Kate.

'Look,' I say. 'I'm really tired. Can you just go now?'

The colour floods his cheeks again.

'Honestly, we're going to sort this out like you want, only I need you to go now. I'll text you when I've heard from Becks.'

'Alright,' he says, walking to the door. 'Don't mess me about anymore, Azza. I mean it. I'm moving back here, whether you like it or not. How amicably that happens is up to you.'

I stare out of the window and ignore him. I hear the door shut and his feet on the stairs. Moments later he comes into view on the street, looks up at me and waves before opening his car door. I don't wave back or smile or anything, I just walk to the couch and start making up my bed. I could have moved into the bedroom while Becks was away, only it was filled with memories of Nick and some of the good times we had there before I had learnt what he was really like. Do we ever really know someone? How much of themselves do they keep hidden like a monster lurking in the dark that only shows its face when you least expect it.

30

Dream

I'm at home, the old one in Redland. There's music playing; I can't put a name to it, but I feel like I know it. It has a heavy angry beat, and its pulsing hurts my head.

I was busy packing boxes, only I had this bad feeling, so I'm standing amid this sea of half-packed cardboard boxes looking around me, fear prickling in my gut and the hairs up on the back of my neck. What is it, what is it? The music gets louder. It's coming from the hall. The door opens and a figure in a grey hooded top steps into the room.

Turning fast, I run for the backroom.

Hoodie man runs after me. I can hear his growling. I need my mobile, I must take a picture of him for the police – where did I put it?

Tripping over boxes, yelling and leaping, if only I can get to the door at the back, I know I can lock that one.

The room elongates like a tunnel and my feet are dragging through spilt boxes, my belongings scattered all over the place. The music is so loud I feel like my head will explode.

My shoulders are grabbed from behind and I'm dragged backward.

I fall, it feels like forever.

It doesn't hurt when I hit the ground and he's on top of me. I feel frightened and yet aroused. I want him here and now, on the floor amid all this mess. This fills me with shame. When he pulls back his hood I see Mark's face smiling his sweet crooked smile. Then we're kissing and the music is so loud.

'Can't you turn it off?' I ask him.

'What?'

'That music. It's too loud.'

'What music?'

Then over his shoulder, I see a figure coming towards us. Its face is in shadow, hidden by the hood of his top.

31

I thought about Nick and how to deal with everything all the next day, Wednesday. The dream was strange and it haunted me. Because of that everything I did was on autopilot; I saw my service users, put up posters about Sir Lancelot and 'un-stole' several of my hoard. So many thoughts were spinning in my head and I still didn't know what to say to Kate. Despite an uneventful day and a dreamless night I felt just the same the following morning, which is Thursday, make-your-mind-up day.

Thursday morning I visit some of my Clifton clients, then head down Park Street to the library.

Kate is waiting for me by the statue of Raja Roy.

'Hi,' she says, a nervous smile twitching her lips.

'Hi.' Oddly I feel like hugging her, but don't try. 'Let's go to the cafe and get a cake or something.'

I see her relax a little and she walks beside me up the stone steps into the cool library lobby. We walk through the downstairs centre aisle, the smell of books all around us. My heart is racing as I consider what I want to say to her.

We're lucky because the cafe is almost empty. I ask Kate to save seats on the fake black leather couch for us while I get our drinks. A cappuccino for me and fruit tea for her as she says she can't stomach coffee at the moment. I splash out on a couple of fat knobbly chocolate chip cookies and bring them back to the sofa with slow care as they keep threatening to slide off the tiny saucer the assistant has put them on.

'So,' I say once we have both eaten a bit of our biscuits. 'I'm not sure what we're going to do about you and Nick. I've wracked my brain. All I can think is to tell you what I know and maybe between the two of us we will work out what to do?'

'Okay,' she says, sitting up straight, her cheeks taking on the pallor of paper.

'First, let me tell you that no way, no how, do I want anything to do with Nick. He's all yours.'

The breath whooshes out of her and she gives a nervous laugh.

'Did you know he came over to mine Tuesday night?'

Biting her lip she shakes her head.

'He wants to move back into the flat, whether I like it or not.'

Her eyes widen and I feel cruel. I'm angry but what Nick's doing isn't her fault, and it's obvious she doesn't want this. I try to explain. 'He does own half of it, even though I've been paying for everything since he moved out. He has a right. I can't stop him if he insists.' Seeing tears in her eyes I reach out to touch her arm. 'Has he said anything to you?'

'No,' she says, her voice a small sad sound that's almost a sob.

I know exactly how she feels – exactly. I grip her hand. 'I asked him if he was going to move you in too.' Seeing a flash of hope in those pretty eyes I shake my head. 'At best he avoided answering. Judging by his track record I wouldn't hope for too much.'

Tears spill unchecked down her cheeks, so I find some tissues in my rucksack and give her a generous handful.

Murmuring her thanks, she blows her nose. 'But what about you?' she asks.

'Obviously, I don't want to live with him. I've asked him to wait until Becks gets back. She's on holiday with her boyfriend. Me and her can probably find somewhere together. What makes me angry is that I paid for my share of the deposit on that flat with money my nan saved up for me. I can't make Nick sell up to get my money back. I can ask him to buy me out, but why should he bother? He hasn't exactly bent over backward to help me so far.'

It's her turn to look concerned and she squeezes my hand.

'I feel like an idiot. I thought he genuinely wanted me back, and I was glad about it. Now I know it wasn't me, just the flat he wanted, and a chance to escape his responsibilities. Sorry,' I add when I see her stricken face.

She gives a helpless shrug, then asks, 'Where will you go?'

'I don't know. Don't you worry, something will turn up, and I've got a bit of time. What about you though? You live in a house share. How will you cope when the baby comes?'

'I honestly don't know. I haven't told my parents yet. I'm not sure how they'll feel.'

'Could you move back home?'

She grimaces. 'I'd rather not if I can help it. I'll have to talk to them. If Nick's leaving me I need to know what my rights are. My mother can help me there; she was in family law.'

I raise my eyebrows.

'I know,' she says. 'I think she had higher expectations for me than becoming another single parent statistic.' Her tears start again and I pull her into a hug. Despite my earlier feelings about her, I like her. After all, we've got a lot in common.

'Perhaps you can ask your mum how I can get my deposit back from Nick.'

She gives a sharp high laugh. 'Oh I will, don't you worry.'

When Kate feels strong enough we walk out into the breezy afternoon sunshine. Despite the bright sun, it's cold and I shiver.

'Feels like summer's coming to an end already,' she says.

We hug and she promises to text me any ideas or new information about Nick. We both agree not to share our thoughts with him, not until we have a clear idea of things.

'It'll be hard,' I tell her. 'Because you love him and you want to believe in him. But you've got to think about what's best for you and your baby now.'

The rest of the day goes by without a hitch. When I've finished all my tea time rounds, I hop on a bus to Totterdown and stop in to see Dad. He's looking grey and washed out.

'How was your night out with Beanie?'

'Cracking,' he says doing his best Wallis impression.

I make us each a cup of tea and sit opposite him in the living room.

'Stuff's happening, Dad.'

He raises his eyebrows and slurps his tea.

'It's Nick,' I add.

'When isn't it?'

It's my turn to give him the eyebrow.

'Sorry, love, but he's been nothing but heartache.'

'Well, without boring you with all the gruesome details, let's just say you might get your wish and have me moving in with you. Won't that be fun?'

'Bloomin' boomerang kids,' he says, but I can see it was joy making his eyes sparkle. 'You selling the flat then?'

'I'm going to ask Nick if he'll buy me out.'

Dad snorts. 'When hell freezes.'

'He might have to. I don't know, I'll get some advice on it.'

We chat. I make us some sandwiches from the least out of date stuff in the fridge. Then I set off to what I still think of as home.

When I get in I switch on my laptop and spend some time on Facebook. There are lots of lovely pics of Becks lounging on a beach and drinking cocktails with Greg. I'm glad she looks so happy. I private message her about needing to chat about Nick and the flat and was surprised to get an immediate response.

Becks - What's up, me babbers?

Me - Nick says we got to be out of the flat asap as he is moving in v v soon - WITHOUT KATE!!

Becks - What a shit!

Me - And some.

Becks - Has he split from her then?

Me - Keep it to yourself for now but she's pregnant and he's bolting.

Becks - !!!!!

Me - I know. Don't breathe a word for now as Kate and me are plotting.

Becks - KATE & YOU!!!

Me - I know. Mad. Can't wait till you're back to tell all. You having a brilliant time? Love the pics.

Becks - Amazing time! Just explained to Greg (hope that's OK cause he doesn't count as 'the crowd') & he says I can stay at his till we find a flat or something. What about you? Where will you go?

Me - Dad's.

Becks - Greg says he'll help us move stuff.

Me - FAB.

Becks - Greg says would you like him to 'sort' Nick?

Me - Ha ha. Would be great but best not! Maybe later when all's done & dusted!! When you back?

Becks - Sunday, probably evening once we've got our luggage and everything.

We carry on like that for a bit. I explain more about Kate and just a little about my interview with DI Reid. She makes me laugh with her indignant one-liners. God, how I miss her. Finally, we call it a night and I shut my laptop. After making my bed up I go to shut the curtains. There's a figure standing in a pool of shadow. My street is a quiet one. Not the sort of place to hang out, there's nothing to see as it's purely residential. That's why I notice him. I assume it's a him, but it's hard to tell in the dark. Could it be Nick? I haven't done anything about changing the lock. It seems pointless if I'm going to move out. The figure does seem to be watching my building, or am I being paranoid? I don't want Nick letting himself in. Now I feel creeped out and I can't settle to sleep.

Slipping out from under my duvet I press down the snib button on the door lock which means that Nick couldn't unlock it even with his key. I think so anyway. I know it keeps the latch open so it should keep it closed, shouldn't it? And I put the chain on too, just in case.

Even with these extra measures, I feel on edge and it seems to take ages to get off to sleep.

32

Hunting, sniffing, trapping

He feels so good standing out here; just knowing she's close warms him. It's been a long couple of days. He's missed a lot of work too, but she is worth it. Who cares if his bosses don't like it, there are plenty around they can hire instead. He can find another job anytime. He's good at what he does, and he has all his own tools and transport. He's hard-working and uncomplaining; bosses value that, but they don't own him. He's free, like the wild wolf in his heart.

Yesterday he'd hung about his usual spot in College Green so he could watch for her and had eventually picked up her trail in Park Street. She'd been busy in some of the shops there, and then up in Whiteladies Road and Clifton Village. She'd seemed serious and distracted, keeping her gaze lowered to the pavement and her hat brim down. It made him feel more secure in following her undetected, but he preferred her to be carefree and smiling. When he had her to himself he would explain that to her, that she needed to smile more, but only for him. He'd watched her put up some posters on lampposts and checked what they were about when she'd gone into someone's house. It was a picture of a fluffy cat with an appeal for information with her contact details, including her name and mobile number. Azza, what an unusual name. He took a picture of it with his mobile. When she went home, he followed her there too. He'd stayed outside for quite a while, catching the occasional glimpse of her walking past the first-floor window with a mug in her hand. When the lights in her place went out he'd still stayed outside, searching until he found her Facebook page on his mobile. There was a beautiful picture of her, smiling shyly with a black hat pushed to a jaunty angle at the back of her head. After that, he went home and created a page for himself under a false name. Then he followed as many of her friends as he could. For sure, one of them would follow him back and then he could look deeper into her life – soul deep.

This morning he'd got here outside her place at the crack of dawn and waited until she came out again at about seven. He'd followed her through her work visits in the morning. Then, when she met some blonde girl at the library, he'd waited outside on the Green, eating a sandwich and singing in a low mutter along to heavy music on his iPod. When she came out again, he'd followed his angel to the bus stop in Park Street. He'd managed to keep up with her two days in a row. If he ever lost her, it wasn't a problem; he'd know exactly where to find her.

Smiling he turns up his music so that it fills his whole world, just like she does.

As he waits there in the dark, she comes and stands by the window. He can see the dark gold halo made by her hair, lit up as it is from the low hanging light behind her. She seems to be staring right at him, only he knows that with the scarcity of street lamps here she can't really see him, he could be anyone. His lips stretch over his teeth. If the moon had been full she would have seen him alright.

Now he has her movements mapped he needs to up the chase.

It is time.

33

I still haven't heard from Mark. No text or missed call or anything. That's the first thought I have in the morning so I switch on my laptop again and stalk his Facebook account. He hasn't posted anything for days. It's like he just dropped off the face of the earth. Maybe Reid arrested him? A horrible pang of guilt ripples through me.

I google Bristol Beast and sure enough, there's a news report about a man helping the police with their enquiries. It's so vague, no details about who he is or anything. So it might not be Mark, but if it isn't, wouldn't he have been in touch by now?

I did that; I got him arrested.

Nice one, Astrid. You finally meet someone who seems to genuinely like you, so you get them arrested. Not much chance of a relationship after that then.

It might not be that, maybe he's just too messed up after all the stuff he remembered about Felicia. He might be too traumatised to speak to me?

All these thoughts are chasing about my head, making it spin.

It's Friday and supposed to be my day off, but when work rings, begging that I cover for someone, I cave. I need the extra cash and it's not as if I have anything else to do.

I get ready for work and set off fast walking to my first service user. My mobile's ringtone stops me in my tracks.

Mark?

I dig it out of my pocket. It's Nick.

My stomach drops. For a second I contemplate ignoring him, then with a sigh, I answer; best get this dealt with now.

'Hi.'

'Azza. So, any news? When's Becks back?' His tone's all business; so much for his previous confession of enduring love.

'Sunday evening,' I say.

'So, when can I move my stuff in?'

'Look. We'll both move out next week, but we'll need a bit of time. If I'm to move out I'll have to have some deposit money to be able to rent a new place. Are you going to buy me out, or else we need to put the flat on the market, don't we?'

'I can't afford to buy you out.' Now he sounds like a petulant schoolboy.

'Then the flat should be sold.'

'I'm not selling.'

'If I have to move out, it's not fair if I can't have my share of what I put in.'

'It's your choice to move out. I had the same deal when I moved out.'

'That was different. You were leaving me for another woman.' A woman walks past me and I lower my voice. 'Look, Nick, you chose to leave to be with Kate. It was different.'

'And you're choosing to leave now.'

'God. I can't believe you. You really are…' I'm lost for something loathsome enough to describe him and so I hang up instead.

I'm fuming, only I knew, didn't I, that he'd be like this.

My phone starts ringing again. Glaring at it, I prepare my angry words and then see it was Kate calling. Taking a big breath to calm my fury, I answer. 'Hi.'

'Hi, Azza. You okay?'

'Not brilliant, I just spoke to Nick.'

'Oh.'

'Basically, he's moving in, as you know, but he's not prepared to consider either buying me out or selling at all.'

'Okay,' she says slowly. 'That's where I come in.'

'Oh?' It's my turn to sound surprised.

'Can you meet me today?'

I think for a minute. 'The library, lunchtime, like we did yesterday?'

'I'm working till two, so it would be impossible to get to the centre and back. How about sometime after two but before Nick's back at six?'

We agree that I would text her when I'd finished all my lunchtime shifts. That's usually somewhere around three.

I ring off and continue to my first client, Mr Ali, this morning. He's not a morning person, so it's really a matter of opening up all the curtains and making him a cup of tea while he lies in bed, blinking with his usual slow, confused look in those small dark eyes. I can't stop thinking about Kate. She'd sounded upbeat and excited. I hope I'll feel that way too after we meet, but I'm not holding my breath.

All my morning rounds go without a hitch and then I stop off at the library to have a coffee and write up my EFT notes. Revisiting some I wrote earlier about Mark, I wish he'd get in contact. It's horrible not knowing what's going on with him. And I miss him. This realisation hits me and I feel the shock of surprise. He's got under my skin already. Dreaming for a moment, I imagine his green eyes and his soft mouth kissing mine. Sweet warm kisses that offer the promise of something much more passionate. Heat flushes up my neck. *I think I need some air.*

After meeting up with Kate and hearing her news I'm feeling so much more positive. Her idea worries me though, it could backfire and we'll all end up back where we started. Even though it's Friday and all my friends are meeting at our local, I decided to go home and pack. I can always catch up with them for last orders.

Popping into Asda on my way home I ask if they have any spare cardboard boxes. Armed with a pile, I stagger under their weight for the last fifteen minutes to the flat. I could have thought this through a little better perhaps, but I'm keen to get going.

Packing can be fun and cathartic, I discover. It's slow though, because I keep finding things that stop me in my tracks, the memories they invoke flooding through me. After finding a minuscule red and jewel-encrusted thong that Nick gave me on my first birthday after we moved in, I pop open a beer and giggle at the memories of it. He'd put it in a beautiful box and given it to me when I'd just come out from the bathroom wrapped in a towel and still damp after a shower, we were meant to be going out for a birthday meal. I'd dropped the towel, slipped on the thong and gyrated around our living room doing my version of belly dancing. I don't usually do stuff like that, but I'd just had more than enough Prosecco to give me rude bravery. Nick was laughing and tried to grab me so I'd run to the couch, jumped on the arm of it and was working my hips in a rough figure of eight, my arms like snakes above my head, when the wild hoots of a car horn had snapped my head around to see a carload of lads. They were waving at me out of their vehicle window and whistling like crazy. I'd thrown myself to the floor with screams of surprise and Nick had laughed so hard he couldn't stay up straight. The sight of me crawling along the floor to yank the curtains shut had just made it worse. We never made it out to dinner.

Even though Nick wasn't exactly my favourite person right now, it feels great to remember the good times too. One day he'll be just a memory and I hope I'll be able to make the best of that. All these angry thoughts and painful memories just made me sad. That decides me, anything I find that makes me sad goes in the bin – that feels good.

I clean the kitchen, the living area, and the bedroom. All the little thefts except one – a tiny sit-up-and-beg ladies bike complete with wicker basket with a minuscule Toto type dog sitting in it – had been returned. The little bike had come from a shop that was now closed down, so I figure I'll keep this one piece – which I quite like anyway – as a reminder of my slide into crime or whatever it had been. I'll give a tenner to charity in payment. Hopefully, that'll redress the balance. This mini bike is my totem of something bigger I've overcome. The only room I haven't done is the bathroom. Everything in it is still in use anyway.

I've boxed up or made tidy piles of Becks' stuff for her.

Putting on some rubber gloves I wash out the kitchen cupboards. I want to leave it looking nice; not for Nick's sake though.

Once I've finished cleaning it's pretty late. Not much point going to the pub. I open another beer and sit on the couch with my laptop. Another hour gets sucked away by Facebook before I make up my bed and go to sleep.

34

Dream

I'm not sure where I am. Standing in a long grey corridor with the sounds of children echoing off the walls, only it's empty, not a child in sight. The children fade to just a single sound: a baby's cry that is then cut off with the abruptness of a slap. Now I hear footsteps, a strong steady rhythm in hard workmen's boots. The strip lights on the ceiling buzz and flick enough to set off a fit. Someone walks around the corner at the far end of the corridor. It's the man in the grey hooded top. He's carrying a large brown cardboard box. In it, there's something for me. I know this in the way of dreams, that I don't know why I know this, I just do. I want to run but I can't, because of the box. He stops in front of me and puts it down at my feet, his grunts telling me that it's heavy. He steps back from me and stands watching, the hood of his top shows nothing but a blackness within.

Something shuffles about in the box. I think I detect fur and maybe claws scraping against the side.

Squatting down I start working loose the tape securing the flaps on the top closed. As I peel the long line of tape the two flaps bulge and then burst, releasing the head and shoulders of a huge grey wolf. Its eyes fix on mine and its lips curl up to reveal long yellow teeth. The growl I now heard rises deep within its chest. I'm transfixed, its muzzle inches from my face, its stinking hot breath inescapable.

I wake in darkness, with a thumping heart and dry throat.

35

Even though Becks had said Greg would help with moving stuff, I feel eager to get out of the flat; it doesn't feel like a good place to me anymore. I ring a local taxi firm and load my suitcase plus three full cardboard boxes into it before heading off to Totterdown. As I had managed to beg today off work, I think I should make the most of it for moving. Southville isn't that far from Totterdown, so thankfully the taxi ride didn't cost too much.

Dad comes out to the vehicle and helps bring stuff in. We take them up to my old bedroom. Maybe this is a backward step, but I'm confident it's only temporary. Then we sit in the kitchen together and have a cup of tea.

'You permanent then?' asks Dad.

'I'm going back to the flat tomorrow. Becks will be back and I want to see her.'

'Best get some shopping in,' says Dad, looking around his kitchen.

I laugh. 'I'll do that, Dad. God knows what you'll buy. What do you fancy for tea tonight?'

His face brightens. 'Could you make your Bolognese?'

'Sure.'

Reaching across the table he pats my hand. 'It's good to have you home.'

'Don't get too comfortable 'cause me and Becks will be looking for a flat or house share soon as.'

He smiles. 'However long, place is yours.'

Really, I wish he'd join a dating agency or something. He likes company and home-cooked food. He's only fifty-one and as far as I know, there's been no one significant in his life since Mum left. His sadness made him look closer to sixty. It's time he put the past behind him and moved on.

'Why don't we go out for a drink later?' I ask him.

'Oh, okay. Not one of those noisy Park Street places though.'

'God, Dad, you sound like a grandpa. Let's go see a band.'

'Now you're talking.'

Saturday night, there was bound to be something. Getting my laptop, I open it up on the kitchen table and connect to Dad's Wi-Fi. It's slow, but just about usable.

'There's an indie all-girl band describing themselves as 'country sleaze' called Goat Girl playing at Thekla tonight.' I bring them up on YouTube and we listen to a track.

'I like them,' says Dad, nodding.

When I go to book tickets I see it's sold out. I put a shout-out plea on Facebook and then go up to Dad's bathroom for a pee. By the time I get back to the kitchen table I'm surprised but happy by the quick response. A guy named Joe has some tickets for friends who now can't go. Two minutes later and I have arranged a meeting with him at seven in Watershed's lobby. Social media is a wonderful thing. I grin at Dad. 'Get your glad rags on, Cinders, you shall go to the ball!'

He laughs, which crumbles into a coughing fit.

‘First some shopping for those boring necessities. Why don’t you come with me and clear those lungs a bit?’

We amble together to the local shops. It’s a nice gusty day and I feel excited about the evening ahead. We haven’t gone out to see a band together in years. He’d taken me to stuff right from when I was quite young. Bristol is good like that, plenty of live music. We’d go to festivals too, like Womad and the small one at Ashton Court. One mad muddy summer he’d taken me to Glastonbury. That’s when Mum was still with us and even though I must have been quite little, I still remember it. It was amazing, even the disgusting bits, like the toilets. I managed to get lost for what felt like hours in a sea of crazy happy adults. Some young women found me and took me with them, painting my face and feeding me lumps of homemade fudge, crumbly and sweet. I don’t know how they eventually got me reunited with my parents but I remember Mum was crying, hugging me and hissing angry words at Dad. He seemed glad to see me and not so het-up like her. I think she was the one that did all the worrying for them, as a couple. After she left he just sank into his emotions, only showing up when the music started to play. I guess that’s why music has always been an important connection between us, it’s our private language of intimacy: when he lifts the blinds and lets me see inside.

When I’d got to my teens, I’d preferred to see bands with my friends. Hot sweaty nights mosh pitting at the O2 Academy and fake IDs to get into Wetherspoons and all the other bars that hosted live music.

Going out with Dad would be a treat I’d long neglected.

When we get back I make a Bolognese sauce and leave it simmering while I go upstairs to unpack and choose what to wear tonight.

We eat early at half five. I want to leave in an hour to be sure of meeting Joe at seven, and who knows with the local buses how quick we'd make it into the city centre. I put the empty plates in the sink and run upstairs to change. Ripped jeans and a boat neck black and white striped top. DMs for my feet. I've had enough of squashed toes in overcrowded clubs over the years so DMs are the perfect solution. Step on my toes all you want, I won't feel a thing. I put on a few dabs of the Romanian perfume and clatter down the stairs shouting to Dad to get going.

He comes out to the hall and looks me up and down. 'Something's missing,' he says, his tone critical. 'Ah.' Reaching up he grabs a charcoal grey trilby off the coat hooks and plonks it on my head. 'Better.'

It's a bit big, but I like it. We leave the house and walk arm in arm for the bus stop.

We get off the bus at the Prince Street stop, just before the centre, and walk across Pero's Bridge. There are so many locks now on its metal mesh sides. Dad and I linger and read some of the inscriptions etched or handwritten on them; many declarations of enduring love. A week ago I couldn't have looked at them; now I enjoy seeing how close two people feel about each other. Staring over the railings, I gaze at the water steps backing onto the floating harbour at the city centre. The long wide staircase sparkles with the water cascading down them. It's a warm evening, the earlier wind has died down, and people are swarming about the edge of the steps, their shouts and laughter carry clear across to me. Someone is playing a stringed instrument near the other end of the bridge. My eyes follow the sound and I just glimpse Moussa playing his kora on the quay outside the Pitcher and Piano. Dad and I walk across the bridge and watch Moussa for a moment, his kora held upright in his lap is so different from any other instruments I've seen. I can only describe it as being a bit like a sitar, but the sound it produces is completely different. He looks up and nods a greeting, his slow smile expressing the bliss of an engrossed musician. I return the gesture. I have no idea how old he is; he's delicate-boned like a fine ebony carving, no grey hair, and hardly any wrinkles, only he seems ancient and ageless at the same time. When he speaks, his voice is the soft whisper of dry grasses blown in savannah winds. He's just always been about, either here – his favourite busking spot – or walking through Southville. The music he plays is harp-like but with the tumbling waterfall sounds of places a girl like me can only dream of.

Leaving Moussa to his music, we turn right and amble down the covered walkway beside the water. There would have been stalls here earlier. Now they're packed away leaving the space free for night revellers, and there are plenty of those. Each gap between the sturdy square brick pillars that support the overhang of the building above, houses a gaggle of drunks or a homeless person with their few belongings huddled around them. There are so many homeless in Bristol. Is it a sign of our fragile economy or do they travel here because they prefer it to other cities? They seem to be a constant reminder of a threat that hangs over all of us – remember, this could be you. There are quite a few women amongst their number too. If I have spare change, and I don't often have any, I give it to the women. Generally, they're about my age and I can't bear to think how they got to this point.

We're heading for Watershed. That's where Joe said he'd be with a group of friends. He said he'd nip down to the lobby at seven. We're a bit early so we start poking about looking at the programmes of upcoming movies. Watershed is an arthouse cinema as well as bar and restaurant so it's generally full of well-heeled trendies looking for a more upmarket night out.

I've never met Joe before, we're just Facebook friends, and I don't know if I'll recognise him. His profile shows a bloke in his mid-twenties with a big shock of frizzy dark hair. I'm hoping this feature alone will be enough to find him by. At the clatter of loud footfalls on the stairs, I turn and see a body rapidly develop into view. The hair is unmistakable.

'Joe?' I ask.

He grins, 'Azza, great to finally meet you for real.'

He bounds forward and shakes my hand, then Dad's when I introduce them. His loping happiness is infectious and by the time he has sold us his two spare tickets we're all laughing.

'Well,' he says. 'I guess I best get back to my mates. See you at the gig. Laters.' And he's bounding back up the stairs before I can voice my thanks.

'Shall we go straight to Thekla, or get a drink somewhere first?' I ask Dad.

'A drink, but not here.'

We leave and walk along the colonnade to a bar just before the centre. It's called No.1 Harbourside. I've been there quite a few times so I know why Dad likes it – they have craft ales. I like it because you can have tea and cake just as easily as alcohol so it's like a boozy cafe. But I don't want tea and cake now.

We both sit down at a small wooden table with a pint of ale each. I let Dad choose for me as ale is his territory. Conversation is almost impossible because of the noise levels of an enthusiastic Saturday night crowd. We sip and smile at each other soaking up the atmosphere. Me and Dad have that in common, we don't need to talk to have a good time.

After our pints we head off towards Thekla, retracing our steps over the bridge to the other canal where the boat is permanently moored. It's a big ugly grey and black hulk that is so much fun as a venue. We show our tickets and get the back of our hands stamped at the door. Goat Girl is due to start at eight. Once their set is finished it will be a normal club night on board, with the opportunity to dance till almost dawn. Probably too much to ask of Dad, but I hope to get a bit of dancing in before we head back home.

Once down in the big belly of the boat, we settle on one of the benches fixed to the sides round this lower deck level. With a pint each, we watch Goat Girl set up on the stage area. Everything is painted black down here and no outside light penetrates. It's easy to lose track of time. The place is filling up fast so I'm glad we have our drinks in already, although I have a good beer buzz building up so I'd better watch my step, I don't want to overdo it.

When Goat Girl hit their first number, Dad and I work our way through the crowd for a better view. Three guitarists and a drummer; all young, pretty and relaxed, who look for all the world like they're just there to have a good time. They could've been anyone, not rock starry at all. I love them. Pint in hand, nodding my head to their electric slow style, I peek a glance at Dad and see he feels the same. Does he miss being the one in the spotlight? He must do, but he makes no effort to be there.

Goat Girl did five more numbers then took a beer break before doing five more. We all shouted and stomped our feet for an encore – which we got – then they packed up and left. Dad went to sit down back on the bench when the regular club music started. I nipped to the toilet and was making my way back to find him when I bumped into Joe.

'Azza!' He grabs me by the arm. 'Come meet my crew.' Holding my hand he pulls me along to a small gaggle of young men standing at the edge of the dance floor. The music is so loud here that we're forced to shout introductions and to share our mutual admiration for Goat Girl. Someone bought me a drink and then we're all dancing. The floor is packed with so many people jostling and wriggling in time to the beat. Spotting Dad still on the bench I take my half-finished pint over to him.

'You okay?' I shout.

He nods. 'You enjoy yourself.'

'You sure?'

'I'm fine. Go on, have fun.'

I give him my drink and work my way back to Joe and the lads. The music takes me and closing my eyes I let my hands snake above my head as I cross over to a primitive instinctive part of me that knows nothing but the rhythm.

Hot breath on my face, the scratch of bristle on my cheek. My eyes snap open.

A man is leaning right into my face. Strobing lights flash him like a monster in a thunderstorm. White death mask face, bright saucer eyes.

Gasping, I step back, clutching my arms around my chest.

His hands grab my arms in a painful grip of steel, pulling me towards him.

Shouting, I struggle and feel my hat falling off as he seems to shake me.

He pushes his face in my hair and I hear his deeply inhaled breath.

Oh my God, he just sniffed me.

Screaming and struggling, the strobing lights disjoint the bodies around me.

No colour; just black, then white, then black.

On-off, on-off.

Sound so loud I couldn't even hear my own screams.

Only his mouth, so close to my ear, his breathing: I can hear that. The long-drawn in breaths, in through his nose then out through his mouth.

Kicking wildly, I feel my DMs connect with his shins.

Sharp pained intake of breath, then a growl, menacing and deep.

It's him! Oh God oh God oh God.

I'm rigid with fear, paralysed by that sound. Animal, yet so familiar.

'Hey!'

A shout in my other ear. People are all around us; yelling, pulling.

I'm released. Joe is holding me. 'You alright?'

I look around desperate. Where is he? There are too many people.

Joe and his friends lead me to the relative quiet of the bar area. Someone gives me back my hat, miraculously found on the dance floor. They all talk at once, wanting to know what happened. Questions fire all around me. Who was he? Did I know him? What was he doing? Creep.

Their voices wash over me. I can't explain. I don't want to explain. Exhaustion is all I feel. It swamps over me with the suddenness and rattle of a shop's drop-down shutter. I need to go home.

Thanking the guys for everything, I find Dad and usher him to the door. I don't want to tell him what just happened; I don't know why, I guess I don't want him to make a fuss, or to ruin his evening. It must be late, there are quite a few people leaving. Some mill about in the car park, smoking and shouting, their hearing shot after the loudness of the club.

Looking around me, I realise he could be anywhere. He could be any of the blokes standing around here. I only saw a stark white face with staring eyes for a second of time – it literally could have been anyone.

'Let's get a taxi,' I say to Dad. I'd seen at least two drive past since we clambered off Thekla and I'm too freaked to catch a bus. Luckily he agrees and we walk across the car park to the pavement and hail the next one we see.

36

Hunting, Sniffing, Trapping

He'd been waiting around since early this morning, keeping an eye on her front door, when a taxi pulled up outside. Moments later there she was, his angel, loading boxes into it. Then she was gone, driven away to a destination unknown. *Why?* The not knowing hurt and angered him. Where did she think she's going?

He set off then, walking to College Green. Whatever it is she's doing, he's bound to catch up with her there.

Sitting on a bench at the edge of the Green, his sense of anger and frustration grows by the minute. *What if he'd lost her?* Maybe he'd been wrong and she'd seen him waiting outside her home last night. Maybe she's gone, and he's lost his chance forever. He checks his new Facebook account on his phone. A couple of her friends have accepted his friend request. He checks her account and sees she made some updates last night. Something about going to stay with her dad.

He has no idea where that is and everything inside him cries out to know. Otherwise he will lose the control.

All morning he waits on the bench, watching for her at the library or at the bus stop on Park Street. Every half-hour he checks her Facebook page. When it all gets too much for him he leaps up and paces round the circumference of the Green, putting his music up high to block out the rest of the world and the buzzing that swarms his head, turning the world into the grey of metal.

He *will* find her.

Then when he checks Facebook again he sees she's posted a message and someone called Joe has responded.

Joy swells his heart: the chase is on.

He looks up Thekla and Watershed. By six-thirty he's waiting close to Watershed, leaning against one of the wide brick pillars, invisible amongst the throng. Just before seven, his efforts were rewarded; there she is, his angel looking happy and beautiful arm in arm with some shabby old man. That's probably her father. Even so, he doesn't like the familiarity between them and his lip curls in disgust.

They go into Watershed and he watches them through the exterior glass walls, all lit up with super bright lighting, walking about inside looking at the shelves and chatting until a tall young man with stupid afro type hair comes down the stairs to greet them. The three perform a silent pantomime of happy smiles and chatter before they part, Stupid Hair up the stairs – *that must be Joe,* he thinks – while his angel and the old man exit the front door to walk down to a noisy bar nearby.

He stays hidden outside, completely focused on her until they come out again. Then he follows them to Thekla.

That's as far as he gets, at first. He's told at the door that he can't get in without a ticket for the band, and that's sold out. He can come in later when the band is finished. No problem, he would wait. He watches other people get turned away too. And others, like Stupid Hair with some loud friends, waving their tickets and all talking at once, go in there, through that narrow door into the bowels of the boat like he longs to do.

Then after a couple of hours, a group of young women comes out carrying black instrument cases. He assumes that was the band and goes forward to the bouncer who's now happy to let him in. He pays and has his hand stamped before descending down a narrow shaft of a staircase. A sense of excitement rises up with each step down into the dark, with the enveloping heat and loud throbbing music. This is a place he feels he belongs: dark and loud, with an edge to it that raises the hairs on his neck. The smell is strong – animal sweat and spilt beer.

Going to the bar, he buys a double vodka and knocks it back in one. The fire of it runs down his gullet and brings him a fierce joy. He'd just ordered another one when he sees her, his angel, cross past the bar towards the heaving dance floor. His heart leaps, but before he could follow Stupid Hair Joe steps out of the crowd by the bar and grabs her. He actually touches her! Grinding his teeth, he downs his drink and follows them and a group of men as they move to the dance floor. He watches them all leaning in towards his angel, all too close and too intimate. When she breaks away from them he follows, hoping he can get a chance to speak to her somehow. Only she goes to the old man and then back to the young men. They're all dancing like some primitive group with her, their goddess, at their centre.

He keeps back a bit, watching her through the writhing figures. She shines. The white stripes of her top are mesmerising hot white bands under the club UV lights. They follow the curves of her body and roll with each move she makes. With her arms above her head and her eyes closed she undulates and swings her hips like an exotic dancer. She draws him to her; he can't bear anyone else to be close to her. Gradually, he works his way forward until he's standing in front of her. Leaning in close, he drinks in the intoxicating scent of her, his cheek brushing her silk-soft one.

Her eyes shoot open, wide in fear. For a moment they're held together in a ticker tape of flashing lights that make it all so unreal. Instinct makes him grab her and she struggles, her mouth opening and closing but he can't discern the sounds she might be making above the deafening music. She must have kicked him, as a sudden pain in his leg wakes the beast. Its growl rumbles up his throat, the flashing lights maddening its senses.

Someone pulls him from behind. He fights for a moment, but there are too many of them. Instead, he runs.

He weaves fast and out through the crowd; up the narrow staircase, uncaring who he shoves aside, and out into the sharp night air.

He forces himself to slow down then, as there are others waiting around in the car park. Noisy drunks stumbling around the cars, he doesn't want to be noticed by any of them. There's a large dark coloured van and he stands behind it, watching Thekla's doorway from over the bonnet.

She comes out not long after. She's with the old man again and together they hail a cab. He watches, bereft, as she climbs in and is carried away into the night.

And now he's alone; suffering pain, anger, and frustration at the loss of her. He'd been so close, he'd actually touched her. Why had that chance slipped away so suddenly?

Loud voices spilling out from Thekla pull his attention.

'What a creep!'

It's Stupid Hair. Anger bubbles up inside him and he clenches his fists.

The young men from the dance floor stand in the car park, sharing out cigarettes and talking about him like he's some monster. Their voices are excited, almost shouting as they relive the moment when they'd saved their beautiful princess from the freak.

Stupid Hair is the loudest.

Then they slap each other on the back and hug goodbye and wend off their separate ways.

Stupid Hair is alone.

He follows; hood up, hands in pockets.

Stupid Hair saunters, smoking his cigarette and humming.

He follows Joe along a few streets and into the cobbled edges of Queen Square. It's late now and most sensible people keep out of this shadow soaked place in the dark of night.

Not Joe, though. He walks across the big expanse of the square, the crunch of his shoes on the gravel path the only sound. Because those who don't want to be heard walk on the grass, don't they?

Quickening his pace across the lawn he gets closer and closer to Joe. Desire is rising up inside him. Joe and his friends called him a monster – they have no idea. A grin stretches his lips.

Joe steps on the grass and is heading over towards the darkest patch of the square when he makes his move. He leaps, slamming into the back of Joe's knees and toppling the boy before he knows what has happened. The cry of surprise is knocked out of Joe as his belly hits the ground.

He knows he needs to act fast to make the most of his advantage.

Grabbing Joe's ridiculous hip hanging jeans, he yanks them down along with the underpants beneath them. He spat a generous blob on his hand and smears it between Joe's buttocks. A hoarse yelp escapes from the man beneath him so he grabs a handful of that thick springy hair and pulls while using his other hand to guide his rock hard penis into Stupid Joe's anus.

It's so tight at first, it's almost too painful as he forces his way in.

But not as much as it's hurting Joe. Joe's cries bring the beast up, consuming him with its red hot presence. Hunching over the boy's back, the beast yanks Joe's head further back and bites into his ear, growling with guttural anger.

Joe screams, and with each thrust, he screams again. And with each scream the beast bites whatever flesh is closest.

By the time the beast has shouted his ecstatic moment at the stars, Joe's ear and shoulder are a ragged bloody mess.

As the beast recedes back into the depths of his consciousness, he withdraws from Joe. Glancing down he sees that his fast softening penis looks as if it's been smeared with black paint, as did Joe's buttocks.

Funny how different blood looks in the moonlight.

37

I didn't tell Dad. What should I say; some weirdo growled in my ear? Big deal. I couldn't tell anyone; what difference would it make? If anything, the police were more likely to think I was being a drama queen and making stuff up. I couldn't give a description as I only had an impression of a man who was probably white, with big staring eyes. Everyone knew, from Becks' description, that the Bristol Beast sniffed people and that he growled. Last night could have been someone having a laugh. Not that I'd found it funny.

Even though it was Sunday, I had service users to visit, but not until lunchtime, thankfully.

Getting up late I find my head is groggy from too many beers and my ears are still ringing, so I go and make myself a coffee before going to find Dad in his office.

'That was fun last night,' he says looking up from the Sunday papers spread out over his desk.

I nod. 'Should be you on the stage.'

'Well…' He shrugs.

I want to ask why he never tries anymore. No gigs, no girlfriends, almost no social life. But I haven't the heart to drag up his well-buried feelings.

'Anything exciting in the paper?' I ask instead.

'Yes.' He flicks back to the relevant page to show me the headline – 'Bristol Beast Attack in Queen Square,' he reads out the huge headline. 'Late last night a young man was attacked and sexually assaulted in Queen Square.' He looks up at me, his eyes strangely enlarged by his glasses. 'Raped apparently, poor bloke. You don't hear about that often, men getting raped I mean.' Dad shudders. 'What a world.'

'How do they know it was the Bristol Beast?' *Queen Square is only streets away from Thekla.*

'Just says, the police reported it was the same MO – whatever that is – as the other attacks. Growling and biting. Apparently, he likes to smell them and if they don't keep still, he bites. Damn right I couldn't keep still if some bugger started sniffing me. Just weird, that is.'

'Well it's not exactly normal to bite or rape people is it?' I snap and he looks surprised. 'Sorry, Dad, I never told you. The same guy attacked Becks.' When I see the look of horror in his eyes, I quickly add, 'He didn't hurt her, and she managed to get away.'

'Where was that?'

'East Street.'

'God!'

'I know. It's good we're moving.'

'I think you should stay here. There's probably room for Becks too if we shuffle things around a bit.' Worry lines furrow his brow.

Putting down my mug, I wrap my arms around his neck. 'I'll be fine, Dad. I am careful, I promise you. Look, I need to get a move on. I'll be late for my first appointment otherwise.'

'When are you back?'

'I'm meeting Becks at the flat this evening. She's going to stay at her boyfriend's until we find a place, so I guess late. Probably around half eleven?' Seeing his expression I add, 'Please don't wait up. I've got appointments first thing and I can't be too late, so don't worry.'

Giving him another quick hug goodbye, I go off to rinse my mug before grabbing my rucksack and hat – the striped beanie – and head out to the bus stop. My first appointment is in Clifton and most of the afternoon is in that area, so I won't get to the flat until after four. I know I need to call the police. If there had been an attack in Queen Square it seemed more likely that the person in the club had been him. Today being Sunday I wonder if Reid will be there. Sitting on the bus I get out his card and call him. It rings for an age and then a man answers introducing himself as PC Morris.

'Inspector Reid?' I ask.

'The inspector is currently away from his desk. Can I be of assistance?'

I say who I am and why I'm calling. He gets me to explain everything that happened last night, making me describe the events at Thekla twice. Then he thanks me and says that Inspector Reid would most likely be in touch as soon as he is free.

Well, I've told them what I know. I don't suppose it'll make much difference, but at least I can stop hashing it through in my head.

Letting myself into the flat I look around me. It seems alien, too clean and empty. All ready for Nick and my new tenant. How I wish I could see the look on his face. I hope it works out.

Getting a bin bag from some I'd left on the counter, I put all Becks' wash stuff, towel and dressing gown in it. Now I have all her stuff piled up on the kitchen counter and the rest by the door, I'm amazed how little we have. Then the intercom buzzes.

'Hi?' I call into it.

'Kate,' came her crackled reply.

Smiling, I buzz her up.

I have the door open as Kate and her parents come up the stairs. Each of them carries a bundle of bags and boxes. Welcoming them in, I direct them to put the stuff in the bedroom.

'Okay,' says Kate's Mum shaking my hand. 'I have drawn up a contract for you and Kate to sign, assuming we're happy with everything.'

'What if it doesn't work out?' I ask giving Kate a worried glance.

Her mum shrugs. 'We'll deal with that when we come to it. This is a six months' tenancy agreement. It's just a bog-standard one that I obtained from a colleague. It protects you both. I'm Kate's guarantor so that's double protection for you should she default on her payments. After six months we can review the situation. If Nick and Kate are alright and choose to stay together we're prepared,' she glances round at her husband who gives me a nod, 'to help her buy out your share of the flat. If it's not working, it's within your rights to insist you both sell, in which case we will still buy your share. With this possible outcome in mind, I am preparing a document, in my capacity as Kate's legal adviser, which will map out what happens to his share. I can't be totally assured that everything will come out in her favour, but I feel quite confident that a substantial proportion of it will come to Kate to help support her and her baby, or that we can, at the very least, make life very difficult for him.'

An infectious grin passes between the three of us women. Kate's Dad, I notice, just looks grim. Either way, Nick is going to have to work hard to stay in this family's good books.

'Nick?' I ask Kate.

'He thinks I'm on a break with my parents. This is just some of my stuff. I'm going to go back for the rest of it when everything is more settled.'

'I'll text him tomorrow and tell him me and Becks have moved out. I expect he'll come right over.'

'Believe me, I'm ready for that,' says Kate with a look of steel.

I think I underestimated you, I think, *and so did Nick.*

I show them the ins and outs of the flat, plus any paperwork, like the utility bills which I have put in a tidy pile in one of the kitchen drawers. I'll ring the service companies tomorrow to put it all in Kate's name.

We have a cup of tea while I read through the contract. 'Becks gets back with Greg soon, so either of them can witness our signatures,' I say.

Kate's Mum, who I now know as Charlotte, nods. 'I can't thank you enough, Astrid, for what you have done.'

I look at my feet, embarrassed. She takes hold of my hand, forcing me to meet her eyes.

'Kate has explained everything, and I can tell you that your attitude to the situation is nothing short of remarkable. I know, I've seen it all first-hand. People can be eaten up with pain and anger. Nick's behaviour has been reprehensible, beyond reproach, but you have given both Kate and him a chance at happiness.'

'That's if the stupid boy can see what he's about to lose,' adds Kate's dad, Toby, putting an arm around his daughter.

'Either way, I hope this arrangement we have put in action today can ultimately benefit you all,' concludes Charlotte.

I shake hands with them both and accept a cheque for the deposit, plus the first month's rent before they each give Kate a hug and kiss and clatter off back down the stairs.

Kate and I sit on the couch to chat and wait for Becks. She seems nervous, fiddling at a small silver chain around her neck and laughing too much at nothing in particular.

'Are you going to be okay?' I ask.

'Actually, I'm more frightened about seeing Becks. I bet she hates me.'

I laugh. 'You weren't her favourite person, but I bet she'll just love for you to pull this off.'

Kate bites her lip. 'Mum says I have rights. That Nick will be forced to provide for me and the baby, only I can't stop imagining all kinds of stuff.'

'Your parents are good people. You're very lucky. I think they'll look after you whatever the outcome. After everything he's done, are you sure you even want to be with him?'

Kate looks down at her hands and then up again holding my gaze with the pain shining in her eyes. 'I know it might sound weak to you, but I love him. I've tried to imagine getting on with my life without him and I just can't. Perhaps I'm fooling myself, only I have to give it a try.'

'Hi, hi, hi.' Becks' voice at the door and her open-mouth surprise as she enters and clocks Kate sitting with me, has us both breaking into a shaky laugh. Greg is close behind her so Kate and I rise together to greet him.

Becks pulls me into a hug whispering, 'Explain,' in my ear.

I show her the contract, which we then make Greg witness, and explain how Kate is now my new tenant, with a view to buying me out – fingers crossed – in about six months.

'Wow. You amazing tricky bitch,' says Becks looking Kate up and down. 'I love it. Promise you'll meet up and tell me and Azza how he takes it.'

Kate looks uncomfortable so I pull Becks into the bedroom on the pretext she checks I haven't missed any of her stuff.

'Be gentle,' I say in a lowered voice. 'I know it's sneaky.'

'He deserves it.'

'But she loves him all the same, so she's hoping he'll come round to the idea.'

'And they can play happy families.' She snorts and shakes her head.

'Becks,' I warn.

'Okay, I'll be good. But still—'

'Becks.'

'Okay, okay.' She holds up her hands, admitting defeat.

We do a round of the bedroom and can't find anything I'd forgotten.

Back in the living room, I give Kate my keys and then Greg, me and Becks carry everything down to his roomy Volvo estate.

Looking up at the window, I see Kate gazing down at us. It gives me the strangest feeling. My rival finally has it all: my man, my flat and the baby I'd wanted so badly – and yet all I feel is free. I hope it works out for her, I really do. I give her a brief wave before climbing into the back seat and squash in beside my last few bags and boxes.

Following my directions, Greg drives to Dad's house while Becks keeps up a stream of chatter. At first, it's about Nick and Kate, and then about their amazing holiday. I can see she looks tanned and happy; Greg must be good for her. Hopefully, this will be a relationship that lasts.

Finally, she asks about Mark.

'I haven't seen him since the Monday you went away,' I say.

'Why, you two had a spat?'

I'm not sure how to answer. I can't explain without damning him to Greg and maybe creating suspicions where they don't belong.

'I… I think I upset him.' Is the best I can come up with.

'How?' She's half turned round in her seat peering at me between the two front backrests. Eyes wide, fascinated. Gossip's her bread and butter.

I widen my eyes at her and flick my gaze at Greg's head.

'Okay,' she says, sitting back round. 'I'll get you later. Meet up for a proper chat.'

'Okay,' I say, relieved.

'We need to talk about flats too. As much as I love spending time with you,' she adds, rubbing Greg's thigh, 'I need my own place, so I can spread out a bit.'

He gives a deep chuckle and I sense a private joke between them – *please!*

Slapping his leg she shouts, 'Oi you, my make-up an' all.'

'I haven't started looking yet. We definitely need to get that on the go,' I say, ignoring the innuendo going on between them.

'Definitely,' says Becks, giving Greg's leg another slap.

When we get to Dad's, Greg and Becks help me carry all my stuff in. It isn't that late, only half nine, so they stay for a quick chat with Dad before heading off to Greg's place in Redland. Becks texts me a bit later to say she'll scout out some properties, and maybe we can meet up at the estate agents near the top of Park Street tomorrow afternoon. She adds that she's expected to start work again pretty soon so we should make the most of her free time for house hunting.

Despite all the bags and boxes cluttering my room, I go to sleep feeling light and free. I'm done with the past and ready for a new exciting future.

38

Dream

This dream is the same as last night. The man in the grey hooded top carrying a large cardboard box. Even though I know it contains a wolf, I still open it; only I don't wake up when its head and shoulders burst through the lid. We stare at each other, its low growl sending goosebumps up my arms.

I scream as it leaps out at me; snarling, teeth bared.

Turning, I run up Mrs P's spiral staircase.

It goes on and on forever, with the wolf's harsh panting breath and the sound of its claws scrabbling on the stone stairs far too close behind me.

39

I'm up early and ready to go to work in plenty of time this morning. I'm due to visit some service users in Clifton, so I think I'll pop into Mrs P's. The idea creeps me out, but I have to do something about Sir Lancelot. Reid hasn't called me about my encounter at Thekla so I guess it wasn't that vital. No one has called about the cat, but I'm hoping that if I leave some food out on the doorstep it might encourage him to stay near his home. The dream I'd had was so unsettling, almost identical to the one before. Stuff must be getting to me. All the moving, and Nick and Kate. I need to lighten up a bit. If I can afford it, a holiday or at least a few days off would be good. But who am I kidding? If I'm serious about finding a new flat I need as much work as I can get to earn the money for it.

After seeing some of my regulars and getting them up for their breakfast, I go along beside the Downs and then the leafy avenue to Mrs P's building. The wind is up this morning and the canopy above me roils and clatters about, sending twigs and leaves onto the road. I'm grateful for my beanie hat as the first stings of rain touch my face, pushing me to hurry faster and unlock the key-safe by the front door. I stand in the open doorway for a couple of minutes calling for Sir Lancelot. Nothing, no cat, just the wind. Shoving the heavy door closed behind me, I run up the first flight of the spiral staircase, the wolf in my dream nagging at the edges of my thoughts, pushing me to run faster. Despite this, by the top, I'm trudging and out of breath.

Her flat seems lonely. The rain has got heavy now; droplets smash against the windows in a discordant tattoo. The deep sill outside the living room is empty. Sensible gull is probably lurking somewhere dry. Although it's a sea bird, wasn't it? Shrugging I get some dry cat food pellets and put them in the cat bowl. I take this back downstairs and set it down on the top step as close to the front door as I can. There's an overhanging stone lintel above that will save it from some of the weather.

Heading out into the rain, I run for the nearest bus shelter. The next bus takes me down to Park Street. I have some lunchtime appointments around this neck of the woods for the next couple of hours. I text Becks to meet me at the estate agent's at two. Then I message Nick. I say we have moved out and our keys are in the flat. After that I set my phone to silent; no need to answer his calls.

Lunchtime visits done, I grab a sandwich from Sainsbury's and eat it as I walk to the estate agents, checking my phone as I go. One text from Becks confirming she'll be there at two and three missed calls from Nick. Grinning, I take a big bite of my sandwich, relishing its soft fullness in my mouth.

As I get to the estate agents I can see Becks is already inside, a pile of prospectuses in front of her and a trim smartly dressed woman across the desk from her, tapping at her keyboard.

'Azza,' Becks calls across the office as I enter. 'This here's my friend, Astrid,' she tells the woman opposite her.

The agent stands and extends a manicured hand. 'Isabel,' she says.

I smile and shake her hand before taking the seat next to Becks.

It takes an age, finding some flats to match our meagre budget, and to input our details into her system. It seems that most places won't become available for at least a month. The deposit and first month's rent are mammoth. At least I have Charlotte's cheque, already deposited this morning, to be able to pay for this. The flats on offer seem lovely, but as Becks says, the camera shots probably make them look a lot bigger than they actually are. We make a date with Isabel to meet at two the next day at the first address we want to see; a fairly new development round the back of Temple Meads train station. After that, she will drive us to see some more.

Back out on the street, Becks and I walk down Park Street, chatting and catching up on all our gossip. At least the rain of this morning is holding off, but the clouds look dark and threatening.

'Let's get a coffee,' says Becks, and I follow her into the Boston Tea Party cafe. Becks gets cake too and we carry our drinks and her snack upstairs, taking a moment to choose from the many wooden tables cluttering the high ceilinged room before settling down at one by the window. I like the huge paintings they have here. Roughly depicted portraits of unsmiling, yet composed characters. Somehow the artist has managed to make them look like an incredibly talented child has painted them.

As we sip our drinks I look out of the window, watching all the people marching in gaggles up and down the street. Those going up lean forward, compensating for the steepness of the hill.

'Come on, spill,' says Becks.

'Uh?'

'You and Kate, you and Mark. Honestly, I leave you alone for five minutes and the whole world goes mad.'

Laughing I tell her all. It's a lot, just for one week. Hopefully, everything will calm down now. I moderate the bit about Mark, patient confidentiality in my mind, and just say he got over-emotional and had to leave in a hurry. I stop her questions about him by moving quickly on to Kate's visit and my subsequent burst of destruction.

Becks looks impressed and bites into her cake. 'Mad crazy lady,' she says, her words muffled around a full mouth. 'And Mark's not contacted you since?'

'No, but I'm worried that might have something to do with Reid.'

'Uh?'

I explain about my experience at Mrs P's and my later interview at the police station. Becks says 'Shit' and 'Bastard' when I tell her that Reid suggested I was making it all up. And then I explain how Reid had wanted to know anyone we had both associated with recently, people who are new to us, and how I had mentioned Mark.

'No way was that thing Mark. I would have recognised him, wouldn't I?' says Becks shaking her head.

'I know. All the same, how would you feel if someone accused you to the police?'

'You didn't accuse him, you just said he was someone we both know so they could, what's it called, him from their enquiries.'

'Eliminate. I know, but Mark might not see it that way. Oh Becks, I feel terrible. I think I really liked him, and I was so sure he liked me.'

'He'll be back. I'll get Greg to sound him out.'

'Don't tell Greg. Oh God, I shouldn't have told you,' I say, literally wringing my hands.

'I'll be subtle I promise.'

Inside I cringe. Becks isn't known for her subtlety.

'Promise,' she says, grabbing my hand from across the table.

'Okay, but don't say too much to Greg. Please.'

'One hundred per cent,' she says, her eyes wide and innocent as a child's.

'God!'

I tell her about what happened at Thekla and how I rang the police about it.

'Really creepy,' she says. And, 'God! Fuck's sake,' after hearing about the attack in Queen Square.

We chat about her holiday and her feelings for Greg, which seem to have got even bigger since their holiday. I quash a tinge of jealousy. I'm happy for her; I just wish I could be saying the same about my love life.

Cake and coffee finished, we head out into the street, and after a big hug, off to our separate homes. Sitting on the bus to Totterdown, I stare out of the window. Bristol looks as grey and gloomy as I feel. Stupid. I have so much to be happy about. I need to shake off this gloom. Hearing my mobile buzz, I check my messages. Someone has found Sir Lancelot! Finally, something good. I try ringing them but they don't pick up so I send a text. After that, I keep checking my phone for a reply, eager to know if I can arrange to meet them and get the cat. I can see from my call history that I have a missed call from DI Reid. I try the number he gave me but can't get through. No doubt he'll see my missed call and get back to me. I expect he has much more to deal with than my ramblings about flashing lights and a creepy man. Also, I don't want to keep ringing him in case I miss a call about the cat.

40

Hunting, sniffing, trapping

He's so happy, he can't stop smiling. She even tried to ring him back. He'd stared at his ringing phone, his heart beating the fastest of tattoos, but he couldn't answer, his mouth had been too dry for words. He wouldn't call her until he has his story straight. No mistakes this time. He would be vague and not say too much, not give her the chance to ask too many questions.

Lifting the large cardboard box onto his kitchen table he begins to load it with the things he'll need. Cable ties, rope, and some tools. Best to have everything to hand. Who knew what he might need on the day?

41

It's the next day, Tuesday morning that the call comes. I'm walking through Bedminster on my way to one of my service users and I hear my mobile ringing. At first, I can't understand him. His English isn't very good and it's laced with an accent I don't recognise.

'Ello. I have cat. Cat you lose.'

'Cat, Sir Lancelot?'

'Sorry? Cat you lose, yes?'

'I lost a cat, yes,' I say, beginning to grin. This conversation reminds me of the old *Fawlty Towers* re-runs that Dad likes to watch.

'I have cat. Please, can I… Can you cat back. Is big. I not like cat much, I…' He seems at a loss to explain, then says, 'I like this.' He makes what sounds like a sneeze. 'Cat not good me. What I do him? I bring you, please, you tell me.'

I think it's best, if he's willing to bring me Sir Lancelot, that we meet at Mrs P's. At least I can put it straight into the flat without the risk of losing him en route.

So I give him Mrs P's address. I say I will text it to him too and thank him over and over.

'It's okay. I happy you happy. Indeed, I very very happy. I be at address one o'clock, is okay? I sorry, can only be one o'clock, after busy. Very very busy. Much big busy.'

So I might be a bit late meeting Becks and Isabel at Temple Meads, but that shouldn't be a problem. This is important; I need to get that cat back. It's twelve now and I have two more lunchtime appointments. I'll have to get a move on.

It's twenty to one when I hop on a bus for Clifton. Finally, I'll get that bloody cat back where it belongs. I have my alpaca hat on today and I pull on the thick plaited strings that hang down from either side of my chin, grinning like a loon. One less thing to worry about.

By one, I'm waiting in the downstairs hall at Mrs P's, sitting on the bottom step of the spiral staircase with the front door open, watching the car park. I hope he'll be on time so I can get to Temple Meads. Just in case I send Becks a text – 'Got to see a man about a cat. Might be a bit late'.

A white van pulls into the car park and a man gets out. At the sight of his grey hooded top, my heart begins to race. *Stop it*, I tell myself and raise my hand in greeting as I rise and walk out to meet him.

'Hi,' I say.

Ignoring me he goes to the back of the van. Opening it he takes out a large cardboard box. 'No,' he says when I try to take it from him. 'Is heavy, I bring.'

He strides to the entrance and steps inside, turns and waits for me to join him. As soon as I'm inside he puts the box down and pushes the door shut with a bang. My heart leaps with the sound.

'Hey!'

'Is better, maybe cat…' and he makes shooing motions with his hands. 'Be gone again,' he says grinning, showing a set of mismatched yellow stained teeth.

'Um,' I say stepping back a little. 'Where did you find him?'

'He make noise in bush. I walking and find cat there.' He gestures towards the Downs, which makes perfect sense as it's only a few streets away. 'I see poster about lost cat. I pick him up and take him my home.'

'Let me just check.'

The sight of the box, so like the one in my dream, has given me the jitters. *Stop it,* I tell myself, *am really expecting that there's a wolf in it?* But I need to see, and also I have a sudden thought that maybe this odd man has brought me someone else's beloved pet and that it isn't Sir Lancelot at all. As I approach the box, something changes in his expression. His thick dark eyebrows, they're almost one black line across his forehead, drawn down at the centre in a deep frown.

'If… if that's okay?' I stammer.

He doesn't answer, just steps away from me, putting his back against the door.

With fear stabbing my gut, I bend down and prise open the box. 'What?' I say looking at an assortment of tools and rope, but no cat.

As I straighten, he raises his hand and I flinch back. A smile thins his full lips as he pushes home the upper bolt on the door.

'What're you doing?'

'Please,' he says. 'Calm. You okay. I not hurt you.'

Turning fast I leap for the stairs, my only choice, and run.

His laboured breaths close behind me. His work boots, loud slaps on stone.

Risking a look back, I can't see him. But I can hear him.

Ragged breaths.

Slamming boots.

Shouts in a language I don't understand.

My screams, echoing around this tunnelled space.

Racing heart, jagged breaths.

The door.

I jump up the last curved flight and fling myself through the flat's glass panelled door and slam it behind me, pushing home the tiny bolt. Through the rippled glass I see his figure come in to view, distorted and refracted.

Run.

Running up the hallway I scream when I hear the crash of the door smashed in.

Hide. Where?

I hurtle into the bathroom and slam the door, the sound no doubt telling him exactly where to find me, and search madly for a lock.

No lock.

No lock policy with the old and infirm, stupid health and safety.

There's a sudden pounding on the door and I jump with a scream.

Whimpering, I press my back against it and brace my DMs onto the linoleum floor. Each crash of his body translates straight into mine until, sobbing, I'm thrown across the bathroom as he slams in and grabs my shoulders, turning me to face him.

He's breathing hard, his dark eyes wide, nostrils flared as we stare into each other's eyes.

'I. Not. Hurt. You,' he says, each word punctuated with a gasp. 'Just talk.'

Just talk. Crazy way to get a conversation. I almost laugh. 'I can't.' My words shiver out as my teeth are chattering. 'Too scared.'

He lets go of my shoulders and steps back into the doorway, his hands on his hips, still trying to catch his breath. His round face is red from the exertion and a trickle of sweat runs from his close-cropped dark hair, tracking a silvery line down to his eyebrows. He wipes it away with the back of his hand.

'Okay. You okay. I not hurt you. Just talk.'

My heart's beating so hard it almost blocks his words. *Calm, think.* I force myself into long slow breaths until I could speak. 'Please, I need some water.'

He indicates with a jerk of his chin the sink to my right.

Flooding water into my cupped hands I bend to drink, peeking through my lashes left and right to see if there is anything I can use. Nothing, just plastic bottles, soap, and a flannel. No razor or hard heavy objects to fling at him. Turning back to face him, I wait, arms tightly wrapped around my chest. Who is he? What does he want?

'Come,' he says. When I don't move, he steps back a little. 'Come. We sit, we talk.' When I still don't move, he gives a grunt of impatience and comes back into the room and grabs my wrist.

'No no no no,' I scream, holding onto the sink with my free hand.

Wrapping his other arm about my waist he jerks me to him and holds me tight against his body. I can feel his face and hot breath through the wool of my hat, and then I hear his deep inhalation as he presses his nose against the top of my head.

No no no no screams my mind, but my body goes rigid.

With frightening ease, he half lifts half drags me into the living room where he pushes me down to sit into the couch. He sits down beside me, keeping a constant grip on my wrist.

'Azza,' he says. When I don't respond, he jerks at my arm, squeezing my wrist hard so I cry out. 'Answer.'

'Yes.' It comes out as a shriek.

The smile is back on his lips. 'Good,' he says, his voice almost a purr. 'Is not English name?'

I stare at him. What game is he playing?

'Wh… what's your name?' I hate the thin weak sound in my voice, but I must get him talking somehow. Engage him, to see me as human, isn't that what all the advice says, so maybe he won't want to hurt you – too much.

His smile grows to show those dreadful stained teeth. 'I am Dragos.'

Dragos, this sounds familiar. I just can't remember why my brain is fogged with fear. 'Where're you from?'

'Romania,' he says.

Now, something explodes through the fear as brightness in my brain – Romania, Dragos. Dragos was Mark's friend at the orphanage. Although it was probably a common name there. 'Why are you here? What do you want?'

'I see you all time. I want talk with you. You special.' His smiles his terrible smile and I shiver.

'Have you been following me?'

'*Da*,' he says nodding, clearly pleased. 'I see you all time. We be friends, yes?'

'Was that you at Thekla?'

His heavy brows draw down.

'On the big boat,' I explain, 'with the music, did you…' I'm finding it hard to find the words without sounding offended. If I want to gain his confidence I have to stay neutral. 'Did you… touch me? Was it you who tried to dance with me on the boat?'

'*Da*,' he says, nodding.

So it was probably him who attacked the man in Queen Square. I blink at tears blurring my vision. 'Did you chase me, here in the car park last week?'

'I nearly get you.' He wags his finger at me, grinning. 'Fast, you very fast.' He gives a short bark of laughter as if this thought amuses him. 'And you smell good.' Leaning over he pulls my hat off my head and presses it to his nose. Eyes closed, he inhales a deep breath.

I watch, mesmerised, as he stays like this for several minutes engrossed in tightly squeezing my hat and inhaling its aroma. Maybe this is my chance? I shift forward, and his eyes open, freezing me to the spot. He has a glazed look like he's stoned. Putting my hat down beside him, he pulls me slowly towards him until his face is touching mine. His breath is strong and revolting so that I instinctively hold mine. Then his nose brushes my cheek as he moves across to bury his face in my hair.

He breathes in deep and murmurs, 'I like too much.'

I don't move a muscle. I can't. When he changes to the back of my neck I almost scream. The feel of his mouth there, at the back of my neck, sends goosebumps down my arms. His free hand brushes my hair away so he can get closer to my skin. The body odour that rises from him makes me want to gag. It's all I can do to keep still; my body begins to shake and shiver. God, what if that made him angry?

'So sweet, your scent is sweet like honey and milk.' He nuzzles behind my ear. 'Mmm,' the appreciative sound he makes becomes deep like a growl.

'Please, Dragos.'

He stops. His body still and I sense his tension.

'I… I need to pee. I need the bathroom.'

He sits back and looks at me, his thunderous expression showing how much I've upset him.

'I'm so sorry, but I need the bathroom. Please.' Hating my pleading, and trying to stop my teeth from chattering, I know it's useless but it's all I can think of to stop him smelling me like that.

And to halt the excitement I feel emanating from him.

'*Da*, okay,' he says, only his face says that he's anything but okay with me needing a wee.

He escorts me back to the bathroom, patting down my pockets and taking my phone. Nodding he puts it in his pocket, then he shuts the door, leaving me alone to do my thing.

Looking around me I try to think. The window is small and high up behind the toilet. Putting down the seat I climb up. Looking out I can see into the large well-kept garden of the property beside this one. Nobody in sight. What if I write a note on some toilet paper and throw it out the window? Who in their right mind picks up old toilet paper? If I shout he will hear me. Maybe it would be best if I climb up and throw myself out somehow. At least I won't have to go through what others have suffered at this man's hands. I start to climb up and get my head and shoulders through the narrow oblong hole. Staring down at the hard unforgiving space below I know I can't, not like this.

There's a yell behind me and hard hands are pulling me back.

'No, you not do that.'

His face is twisted in pain and anger.

I start to cry. That's easy, the tears have been just waiting to come. He lifts me off the toilet seat and carries me like a child back into the living room. Sitting down he holds me in his arms as I cry.

'Hush hush,' he says stroking my hair. He begins to hum a tune under his breath and my tears almost stop in shock. It's her tune, the woman from my dream. Self-preservation keeps me still. He hugs and hums to me until I begin to drift, all the fear and exertion taking me away from the horror of the monster that holds me.

42

Dream

I'm creeping with slow infinite care through a dark cave. Its walls and roof press in around me so that I have to duck to avoid hitting my head. The walls are damp and cold to touch. Ahead I can hear a sound – it's breathing. Enormous animal breaths. Something skitters beneath my feet and I cry out looking down to the grey concrete floor. What was it? Bending down I try hard to make out what it was in this arid rock space. Something smooth with a little shine. Reaching out, I touch it with a tentative finger, rolling it away from me. A small glass marble. I can see more of them lining the floor ahead. Now as I walk, they slither and slide beneath me, hundreds of them. The only way to walk is by slowly gliding my feet through them, or I know they'll make me lose my footing. The sound of them is musical, skittering and clinking against each other, the glass flickering in the low light around me. I'm cold, so cold I can't stop shivering, the noise of my chattering teeth echoes that of the tinkling marbles and my breath is like smoke puffed out before me. There's light up ahead and I need to get towards it. But the animal breathing is getting closer too.

Peeking around a corner I see that the cave opens up into a huge cavern that is piled up with a mountain of marbles. Lying on top of this is an enormous black dragon. It's asleep, at least I think it is, and the loud breathing is coming from it.

Something moves across at the back of the cavern. It's Mark. He's making his way, with slow sweeping steps, across the river of marbles towards me. I wave and he holds a finger up to his lips – shhh. I nod and we slide our way through the glass towards each other. He hugs me and I whisper into his ear, telling him how much I've missed him.

Around us, the marbles start moving in a glittering tide.

Looking up I see the dragon's huge eyes are open, its yellow gaze trained intently on us.

Turning we try to run, but the rolling marbles underfoot make fast movement impossible. We can only slide through them as they rise up our legs in a glinting wave.

With a shout, Mark falls. Glass engulfs him as the huge black beast slithers down the mountain of bright orbs and stops right in front of me.

I'm frozen with fear, rooted to the spot. It bends its long neck and puts its nose into my hair and inhales deeply.

My scream leaves my throat in one long piercing shriek of fear.

43

'Hush, hush.' Dragos is trying to hold me still. The scream in my dream is loud in my ears.

Snapping my mouth shut I stare at him.

'Better?' he asks. 'You sleep like baby.' He smiles and I shiver. *How could I have fallen asleep with this monster beside me?* 'Better?' he asks again and shakes me a little when I fail to respond.

I nod. Fear has stolen my voice again.

'Now is late. I hungry. You hungry?'

I wasn't; if anything I felt sick, but I nod.

'Good. I have food in van. You stay here.' He gets up and looks at me, speculating. Digging in his back pocket he pulls out a bundle of thick white plastic zip ties. He wraps one around my wrists locking my hands together. 'Come,' he says and drags me back to the bathroom. 'Is best place,' he says as he pulls a short length of slim silver chain from his pocket. He uses more zip ties to fix me to the radiator with a chain for some freedom of movement. 'Here you have everything, water, toilet. Maybe bath too,' he adds giggling. 'Be good girl. I be back quick quick.' Smiling at me he does an oddly childish hand wave, his thick fingers opening and closing like a fat pink sea anemone before disappearing out of sight.

God God God. Quick, think, what can I do? I try clambering on to the toilet seat but the chain is too short to get my head up to the window. I pull and twist at the zip ties achieving nothing but chafing red rings on my wrists. Then I try chewing through them. It's hard and I can only use my front teeth, but if he gives me enough time I feel like I could bite through. Actually, I've made quite impressive dents in the plastic when he appears in the doorway. He checks my wrists and tuts. There's the glint of a large hunting knife in his hand suddenly and I shrink back, cowering against the plastic bath panel so that it buckles in against my weight. He jabs it at me and giggles when I scream.

Shaking his head, still laughing, he leans down and grabs my wrists.

I squirm as the knife comes close, but he just cuts through the plastic and pulls me up to standing.

'Come,' he says dragging me behind him to Mrs P's small kitchen.

The table is laid like a restaurant. Pink flowers in a glass jug, a tall silver candlestick with a lit red candle stuck in it and a bottle of champagne beside it. Two floral patterned plates are placed on either side of the small pine table. Each plate is laden with a mountain of assorted deli foods: smoked salmon roulades, slices of ham, various salads, seeded rolls and chopped tomatoes slick with oil and herbs. The song 'Be Our Guest' from the banquet scene of Disney's *Beauty and the Beast* unexpectedly floods my brain. Laughter threatens and I squash it down before madness overcomes me. He must have picked one of everything.

'Sit,' he says pushing me towards a chair, and then he sits down opposite me. He gestures at the spread. 'All for you.' He beams, brimming over with pride.

I feel sick. Flowers, candle and champagne – what is this, a proposal?

'Eat,' he says stuffing a forkful of the pile in his mouth. 'Mmmm.' Breathing with loud grunts I watch as he visibly churns his mouthful like hell's washing machine. 'Eat,' he says pointing at my plate with his fork.

Picking up my knife and fork I push the food around my plate. Maybe I could slip the knife in my pocket?

'Ah.' He reaches across and grabs the bottle of champagne by its neck.

I watch as he wrestles with the foil and then the wire, his brows lowering with frustration.

'Um,' I start and then silence when his ferocious glare shot to me. 'You, um, twist that wire bit there.' I point a trembling finger.

Looking down he grunts and works at the wire before yanking off the cork with a bang that makes me squeak. Laughing he hurries the mouth of the bottle over his tumbler to catch the over-spilling froth. Then he fills my glass. He holds up his glass towards me, indicating we should clink them together. '*Noroc*,' he says forcefully knocking his glass into mine before downing his drink in one. He gives a loud burp, giggles and refills his glass.

He says nothing then, while he eats, the noise of his chewing filling the small space of the kitchen. I know I should try and eat something, I haven't eaten since this morning, but I can't.

Grunting, he points his knife at my plate so I put a small forkful of salmon in my mouth. But my mouth is so dry and the fish slimy so that it sticks and I can't swallow it down. I start to cough and gag. He's over to me in an instant thumping my back. Forcing my glass into my hand he pushes it up towards my lips. I sip. God, horrible warm champagne burns inside my mouth, but it does the trick and I can swallow back my mouthful of food.

Sitting back down, he looks at me. 'Okay, we talk now,' he says. 'Tell me, what is this place? I see here, always. Is not your home?'

'It's one of my service user's.'

'Eh?' He curls one side of his mouth and squints at me. I could see something green stuck between his teeth.

'I'm a carer. I look after people in their homes.'

'Where this person?' He points at the table.

Think quick, what was best – say Mrs P will be back any minute? No, maybe he'd want to move me somewhere else, or kill me. 'She's in hospital. I'm looking after the place for her.'

'And cat,' he says nodding and grinning.

Yes, and the fucking cat I lost because of you.

'When home, this person? When home from hospital?'

The phone starts ringing in the sitting room. We look at each other like guilty children. He gets up and goes into the hall. Unsure what to do I follow. We stand stiff and awkward staring through the living room doorway at the phone. He swings his head like a caged animal looking from me to the phone on the small side table by Mrs P's chair. I can feel his indecision whether to risk answering. The answerphone kicks in with an automated BT voice requesting a message. Then when I hear the message I feel like laughing and screaming at the same time.

'Hello. Mrs Percival. This is Pet Care vets, Hotwells branch. Your cat, um.' There's the sound of shifting papers before the woman's voice continued, 'Sir Lancelot.' She gives a little laugh. 'I love the name. Sir Lancelot was handed into us by a local person who found him and thought he might be lost. We found your details from his microchip. He's doing fine and enjoying lots of attention from all of us here at Pet Care. Please give us a ring on,' and she reels out a number at speed before saying goodbye and cutting off the call.

'When woman home from hospital?' Dragos says, looking at me with his brows lowered into a dark angry line. I guess the call must have shaken him up, reminding him that the real world was forever drawing in.

'She broke her hip. I don't know how long but she's only been away about a week so far.'

He nods and then smiles. He goes to the phone and unplugs it before wrapping the cord round the unit. 'Come,' he says and drags me into the bedroom. Coldness floods through me as I stare at the large pink quilt on the bed. *Please no.* But he seems only interested in unplugging the second phone that stands on the bedside table. He takes both phones and forces me to follow him to the hall where he stuffs them in a large green canvas holdall he must have brought up earlier with all the foodstuff. Then he marches me back into the kitchen.

Seated again, he salutes me with his glass before knocking it back in one. Refilling it he says, 'Azza, I so happy I find you.' He leans over the table towards me and I work hard not to shrink back. 'You very clever. I had to watch and follow. I want to know you, all about you. Why you always in library?'

'I like it there.'

He squints at me.

'It's quiet and peaceful,' I add.

He nods with a sage expression on his face but then that is replaced by another emotion. 'Why you do this?' He starts tapping on his head and face.

Oh. 'It's EFT. It's a way of helping people,' I add when his look of confusion deepens.

'How help?'

I start to tap through my routine. 'While I tap, like this, I say a sentence about something I want to change. If I have a headache or a sad feeling.'

'I sad sometimes,' he says.

Not surprising really, all things considered, with what you get up to you should be in a shit load of sad. 'Really, why are you sad?'

'I miss home, my country. And I miss Felicia so much it hurt here,' he touches his hand to his heart.

'Felicia?' *It couldn't be, could it?*

'She special to me, like you.'

I hold onto my chair to stop myself from bolting from the table. What happened to Felicia? 'Is she… is she your wife?' It's almost too hard to ask. I need his answer, but loath to know at the same time.

He laughs, a sharp barking sound. 'A little like wife, *da*. Like mother too. I love her too much.'

'So is she back in your home town, in Romania?'

'I lost, maybe she dead. But she live inside me always.' His eyes are bright. He looks almost handsome then, with his stark dark features and bright burning eyes. 'That's why I love you,' he says reaching across the table and gesturing that we should hold hands.

My hand shakes so much as I reach out to him that he laughs.

'No scared, I love you, Azza. I want you love me. We can be happy together, *da*?' He lifts my hand in a salute. 'Drink.' He grabs his glass with his free hand and taps it against mine.

My free hand shakes as much as the one he holds captive. Raising my glass to my lips I hear it rattle against my teeth as I take a big gulp. It helps, the alcohol calms me a little and dulls the pulse of adrenaline that's stopping coherent thought.

Think, what can I do? 'What if my friends miss me? My dad is expecting me home tonight. He'll be worried.'

'You grown woman. He think you met some nice strong man.' He grins.

'Not my dad. I always tell him if I'm going to be late, or if I'm stopping out. Otherwise, he gets too worried. Please let me ring him.'

Dragos lets go of my hand and sits back. His brows drawn down and I feel sure he's weighing up his options.

'Okay,' he says in an abrupt tone, full of business.

He takes my phone out of his pocket. 'You text him. I see.' He points at his eyes with two fingers and then down at the phone.

'I need to ring his landline—' I start to say but he cuts me off by shaking his head and holding out my mobile. I see I have a host of missed calls and messages. I don't dare open any of them, I just scroll to Dad's mobile and start to text – 'Hi. Stopping out with the friend who found Mrs P's cat. Don't worry, even the Cramps were teenagers, I'll be back soon as.'

He grabs the phone off me and reads my message with slow deliberation. 'Why you say about cat?' he asks.

'I told him. I was just so happy the cat had been found that I rang him and said I was meeting the kind person who had found it.' I'm rambling on, not properly thinking my words through.

'Take out cat bit,' he says.

Nodding I delete that and pass him back the phone. He re-reads it and grunts. 'Is good, *da*.' He presses send before turning off the phone and putting it back in his pocket. Then he grabs my wrist and pulls me to my feet. 'Come,' he says, tucking the champagne bottle under his arm and picking up his glass. 'You,' he says jerking his chin at my glass, 'Come.'

I grab my glass and trail him to the sitting room.

We sit together on the couch and he refills our drinks. Then he takes hold of my hand and holds it to his lips. I try to pull back, but he holds it firm, looking at me through half-closed eyes. He kisses my palm before pressing his nose to my wrist and inhaling with long deep breaths. His eyes close with a slow languor. 'Ahh,' he breathes and again takes a long inhalation. Pulling my arm towards him he pushes up my shirt sleeve and moves his face up my arm, inhaling like a seasoned cocaine addict. He stops at the crook of my elbow and his lips press into my skin.

Oh God, I think I'm going to scream. 'Tell me about Felicia,' I blurt out.

His eyes snap open, pinning me with their intensity; his pupils are so dilated they're like twin black moons, shining like the marbles from my dream.

'What did she look like? Can I… can I just have a sip of my drink?'

With reluctance he lets me go and straightens up on the couch. We both pick up our glasses. He drains his and I just sip mine. How I want a big gulp of alcohol right now, but I have to stay focused and keep my head clear.

'So tell me about her. I want to know everything. Why was she so special to you?' I ask.

Leaning back against the armrest, he regards me for a moment, his face blank. Then he seems to relax. 'She is mother to me, where I grow up, at the orphanage. Is terrible hard place. Felicia is like light where there is just dark.' He smiles, his expression tender. 'Felicia choose me. I her special one.'

'So she was one of the staff?' I remember the uniform-clad stern-faced women I'd seen on Google Images. The cold stares out from black and white photos of dozens of shaven-headed children cared for by a few overworked women. Was Felicia like this? She must be the same Felicia that Mark had talked about. Surely that was too great a coincidence?

'*Da*, Felicia is matron. She love me because I is good boy. I get what she needs.'

'And what's that?'

'Play, um, what is word? Play friends? I get children for Felicia to play with. I very good hunter. Too much strong.' He grins with pride.

I feel sick. Somehow I don't think Felicia's playing had much to do with toys.

'Felicia show me how to play.' He grabs my hand again and brought it to his lips.

'Tell me,' I squeak, pulling my hand back and lurching for my glass. 'I want to know all about it.' I gulp back a slug of champagne and smile. 'It sounds fun.'

He giggles. 'I tell you, is our secret, okay? Felicia tell our playing is secret, not say others. She gone now.' For a moment his face clouds, then his gaze focuses on me again. 'I tell you.' He grins. 'We play hunting. We are wolves. Felicia is momma wolf, we are cubs.'

'We?'

'There is other cub. He not good like me. He cry, he cry too much. Felicia not like that, cry cry cry, she angry.' He draws his brows down in demonstration. 'She not nice angry. Too much hurting,' he says and I see the pain and sadness harry across his features. 'Marku too little, I help him sometimes. He my little cub brother. We are pack.'

'Marku?' *So!*

'*Da.* I love him too much. They take him away. I sad, I miss.' His face looks lost.

'Where did they take him?'

'Here, England. Felicia say people come and choose forever child and take England. No one choose Dragos.' The sadness again swamps his face before he brightened. 'So then Felicia all for me. I her only cub. I do all hunting.'

'What is the hunting? It sounds exciting.'

He grins, bouncing a little in his enthusiasm as he explains, 'Felicia wait, upstairs, is empty there, no one go up there. Is cold, so cold in winter but is okay. I go to the children. Is best to get a little one, they not fight so much. I take one to Felicia and we play momma and papa wolves, depends,' he shrugs. 'I play, she watch. She show me how. Keep them quiet. Bite keep them still, they must submit. Not bite too much or maybe someone see and ask much too many question.' He shrugs again. 'No matter, no one listen. Matrons all too much busy.'

He honestly has no idea. What he did – does – is evil and he has no clue about the misery he causes. Did Mark do that too? I'm sure now to my very bones that Marku, Dragos's cub brother, is my Mark – the man who can't sleep because of the night demons that stalk through his dreams. Poor little Marku, thank God he'd escaped before he'd ended up like this grinning horror show sitting next to me.

'You want to play?' he asks, edging closer across the couch.

'I need to pee,' I say jumping to my feet. Bolting to the bathroom I'm dimly aware of his clumping steps behind me. Throwing myself down in front of the toilet, I grab the bowl and vomit a violent jet of champagne and the little I've eaten.

'What is wrong?' His voice carries concern. Looking up at him I see he's wringing his hands. 'You sick?'

Oh, you noticed. Sudden anger flashes through me. *Stop it,* I tell myself, *take control and get out of here. He thinks you are Felicia – be Felicia and survive.*

My legs are weak and I find it hard to get back up off the floor. 'Help me,' I bark.

He acts without question, helping me over to the sink. I wash my face and rinse out my mouth. Straightening I look myself square in the eye in the plain oblong mirror fixed above the sink. *You can do this.*

'Right, sit down,' I say, marching back to the couch, without looking at him because I know he will follow. 'Now tell me.' I pat the couch cushion next to me and he sits. 'Why do you think I'm like Felicia?'

'You smell good, special like her. You,' he mutters some words in Romanian. 'You, how I say, you have light, like angel. You have special inside, like Felicia,' he says patting his heart for emphasis. 'Is something I know here, and in here,' he adds tapping his head.

'But Felicia went away, like Marku did?'

'Yes. I not know why. No one say me. One day she gone, no say why.' The sad look creeps across his face again. 'I become big. Have to move to new place for older children. Then Uncle Mihai come. Take me live with him. Work too hard for uncle. Do work for making building. He always angry me. I miss Felicia too much. I run away. I look everywhere Felicia, no find. Maybe, I think, she come England, like Marku.' He shakes his head. 'I come England. It hard to come England, so hard. Work, money, special papers – all too hard. Take so long come England I think maybe,' he shrugs his shoulders, his face crumbling a little. 'Maybe she dead already.' Then his expression brightens. 'But I keep her here,' he pats his chest. 'See.' He unzips his hoodie and pulls down the stretchy neck of his T-shirt to show most of a plate-sized tattoo high on his chest – it's a dark snarling wolf with blood-flecked mouth. *So!*

'When I hunt she inside me. She so strong.' He chuckles. 'She too greedy.' He taps his head. 'I here. Help Felicia to hunt. She is momma wolf. Sometimes she is too strong.' His expression grows worried and he leans towards me to keep his words just between us. 'Sometime I not strong enough to stop her. She is animal inside – too hungry, too angry.'

But that's not real, that's the wildness inside you. Maybe I can do something here? 'Would you like to stop having Felicia control you?' I ask him.

He looks surprised.

'That thing I do,' I demonstrate by tapping my face. 'I can help you.'

'I don't know. Felicia so much strong.'

'Now listen to me,' I say, my voice firm, channelling my inner Felicia. 'You recognise me as being like her, don't you?'

He nods, his expression lax, like a child's.

'So I'm just as strong.' *Just not as crazy.* 'You believe that don't you?' When he doesn't answer I slap the couch making him jump. *Good.* 'You love me don't you?' *God, I hope I'm not pushing this too far.* He nods. 'So prove it.'

He looks frightened now. His nostrils flare and his eyes widen.

I take hold of his hand. 'Don't be afraid because I am with you, okay. Say it – I am not afraid because Astrid is with me.'

'Astrid? Your name Azza?'

I nearly scream I'd said it automatically, without thinking. 'Astrid is my full, proper name. I told you because you are special,' I add quickly. 'Now say it.'

Together we say, 'I am not afraid because Astrid is with me.' I run through the EFT tapping routine, at each point repeating, 'I am not afraid because Astrid is with me,' and at my insistent nods he repeats it too. His eyes are shining as he gazes at me, his hand is hot and sweating in mine. *God, please let this work.* As we run through it a second time, I begin to change the words that he then repeats as best he can in his halting broken English.

'Astrid is with me, I am not afraid.'

'Astrid with me, I not afraid.'

'Astrid will help me.'

'Astrid help me.'

'I have this fear, but Astrid is with me.'

'I fear, but Astrid with me.'

Then I begin to dig deeper. 'Even though I have this fear that Felicia is inside me and I cannot control her, that's okay.'

His hand trembled in mine and I grip it harder. 'Dragos, say it.'

'I… I fear Felicia. I no control. That is okay.'

'It's alright, Dragos, shut your eyes and just listen to my voice. Even though I have this fear,' I tap tap my fingers on the crown of his head. 'This fear that freezes me so I can't move,' tap tap just inside his eyebrow. 'This fear so deep my mind turns to stone,' tap tap beside his eye. 'This fear that Felicia controls me,' tap tap underneath his eye. His body is very still beside me now, his breathing slow and steady. Good, he's relaxed. I finish through that round and start on another.

'Even though Felicia takes control and does terrible things, that's okay.' *Oh God what am I saying?* 'She controls me,' tap tap. 'I am lost inside myself,' tap tap.

Tears start to push out under his thick eyelashes and run down his cheek.

Good, I'm definitely getting somewhere. 'I have no control,' tap tap. 'I am unable to move,' tap tap. 'Unable to speak,' tap tap.

As I say this I'm leaning towards him tapping on the point just under his nose, when his eyes snap open. They regard me with a cold expressionless stare.

It's her, I know it and fear tingles like ice down my spine. The eyes swivel to follow my hand movements as I tap on Dragos's chin. My touch is feather-light so I can jerk my hand away if she tries to bite.

'I am completely lost,' tap tap. A small hard smile thins his lips. 'Felicia has taken control,' tap tap. 'Even though I don't like it when she takes control, that's completely okay because Astrid is with me,' tap tap.

New round.

'Felicia has taken control, but that's completely okay,' tap tap.

'Even though I feel afraid,' tap tap.

'And the fear fills my head.'

'I know I am safe because Astrid is with me and I am completely okay.'

A rumble of a growl starts in his chest. The eyes – her eyes – still follow my every move.

The growl is growing and now I am becoming too scared to move.

His smile widens exposing yellow teeth.

'Dragos, no.' I clap my hands in front of his face and he jerks back shouting a stream of unintelligible words.

He seems to be arguing with himself. Expressions ripple across his face, distorting it into something unrecognisable, like out of a CGI sci-fi movie.

He seems to fling himself off the couch, crawling away from me before staggering to his feet and running for the hall.

I follow and see him grab up a green holdall, jump through the broken door and clatter down the first winding flight of the stairs. He's raving in Romanian, at least I guess it's Romanian, as the animal sounds he's making could be anything. I can hear his descent down to the ground floor. The sound of booted footfalls, snarls and shouts carry and echo; trapped, repeating, round the sound tunnel of the stone spiral staircase.

He has left me up here, alone, but for how long?

44

Hunting, sniffing, trapping

He runs down the stairs, almost falling on the smooth stone and catching himself on the cold metal of the mobility rail that runs its length, before leaping up and on again. He can feel it, the beast, fighting him with every step. It knew what he and Astrid were trying to do, and it's angry, so very angry. He has to get away before it hurts his angel.

Helter-skelter lunging down into the small dark lobby space at the bottom.

Here he stops, hands on knees, bent double to catch his breath. The beast still rages, its heat burning inside his head.

'Hush, hush,' he tells himself. He hums the tune that he remembers from back then, the tune that cools the beast. With the back of his hand, he strokes his cheek and hums until the buzzing recedes and he's almost back to himself again.

Opening the front door a chill gust of wind catches him. It's dark outside – no moon, no street lights – and the air smells fresh. He needs to walk, out there, in the night. He'll walk on the Downs where it's empty and quiet. Only after some time to himself will it be safe for him to return to his angel. But he doesn't have a key. He's seen a small black key-safe box to the side of the front door.

He goes to his van and searches around in his big toolbox for his hammer. Going back to the key-safe he smashes it off the wall with a few strong smart blows. Then he beats the small metal box with punishing repetitive blows until it gives up its contents. Good. Now he has to make sure she can't leave. With efficient speed, he takes the bottom bolt off the inside of the door and fixes it to the outside. He's making quite a lot of noise, but he's lucky, this place stands like an island in a sea of tarmac and bushy planting around the edges. Neighbours are few and far apart in this rich area. If it had been anywhere else, people would have noticed and questioned. He shuts the heavy front door and pushes the bolt home. Now he has his angel secure and safe in this stone tower that is private and only he can enter.

Packing away his tools back into the van, he pulls up the hood of his grey top and sets off out of the car park and up the street towards the grassy expanse of the Downs. Once on those soft damp areas, the moon peeps out from behind the clouds to light his way. It has waned to a cold slice of light and he feels safe and alone.

He's in love. This small slip of a woman, she has done that to him. His smile stretches and he has an urge to whistle. He'd held her in his arms, soothed her. She'd liked the meal he'd brought her, he could tell. Giggling he wags a finger at her imagined face – naughty miss pretending not to be hungry. Women did that. He's heard other men talk about it; on first dates, they pretend to be delicate and only eat little tiny bird-sized morsels. She was probably worried about looking greedy. Silly girl doesn't she know she's perfect to him. And she's strong too, inside. That thing she did – he taps on his face where he still feels the ghost of her fingertips – that thing is something strong. It had brought the beast; he had felt small beside its towering strength. Only this had been different; he'd never felt it like this. When the beast came, he would feel many things alongside its magnificence; fear or wonder, but never this strange calm. It was as if she had climbed inside his head and soothed him. She's so special, his Astrid.

After all this time hunting for Felicia, he's found her, in this other form, a delicate dark-haired woman. And the scent of her – she nearly drove him crazy.

She wasn't afraid of him. No, she was, he'd smelt her fear, but she'd held it and not let it overwhelm her like the others. When they'd squealed and fought, the beast rose and he couldn't hold it back. His angel, her light kept the beast down. *No, she can't*, said a deeper darker voice, *why did you have to run out of there just now?* He shakes his head and knuckles hard punches into the side of his skull. *Shut up, shut up, what do you know?* His angel is brave and wise. Astrid, she had told him her secret name. On Facebook she's Azza. For him she's Astrid; a good name, an old name, from the Vikings. She's his goddess, his angel, his princess, and she will free him from the beast that rages inside him.

They can be together, like other people are, caring for each other, loving each other. They can raise a family together. He hugs his arms around himself. A family – that is all he has ever wanted. He had come to England because that is where his little cub brother had gone. He came here searching for his lost family, his pack, Felicia and Marcu, and he was right. All this effort, working in shitty building work, moving to town after town, it has all been worth it because now he has found her, his one true love.

For now, he'll walk. Let his angel rest and get some sleep. He's too high to sleep. He might never sleep again! Chuckling at the thought, he strides across the Downs. He doesn't care where he goes just as long as he keeps away from strangers. He'll walk like this all night, from one side of Bristol to the other and back again, a lone wolf on the prowl until the dawn birds tell him it's time to return.

And then he'll wake his angel with a kiss.

45

He'd gone. I can hardly believe it. I stand at the top of the stairs and listen to him doing something down there, smashing things about and drilling. Then he slams the front door and is gone.

Creeping down the stairs my mind's on hyper-alert in case he comes back. At the bottom of the staircase, it's totally dark and I feel around the small lobby as if I'm blind. It's so dark here. No window on this level to let in any light, and even if there was, I'm pretty sure there aren't any street lights until you get back near the main road that runs along the Downs. I've not been here after dark before so I don't know where the light switch is. I fumble around by the door, trying to open it. Why won't it open? Feeling the walls, I eventually find the hard nub of a switch.

Bright sudden light has me blinking and covering my eyes with a gasp of indrawn breath. The cardboard box has gone. Has he really gone?

I need to get out, quick, in case he comes back.

But the door won't open.

I pull and pull at it, but it's stuck fast.

Punching and slapping the door, tears are blinding my eyes. What has he done?

Deep breaths, calm. Concentrate on your breathing, be calm and think. All that noise he was making downstairs, was he doing something to the door, to keep me in?

I dissolve again into tears, shaking and crying out and wringing my hands.

Stop it. I slap my own cheek. *Stop that. Take control.*

Breathe…

I start to tap. 'Even… even though I'm scared shitless and… and stuck down here and… and a mad man could come back at any moment, I… I completely love and accept myself.'

My voice echoes, rebounding up the void of the dark spiral staircase and winds around me. It's as if I have Carey with me, helping me through my routine.

'I have this fear.'

'It's shaking my whole body.'

'My legs are weak.'

'I can't think straight.'

And Carey speaks them with me.

It makes me giggle and pretty soon I'm cackling with insane laughter as I run through my EFT routine. But it works, in just one round of tapping, I'm calm and centred enough to think coherently. I sit on the bottom step and just breathe until the strength has gone back into my legs.

Okay, go back upstairs and see what you can find to get you out of here.

I go back up to the flat.

I search every room, looking through all the cupboards and drawers, gradually becoming more frantic – he could come back at any moment and I have found nothing. He has taken the phones and Mrs P doesn't have any panic pulls that most of our service users have. It's probably still on the 'to do' list at Your Home Care, *so fucking sloppy.* Looking at the mess of food on the kitchen table, I suffer a pang of hunger. I must eat, and be strong. If I can't get out then I will need to fight him when he comes back. There is, at least, a small sharp kitchen knife in the drawer. I know because I've used it on numerous occasions, slicing off the plastic on her ready meals. It's nothing compared to the knife Dragos carries, though.

Eating makes me feel better. I am strong. I am smart. I can do this. *Who're you kidding?* No, I can't afford to listen to negativity. 'Step into the positive, Astrid.'

Great, now I'm talking to myself.

Why hasn't anyone come looking for me? Becks must wonder where I am, especially when I didn't turn up to see the new flat. What about Dad? Had he deciphered my message about The Cramps? They're one of the bands we both agreed on. Late '80s, The Cramps song 'Teenage Werewolf' is one of Dad's favourites. Would he make the connection and call the police? And if he did, would they think to find me here? It was a slim chance, but it's something to hold on to.

So I need to consider my options.

I'm stuck up a tower, with no way out. How could I turn that to my advantage?

A tower is like a beacon or lighthouse. Maybe if I turn on all the lights someone will notice and wonder about it? There aren't many neighbours down this road, but the few that are might know Mrs P's in hospital, won't they? Worth a try.

Trotting from room to room I turn on every light. I carry the small knife in my hand. It gives me a feeling of courage and I like the weight of it in my palm.

Brightness all around me. Now what?

I push open the kitchen window that overlooks the car parking area and shout at the top of my lungs, 'Help, help, help!'

After a few minutes of screaming, I stop and listen. Nothing, no one stirs. This is a no through road. Most of the large Victorian houses have been converted into offices and such. The dental practice in the bulk of this building, on the ground and first floor, will be shut now. No one walks down here except to get to one of the buildings, so there's no one to hear me.

I try again anyway.

'Help, help, someone please help me.' My throat is starting to hurt and my voice is cracking from all the screaming. Pretty soon I won't even have this option. I remember something about how people ignore shouts of help, but they'll respond to the word 'fire'.

'Fire, fire, fire!' I scream out the window. That's an idea, I could build a fire. Someone will see it and call the fire brigade.

Enthused I start gathering up things to burn. Where should I put it? Here in the kitchen where it'll be most visible. I pile everything on the kitchen table and hunt about for a light. I don't know how Dragos had lit the candle, which is now out. He must have had matches with him. The stove is electric, so I turn a ring up full and lay a piece of newspaper, which I'd twisted into a tight spiral stick, across it until it starts to smoulder.

I watch, hungry for action, as the paper smokes, turns black and curls away in a small pale flame. With care, I take this over to the pile of debris on the table and hold it against more paper poking out beneath more sturdy things I'd found in the flat. The little flame leaps from item to item; magazines shrinking back to reveal hidden pages where images are bright for a moment before blackening and shrinking up like photographs left too long in the developing fluid; pastel-coloured cardigans fume as thick dark smoke rises up from them.

A sudden loud shrieking makes me shout with fright. The fire alarm. I'd forgotten about that – good, someone is bound to hear it.

The smoke is growing thick and clogging making me cough and wipe my stinging eyes. I begin to choke. Just little coughs at first, but quick as anything my eyes are streaming and it's becoming hard to breathe.

Hey, says a voice in my head, *when this fire really gets going how are you going to get out?*

Oh God! Running to the sink, the shriek of the alarm shredding my nerves, I fill a pan with water and douse it over the flaming table. Horrible thick smoke, even worse than before, blinds me. I stumble back to the sink and refill the pan. I repeat water, pan, douse – like Mickey Mouse in *Fantasia* – until the flames are gone and the smoke is a thin ghost that wavers above the ruined feast. The floor is a slick slippery mess. Black soot is all over the walls and ceiling. I go to the bathroom to wash my stinging eyes. When I see my reflection I nearly scream. Dirty and soot streaked cheeks with black around my nostrils from where I breathed it in and my eyes are bloodshot and red-rimmed. I look like an angry skull face from a horror movie.

Laughter bubbles up and I shake with it, helpless to stop myself as I hold on to the sink to keep from falling. In normal circumstances, I would have taken a shower, but no way was I getting naked with the possibility of Dragos coming back at any moment. Using the hand soap, which gives my eyes a new kind of sting to endure, I wash my face. Looking in the mirror, I can see I'm cleaner, with most of the soot clinging round my hairline. I stink too, the whole place does. Poor Mrs P, what will she come home to? No cat, burnt flat and maybe a murder scene. And it won't be my body on the floor!

Stomping back to the kitchen I find the little knife. The alarm has dimmed down to a drunk bird's chirping. Fucking typical, the battery is running out. I thought all alarms are supposed to be hardwired these days; another note to add to the list of Your Home Care recommendations.

With all the windows open the flat is becoming an icebox. I take a blanket from the bed and settle myself on the couch wrapped in its softness, and jam my alpaca hat firmly down on my head. It adds to my sense of security and the long ear-flaps help cut out the intermittent squawks from the fire alarm. Nestled in my hand is the small knife.

When he comes back I will be ready for him.

46

Dream

Fire. I'm choking. I can hear crying. Who's crying?

'Where are you, I can't see,' I call out.

There's too much smoke, I'm walking through a cloud. Am I flying?

'Astrid, Astrid. Oh my God. What's happened to you?'

47

'Astrid, Astrid. Oh my God. What's happened to you? Can you hear me? Are you alright?'

I jump upright, the knife ready in my hand so that Mark sits back on his haunches just in time.

'Mark!' Flinging the knife from me I throw my arms around his neck so that we both fall together in a heap on the floor.

'No touch her.'

That voice, his voice. I cling even harder to Mark and look up at Dragos striding towards us, his brows in a deep angry line, his breaths ragged. His large hunting knife is in his hand.

Reaching down he grabs my wrist and yanks me up and away from Mark.

'Hey!' shouts Mark, scrabbling to get to his feet.

Dragos kicks him, sending him sprawling with a yell. He points his knife at Mark. 'No move,' he barks.

Mark's eyes widen. 'Hey, I thought—'

'Shut up,' Dragos shouts and lunges at Mark, the blade swiping inches from his face.

Mark scuttles away, his feet propelling him backward across the carpet.

'No!' Shouting and struggling I pull at the arm that held me until he hard knuckles the side of my head and shakes me like a rag doll.

'Who this man? Why he call you Astrid? Is special name for me, only me.'

'I…' I'm too shocked, my mind has locked in fear.

He shakes me again and I hear my teeth rattle.

'What you do? What you do? What this mess? All black. Stinking. I think you die. You stupid.' He rants in a language I don't understand and binds my wrists with plastic ties. Looking about him, his eyes wild, he yanks me to the floor and links the ties to one of the couch's stout feet.

I watch in horror as he strides over to Mark, the knife held out before him. Mark cowers, his hands up trying to fend Dragos off. Dragos kicks him in the ribs doubling Mark up in pain. Then he drops down on his chest, pinning him to the floor. Keeping one knee in Mark's chest he holds the knife to his throat and we all stop. The only sound is our fast rasping breaths.

Dragos pushes the knife and I hear Mark's sharp gasp. The knife is withdrawn leaving a small wound, white for a moment before it fills with red. Blood seeps from the short gash in a stream down his pale neck to pool in the dip of his collar bone.

With a grunt of satisfaction, Dragos grabs Mark's wrists and binds them. He does the same with Mark's ankles. And then he leaves us. I can hear his exclamations from the kitchen at the mess I've made.

'What are you doing here?' I hiss at Mark. His wound looks shocking but I doubt if it's life-threatening. I guess it was inflicted for control. He has his bound hands up tentatively touching at the cut. His fingers, slick with blood, are spreading it over the skin of his neck.

'Looking for you,' he whispers. 'Who the hell is that?'

'The Bristol Beast.'

We stare at each other, silenced by the horror of it all.

'Does anyone know you're here?' I ask. *Please God let him have rung the police.*

'Maybe.'

That's not quite the answer I'd hoped for.

'I talked to Greg and—'

Dragos marches back into the room so Mark and I quickly look away from each other.

He glares at me. 'Why you do this? Disgusting mess, bad. We have to go now. Have stay somewhere else. Bad girl, this place nice. Why you no like?'

I glare back at him. I could feel my fear transforming into anger. Hot red anger.

'Speak,' he shouts.

I turn my face away.

'Speak.' It's almost a scream. He grabs my head, forcing my face round to look at him. When I shut my eyes with deliberate slowness he slaps me, almost knocking my hat off my head.

'Don't!' shouts Mark.

In an instant Dragos is on top of Mark, snarling.

'Stop!' I keep my voice loud and clear, authoritative.

Dragos's head snaps round, his lips curl back from his teeth.

Felicia. 'Dragos, get off him,' I command.

A low growl rose and grew steadily stronger.

'Don't you recognise your cub brother? Stupid. Stop fighting with Marku.'

His mouth opens in an 'O' and he looks down at Mark. Confusion runs across his features. 'Marku?'

Mark looks just as shocked. Then he nods, a slight movement held in hesitation.

'Marku,' says Dragos. He leans close to peer into Mark's eyes. 'Marku!' he yells and grabs him into a hug, babbling in Romanian. I can't see Mark's face. Then he lets go and jumps over to me. 'Is amazing. You amazing.

We family, just like before. Is so good. I so happy.' He's grinning, all his horrible misshapen teeth on display.

'Untie me then,' I order.

He cuts my bonds and rubs my wrists and straightens my alpaca hat, pulling lightly on the side strings and smoothing it down over my ears. 'Sorry, my angel. Sorry I hurt you, but you very naughty. Why make fire?'

I shrug. 'I was cold.'

He giggles.

'Now I'm hungry. Have you got some food?'

'Yes, I walk, long time all night. Then I buy breakfast. I bring but he come, trying to get in.' He cast an angry look at Mark. 'So I leave breakfast downstairs. I get.' He turns towards the door.

'No.'

He stops and looks back at me.

'Marku will get it.'

He doesn't move so I leap fast and slap him hard across the face. I swear for a moment I see *her* staring out through his eyes, then he seems to take control again, shaking himself like a wet dog. 'I can't, Marku might—'

'Now!'

He bows his head and swings round to Mark, the knife in his hand.

I hold my breath, time standing still.

He gets down on his knees and cuts the bonds on Mark's ankles and then shuffles up to cut the ties from Mark's wrists.

Then he stops, his body stiff and unmoving.

'Dragos!' I speak in a loud strident tone.

His body begins to shake. I can hear an incomprehensible muttering that rises into a full deep growl. I see the fear in Mark's wide eyes as he raises his bound hands.

Dragos lifts the knife up, held in both fists.

No, no, no.

I leap.

Sweeping the hat from my head I jam it down over his head and eyes.

Mark grabs his wrists and holds the knife away as I clamp my teeth down through the fluff of the alpaca hat into Dragos's ear.

I bite hard and wrap my arms around his neck.

The air is filled with animal snarling, and my mouth filled with the bitter taste of his blood. With a distant sense of shock, I realise the growling came from me. Beneath me, Dragos is silent and still.

He has done this to me – he has made me like him.

With ferocious anger, I snarl and bite, but he doesn't struggle. He just sinks forward onto Mark's chest.

Mark has the knife. He must have cut the ties on his wrists because he now holds it to Dragos's throat as he wriggles out from under the double beast that the madman and I have become. He staggers to his feet, his face wild and yanks the bundle of ties out of Dragos's back pocket before zip-tying the ankles and wrists of the man prone beneath me.

'Okay, you can get off him now,' says Mark.

But I can't. I can't move. Something primeval has hold of me as I snarl and bite. No sound comes from Dragos, he is completely submissive.

Is this how it was at the orphanage? Is this how a child has been warped into a brutal rapist – worse than a beast?

The power runs out of me then, and I clamber off him and into Mark's arms. We hold each other in silence as we listen to the wracking sobs coming from the man on the floor.

'I'll ring the police,' says Mark.

48

We're on a plane to Bucharest. Mark still holds my hand even though the terrible first ascent has finished and we have levelled out to something that almost feels normal, like being on a cramped bus. After my experience with Dragos, flying in a plane is a piece of cake. I hardly had to tap at all.

I've been seeing Mark for over six months now. He's told me everything he can remember about his cruel years at the orphanage. That's why he disappeared for a week after our last EFT session all those months ago. He'd gone back home to Salisbury to talk to his parents. They'd helped him fill in some of the gaps in his memory. Of course, they didn't know all that had been happening to him under Felicia's ministrations, but they had guessed some of it. With a lot of love and kindness, he seemed to have got better and forgotten the horrors of his past, and they had thought it best to leave it that way, for Mark at least. For the children back in Romania they had worked tirelessly, writing letters and haranguing their MP to get Felicia removed from working with children. There'd been a lot in the papers at that time, about the horrors of Ceausescu's orphanages. Although the dictator was long gone, it took years to sort out the aftermath and some of those still suffering. But the clamour of the press was a substantial weight behind Mark's parents' claims to get the vile matron removed, and they, at last, received assurances that Felicia had been dismissed without pay and was languishing in jail pending investigation. They never did hear anything further. I like to think she got forgotten somewhere, in a dark cell, still waiting for her case to come before the court.

Not long after seeing me, DI Reid had called Mark and arranged to interview him at a police station in Salisbury. That had been surreal and he'd felt confused and more than a little angry, guessing that Reid had got information about him from me. But needing to see me and discuss it all overrode any feeling of resentment.

So Mark had returned to Bristol wanting to explain it all to me, only he couldn't find me because I wasn't answering his texts or calls. He'd gone to the flat and found Kate. She explained that I'd moved out. Then he rang Greg and spoke to Becks. She'd told him about her last message from me and suggested he try Dad's house. So he'd gone there and learnt about the strange text message I'd sent. Dad had been stumped why I'd sent it. He played Mark the song. Then Mark rang Becks and she'd got excited, rambling on about the wolf-like man who attacked her. Only she had no idea where I was, but she thought she might know someone who did. Apparently, it had taken a lot of persuading and shouting with Becks and Greg storming round to the flat because Nick hadn't told Kate about picking me up from Mrs Percival's flat that night, and the loss of the cat. Eventually, under pressure from Kate, Nick had checked back through his old messages from me and given Mark Mrs P's address.

All of this toing and froing had taken ages and it was dawn by the time Mark had driven off to Mrs P's with instructions for Greg to ring the police if no one heard from either of us by mid-morning.

When he'd got to Mrs P's Dragos had been standing just inside the open doorway doing something with the lock. He hadn't wanted to let Mark in, explaining he was a builder doing some work for the homeowner and tried to send Mark away. Mark, thankfully, took no notice and somehow managed to push past him and run up the stairs. He'd been shocked when he saw me; he'd thought I was dead.

After he called them the police were super quick in coming. They'd already had a call from Becks, who couldn't bear to wait till she heard from one of us, so I guess they might have turned up on the off-chance before Mark called them. Perhaps they would have saved us if things had turned out different – well me at least, but probably not Mark – but who knows?

They took Dragos away in one vehicle and Mark and me in another. We gave our account of events down at the station. I found that almost as bad as the twenty hours that Dragos had held me captive. Reliving it all, and not being allowed to wash the stink off me until they had raked every last bit of my body for DNA evidence.

Too many hours longer of that stink of fire, and of him. The torment of knowing I had nearly become like him. That moment when I held him pinned beneath me, his blood thick in my mouth, the power I'd felt and the knowledge that I liked it – that was a shock to me; it still is. I didn't share that with Mark, I took that to Carey and we tapped it out, together. I've had other counselling, provided by my doctor on the recommendation of the police, for posttraumatic stress. It really helped too, but Carey knows me best, so I find the EFT work with her and some Matrix Re-imprinting helped the most.

Mark has been brilliant. He stayed with me through it all at the police station and took me back to Dad's when it was over.

Of course, we still had to give full statements to DI Reid, who was niceness itself. He even smiled at WPC Pettit who I felt sorry for, her face was that red. There were loads in the papers about it all, and a short court hearing, but it was obvious Dragos wasn't in his right mind, so he's gone off to a secure unit rather than prison. The newspaper reports said he would be there for life. The same could be said for his victims, I feel, caged by the memory of what he did to them. I found out through the papers that the man he attacked in Queen Square was my Facebook friend, Joe. That was because of me, I know that, and I can't do a thing about it. It haunts me, despite Carey and all the counselling. Maybe some things can't be washed away and stay with you forever. I can only wish Joe well with all my heart; he didn't deserve what happened to him, but does anyone? I hope he can put it away from him and not let it define him or poison his future.

It's hard to know what I feel about Dragos. He did terrible, evil things; but he'd been made that way, by a twisted and cruel upbringing. Does that make him responsible for his actions? All I know is that I can feel better about myself if I forgive him and let him go from my thoughts as much as I can.

I still get dreams, horrible scary nightmares, only it's okay because I know they're just nightmares – my mind trying to make sense of it all. They aren't one of those dreams, the ones that happen. I don't think I've had any of those since, but who knows? I haven't had any more about Mrs P, whose flat was condemned as unsuitable – possibly due to the mess I made of it. Thankfully she's been moved. I visit her and Sir Lancelot in their lovely new assisted living flat, which is just off on the opposite side of the Downs from her old place. It's on the ground floor so she has no excuse not to go for short walks, and let her cat out occasionally. She still watches her movies and puts food out for the birds, only she has a flock of them instead of that solitary staring seagull.

I feel different now, all grown up. As much as I wished it was before everything went crazy, life is not a fairy tale. I think, because of my crappy childhood, I had yearned for my prince to come and find me so I could live happily ever after. But Dragos has taught me that in comparison to his childhood mine was just peachy – it's all relative really, glass half full or half empty depending on the mind-set I choose.

So we're going to Romania to bury our demons. Mark wants to visit the site of the orphanage. The original building has been pulled down and new homes built in its grounds. And perhaps look at finding his birth mother; he says he'll know if he wants to pursue that when we get there.

And I'm going to visit Mette, my mum, to see what bridges we can build. I'm ready now to let go of the anger about her leaving. I'm lucky because I get to tell her that to her face.

I'm ready to move on to whatever new stuff is coming my way. Kate has bought me out of the flat. I don't know how her relationship with Nick is going, because that's none of my business, and I wish them all the best. I have no idea what I'll do with the money – not property though; I want to be free to do something amazing with it, rather than build myself another cage.

I'm ready with a smile on my lips and a song in my heart – like Carey says, to move into the positive; because, even though it's been hard and I've been afraid, I deeply and completely love and accept myself.

***

Acknowledgements

For the fact that this book exists at all I would like to thank the following people:

Structural edit by Hanna Todd and editor/proof-reader Helen Baggott for correcting all those endless mistakes, and finding all those misplacements and repetitions.

Cover designer Jane Dixon-Smith for yet again producing a wonderful gritty design which perfectly expresses the tone of Bristol through my antagonist's eyes, and for her readiness to try out so many different images and ideas.

My writers group who helped me through the early stages of this novel's growth, giving wonderful critique and invaluable advice; Caroline Mitchell, Sue Wells and Heather Malcolm.

Those precious inexhaustible people who took the time and effort to beta read this book in its raw state and give me back such invaluable feedback; Helen Blenkinsop, Gill Baker, Callie Hill, Cath Bennet, Caroline Mitchell, Helen Chanfi, Trevor Stubbs, Nasreen Ullah and Christine Khalif – I can't thank you enough for your ideas and inputs.

My youngest daughter, who sat patiently while I read the whole book aloud to her (skipping out the more adult moments), and contributed her thoughts.

Sources - My indebtedness to all the informative websites I trawled through on the internet, gaining knowledge about the Romanian orphanages during and after the Ceausescu era and the horror of those times. Also the novels: *Downfall: The Ceausescus and the Romanian Revolution* by George Galloway & Bob Wylie and *Abandoned for Life: The Incredible Story of One Romanian Orphan Hidden from the world: His Life, His Words* by Izidor Ruckel – both books providing invaluable insight a time that should never be repeated or forgotten.

All those fabulous people at ALLi – you were there when I needed you most, giving advice and information I might have taken a lifetime to find.

And to my family, sorry about the mess and hurried suppers. It's not going to get any better.

Jo Ullah

Lightning Source UK Ltd.
Milton Keynes UK
UKHW010924120120
356809UK00001B/2/P